Skylar Mars

and The

Crystal Claw

by Drew Seren

See what Drew Seren is up to.
Visit his website www.drewseren.com
And sign up for his newsletter

Copyright 2018 © MysticHawker Press
http://www.mystichawker.com

ISBN: 13-978-1-945632-24-2

Edited by Cat Lauria
Cover design by Silver Circle Images

1
Running Late

SKYLAR MARS raced down the corridors of Stars' End Academy. Just above him flew his Solar Drake, Filzbalm, whose orange leathery wings were little more than a blur as he kept up with Skylar. Several other students hollered complaints at Skylar as he shot past. He was going a lot faster than he should've, but he didn't want to be late. The head of the reader department, Professor Aduncus, wouldn't be happy if he was late, particularly just because he'd stopped to have a quick shower and change shirts after one of the low-level movers blew splashes of Alorian tomato soup over half of the cafeteria, leaving burn marks on clothes and skin of the non-Alorian students. Skylar endured the minor itching discomfort for a couple of classes, but when he had a few minutes between Galactic History and his free period with Professor Aduncus, he decided to clean up. The shower knocked off the last bits of the overly acid soup, but it left him a few minutes short.

"I have notified Professor Aduncus that we'll not be there on time," Filzbalm announced as they rounded the corner at the end of the hall, leading to the professor's training room.

Skylar let his inward grimace show through his mental link with the Solar Drake. He loved being bonded to the little space dragon, but there were times when Filzbalm's need to treat the teachers at Stars' End with the same reverence he had for The Mother of All Drakes was more than a little annoying. Skylar didn't disrespect his teachers—he just understood they were other sentient beings like himself and could be made to understand that sometimes people made mistakes, or in this case, took a minute or two longer to clean up than they should have.

In the months since their initial bonding, Skylar had tried several times to explain that teachers were like everyone else. Unfortunately, the drake would have none of it and insisted on doing things like telling Professor Aduncus they were running late as opposed to giving Skylar the chance to try to talk their way out of the professor's displeasure with their tardiness.

Skylar slowed to a walk. As he approached the door to the training room, the professor stood right outside the door frame, beyond the shields that blocked his mind from the other members of the school. He was a Tursiops, a race that was more at home in the water than on land, but being mammals and not fish, they were adaptable to both environments. His dark gray brow was wrinkled, and he didn't look happy. Since he hadn't been standing there when Skylar had rounded the corner, and just appeared, Skylar knew he must've been using some kind of mental shield to make himself appear invisible. The professor was a telepath, reader for short, with no mover abilities, so he wouldn't have been able to teleport in.

"Late again, Mr. Mars?" Professor Aduncus pushed open the heavy metal door and stepped inside the room before Skylar could answer.

"I'm really sorry, Professor." Skylar closed the door behind him. Unlike the rest of the station, these training rooms had manual doors since the level of psychic shielding on them made it impractical to use computer automation. Shielding against telekinetics was particularly disruptive to electronics. "I'm sure you heard about the Alorian soup incident in the cafeteria this afternoon. I was one of the ones caught in the spray. I endured the itching as long as I could, then I had to get it washed off." Filzbalm landed on his shoulder as he talked.

The professor looked at Skylar for a moment. "Yes, I heard about it, and I can see evidence of some blistering still on your skin. It doesn't appear that you're having an allergic reaction, so it's just the acidic properties." He pursed his lips. "I suppose it's a legitimate excuse, this time."

He didn't need to mention that Skylar often ran late for their special training sessions. Since Skylar had come into his psychic gifts later than most of the other students at Stars' End, and as a fairly strong reader and feeler, he'd been assigned to Professor Aduncus to get up to speed. Following bonding with Filzbalm, he'd made a lot of progress. That had also been when Skylar had stopped fighting what he was. The hardest part was blocking other people's emotions. Empathy, or feeling, was more instinctive, and difficult to control.

His mother, who'd been killed when Boarisk raiders attacked the planet Hummassa, had always been terrified of psychics and had instilled that fear in Skylar. Adjusting to life on Stars' End had been difficult, surrounded by people he'd been taught to fear, but as his own powers emerged, he'd come to terms with the fact that psychics could use their powers for good.

Even after he accepted his gifts, there were a number of things he was still getting used to, and a lot of his teachers constantly gave him extra work to bring him up to speed. The burden of the extra learning seemed to take up every second of his day. When combined with his sessions with Professor Aduncus and his time on farm duty for stealing a school ship to try to return Filzbalm to Armstrong's Rings, the strange planet where Solar Drakes lived, it seemed he was never running on time— for anything.

"No matter. With your progress, I think we're about done with these special training exercises – at least, until you're comfortable enough with your current power levels to push yourself farther." Professor Aduncus walked to the center of the room and took a relaxed pose that Skylar was expected to mirror.

As Skylar shook out his hands to prep for his exercises, Filzbalm flew from his shoulder. "Next levels?" Skylar still hadn't completely grasped how the definitions of power worked in the psychic community. Everyone talked about being a certain *level* in their given skills. Professor Aduncus was a level-ten reader, which was the highest level of any of the skills. He could easily touch any mind on the station, no matter where he was. Del, his grandson and Skylar's best friend, swore his grandfather was powerful enough to touch minds of people he knew from across a solar system.

"You've mastered the first three levels of a reader, and the first four of a feeler. Once you are comfortable with both, we'll try pushing things, since we know you show the potential to go far beyond most of the other students in the school."

"You have me," Filzbalm chimed in from his perch near the door. *"That gives you a lot more power, even if they don't realize it."*

Skylar didn't reply. Filzbalm's communications were mostly private. Other readers could only hear him when he wanted them to, like when he'd spoken to the professor on their way to the session.

"So, we're going to continue our private training?" Skylar really hoped that wasn't going to be the case. Stars' End was very different from school on Hummassa, but it did have similarities. Any time someone was taking special classes, they were singled out as different. Combined with Filzbalm, that made him a target for the corp-brats and few of the other kids who felt they were better than everyone else because of how high they were in their power ranking.

"We'll have to see. After break, I'll speak with your other teachers and decide if you are ready to join the other students who are starting to work at the next levels. If they think so, I see no reason you shouldn't join them." The professor made the opening sweep of his hand that signaled they were beginning their exercises.

Skylar copied the professor's motion. With that simple movement, his mind started slipping into the quiet he needed to use his abilities without Filzbalm filtering for him. Before he'd bonded with Filzbalm, he'd needed a special dampening bracelet to help block the constant barrage of thoughts and emotions from the other students. The external input hadn't been more than an annoyance until his telepathic skills had erupted when he'd lashed out at their counselor, Ms. Grissom. They'd given him the dampening bracelet to help, but with the little drake, he didn't need it. Filzbalm shielded him from the mental input and protected others from Skylar's occasional outbursts.

"Very good." The professor's thought rang clear in Skylar's head. *"It's starting to become second nature."*

"I've had a good teacher." Skylar followed the professor, moving his arms and legs in simple, circular motions that helped him relax and reach into his mind so he could easily speak to the professor without using his voice.

"Sometimes I think you're too young to understand the subtleties of flattery, then I realize you're just being polite. Even if your mother made you afraid of your gifts, she brought you up well."

"She did her best." It had taken months, but Skylar could finally talk about his mother without his throat tightening up each time. Sometimes he still had

nightmares of the night she died, when their hover car exploded during the Boarisk attack.

"So she did." The professor moved into the next round of movements, Skylar following along.

It had been several weeks since he had felt any physical or psychic fatigue after these lessons. The professor had used a more physical, martial arts approach to his training when Skylar had been resistant to meditation. They'd recently tried meditating again, but when Skylar simply sat and relaxed, he stumbled across memories that made the possibility of relaxation nearly impossible, so they'd gone back to the physical regimen that he responded better to.

"Have you decided what you're going to do over the school break?"

"No." Skylar resisted shaking his head and kept going through the slow, easy movements.

"Although some students stay on station during break, I figure you're tired of farm duty."

"There's farm duty during break?" Skylar hadn't given the upcoming break much thought. Solaria and Del had talked about going to their respective planets and seeing friends and family during the standard Sol-Three month they got off. Since Skylar didn't have any family, and only limited funds, he'd figured he would spend time relaxing with Filzbalm. Maybe get caught up on Galactic Explorers, his favorite game that he hadn't really had the time to play since he got to the school.

Solaria hadn't said anything about her plans, and Skylar hadn't probed her on anything. He figured she'd be going home to Pantheria, an icy world whose natives were humanoid cats prone to warrior-like behavior. Solaria was considered one of the most dangerous students in school, but after Del, she was Skylar's closest friend.

"The various parts of the school have to keep functioning even if classes aren't being held. The staff and students who stay behind normally fill in for the folks who are gone. Since you, Solaria, Del, and Melody have been handling farm duty, I figure Ms. Grissom will assign you to something you're already familiar with."

Skylar didn't bother trying to hide the groan that escaped him. One of the things he had to become accustomed to being around psychics was not trying to hide what he was feeling. Everyone seemed to pick up on everything anyway, and it was actually considered bad manners to try to keep secrets. He'd been amazed he and his friends had managed to keep Filzbalm a secret as long as they did after Solaria saved the egg.

"I was really hoping that would be over when break started."

"But the cows can have the most bovine thoughts." Filzbalm chuckled. The Solar Drake had recently discovered the idea of humor and kept trying out new and strange jokes that often fell flat.

"If you aren't on the station it will be, unless you decide that animal husbandry is something you wish to pursue as a career path. I haven't discussed with Ms. Grissom if your manual labor time is over or not. We'll see." The professor finished the set of movements they'd been doing and paused to get a drink of water from a glass on the table below Filzbalm's perch.

Skylar followed him, and got his own drink from the glass next to the professor's. *"High level readers are wanted in animal husbandry?"* It wasn't something Skylar had given much thought to. If he'd stayed on Hummassa, he might've ended up doing farm work or one of the other more manual jobs and been happy about it. However, after going into space, he wanted to explore the outer worlds. There was so much he wanted to see and experience beyond what a little backwater planet like

Hummassa could offer him. He even dreamed of one day having his own starship so he could go wherever he wanted. He just couldn't see himself settling down to raise cows or some other animal.

"You might be surprised. Readers find all kinds of jobs, feelers even more. But the movers are the ones in growing demand. I haven't seen any evidence of that in your skill set, even if there are mover segments in your DNA. But if you had any active mover in you, you wouldn't have been hit with the Alorian soup earlier."

Skylar had enough to learn without throwing in another psychic skill. Solaria was a mover and made things like zero-g movement look easy, and she could bust down doors like they were nothing, but he didn't want to tackle anything new at that moment. "No thanks."

"I'll put that in your file." The professor set his glass down. *"Now, let's try something a little different. This next set of movements is meant to strengthen your shielding. It's something you still need to work on, particularly when Filzbalm isn't around you."* He looked up at the Solar Drake, who was preening his leathery wings. *"Please don't aid him."*

"I will do as you wish." Filzbalm bowed slightly to Professor Aduncus, then went back to preening.

"Good." The professor strode into the middle of the room and waved Skylar over to stand at his side. *"Now, follow this."* He made a sweeping motion with his hand, in the opposite direction than Skylar was used to. It looked awkward and strange. Professor Aduncus ended the sweep with a hard thrust outward. A soft tingle of energy went out from him.

When Skylar did the thrust, his fingers tingled, and a similar energy came out of him. Like the passive way the other parts of the almost-dance he did to relax his thoughts worked, the new movements triggered something in his mind that sent out protective energy.

The professor smiled. *"Very good. Now follow this."* He did the same movement, then swept his arm in a wide arc after the thrust. A glow of power covered him for a moment, then disappeared.

Skylar copied the move and made his own scintillating arc. It didn't linger as long as the professor's had, but he'd still done it.

"Good." The professor nodded. *"I want you to do that ten times in a row. Let's see if we can get you to hold it a little longer."*

"Okay." Skylar did as he was instructed. By the third time he made the sweeping motion, it didn't feel as strange. Remembering he was supposed to attempt to shield with the motion, he tried to actively think of that as he went through the sweeps and thrusts. The glowing arc happened again and lasted longer each time. On the eighth repetition, he was able to get the arc to become more of a dome, and by the tenth time, he could hold it until he willed it to release.

"You really do have a great deal of natural talent." The professor walked over to the table and finished off his water.

Skylar wiped his forehead, not realizing he'd started sweating during the exercises. He followed the professor over to the table. The water was cool and welcome on his throat.

"You do make a nice shield," Filzbalm said. *"And I didn't help. But I think my shields will still be stronger."*

"But my shields won't get any stronger unless I practice," Skylar reminded him. *"So let me keep practicing. That way if you and I ever need to work together on shielding, we'll both be more protected."* In the school, it was considered bad manners to go around reading minds without an invitation, but that didn't mean

a lot of the kids didn't practice on each other without permission. Every day, he heard at least one person laughing about something they'd heard in someone else's mind. He was glad he had Filzbalm around to help block his thoughts from unwanted invasions, but shielding was what most psychics learned first. Since Skylar had come into his power unexpectedly, his training was a little off.

"Okay, I think we've done enough for one day." When Professor Aduncus used his voice, it indicated that their session was over. "You have a few days before break. If you stay here, we'll need to arrange for Ms. Grissom to continue your sessions. It probably won't be every day, like it is with me. If you find somewhere to go over break, I'll send a dampening bracelet for you to take, in case you need it."

Skylar hated the idea of Ms. Grissom taking over his sessions, even for a few weeks. The school counselor was the first person he met on Stars' End, and they only seemed to interact when something unusual was going on. He had hoped that even if he stayed on the station, he wouldn't have anything to do with the high-level feeler and low-level reader. Even as Skylar was getting used to being around psychics, she still gave him the creeps from time to time with her overly still, observant manners. He was sure she always knew exactly what was going on with him, even when he was shielded.

"Thanks. I'll try to figure out what I'm doing." Skylar finished off his water and set the empty glass back on the table.

"Now, go to your time in the farm area. You don't want to be late for that too."

"You're right." Skylar swung the heavily shielded door open. "See you tomorrow."

Filzbalm flew down to his shoulder as he started off down the hall. *"I wonder if the cows will have any words of wisdom for me today."*

Skylar couldn't figure out where Filzbalm got the idea cows could pass on any kind of wisdom, but he'd stopped arguing about it. He just hoped Solaria, Del, and Melody were all there and they could get their chores knocked out quickly so they could go to dinner. His stomach growled and he felt slightly lightheaded. He was hungrier than normal after his session and couldn't wait for food.

2
An Opportunity Arises

SKYLAR AND Filzbalm made it to the farm section of Stars' End without incident. There always seemed to be something going on in the halls to slow him down, but the route he went was drama-free, for once. It never ceased to amaze him that there was a farming area in the space station. It took up a good portion of the center of the station, with the passage through to space dominating the middle, as was the Z-GBall playing area where the students learned to use jet packs, or mover skills to propel themselves through a gravity-free environment. The first time he'd seen the station, Solaria's uncle Phil had flown Skylar through the middle of it, where the clear metal reinforced by force fields kept the space outside and the atmosphere and occupants inside. It was incredible to be able to see from the station's interior as well, creating a cross between a wall and a ceiling that was either full of stars, or the gas giant the station circled.

Bordering the farm section was a large green zone where trees grew, and a stream meandered through. When classes were out, there were normally a fair number of students there, especially ones who came from planets that were more wild than civilized. Skylar had no idea how many hours he, Solaria, Melody, and Del had spent in the area. In some ways, it reminded him of the unpopulated areas of Hummassa, where he'd lived most of his life. Solaria said it was still more civilized than the vast ice fields of Pantheria, but she did like getting away from the overly techie feel of the rest of the school. He figured Del was there just to spend time with the rest of them.

Nestled on the far side of the park, a series of small buildings made use of the curving dome of the ceiling, which changed its density during the day to act like a planetary sky to help stimulate plant growth and keep the livestock happy. They reminded him of the livestock buildings on Hummassa. The basic rectangular shape, with a pitched roof, and red wood, was the same. When Skylar stopped to think about it, it made him wonder if there was some unwritten rule in the universe that said barns needed to be red to be proper homes for animals.

A flash of movement caught Skylar's attention as he approached the nearest building, where the cows came in from their small pasture twice a day for milking. A pale, lanky form walked out the door carrying a large bag thrown over one shoulder.

"Solaria!" Skylar waved as he broke into a run, dislodging Filzbalm into flight. She was already working, and that probably meant he was late…again.

She upended the bag into the compost heap before turning toward him. "You're late."

He skidded to a stop, as Filzbalm circled her head once before flying into the building where they were going to be working. "Sorry. Had my training session with Professor Aduncus."

"Yeah, and he knows what time we all start this." She rolled up the bag and put it under her arm. As usual, she had on a sleeveless tunic that showed off her light gray fur interspersed with darker gray rosettes. Her long, similarly marked hair was pulled back in a ponytail that she claimed kept her from getting too overheated while doing manual labor in a galactic norm environment. She was constantly complaining about being too hot. Pantheria was a lot cooler than the temperatures Skylar and most of the other students were used to.

"He was trying to hurry me along." Skylar fell into step with her as they went back to the building. "He taught me a new shielding technique."

Solaria huffed. "Let's hope it works better than the other ones he's been trying to teach you. You're still too sensitive to everything around you."

"I know." Even though he'd made a lot of headway since bonding with Filzbalm, there were still a fair number things that got through his shields, particularly the thoughts and emotions of the other high-level students who weren't bothering with control. It wasn't bad enough to consider putting the dampening bracelet back on, but it did get really old after a while.

"Hey, could one of you come over here and lend me a hand?" Del called from the far stall. He stood against the wooden wall with a shovel in his hand, glaring at the cow who occupied the small area.

"Sure." Skylar hurried over to help his best friend—it would help get him away from Solaria's scorn at his tardiness. She was always explaining how predators were never late, and that humans were predators just like Pantherians, even if they weren't as well equipped for the task of bringing down prey.

"What's wrong?" Skylar asked as he reached the stall door.

"She won't move," Del said, pointing the shovel at the cow. "I've tried pushing on her shoulder, yelling at her, scaring her, everything I could think of, but she won't move." He sighed, and the way his forehead wrinkled made him look a lot like his grandfather, Professor Aduncus. Although Del had a full head of dark blue hair where the professor was bald, his smooth, gray skin was an almost identical shade to his grandfather's and their black eyes had the same intelligent sparkle.

Skylar frowned at the cow. When his reader powers first flared to life, he'd come back to himself in the barn, with a couple of cows thinking about how much they wanted him to feed them. It had been very surreal. He hadn't been used to hearing the thoughts of others, let alone the thoughts of cows, who he'd always just thought of as a source of food. Since then, he'd had an indifferent relationship with them. They liked him, but he resisted getting too close, knowing they were food there on the station and he might end up eating them.

The cow currently facing Del down had a series of brown and black spots on her forehead. She was the one most likely to give all of them problems. She was also the one who led the herd, and seemed to take her position very seriously.

Skylar stared into her large sad eyes as he sent his thoughts at her. *"We would appreciate it if you'd go out to the pasture for a little while. You'll be fed after we get done cleaning."* It was the same pattern every day, and he never could understand why some of the cows remembered the way things went, and some refused to.

"Yes, I am waiting to be fed. I should be first. Also I am in need of milking."

"And that will happen as soon as we get the place clean enough. If you continue to slow us down, we'll never get it all done."

She huffed. *"If you won't feed or milk me, I suppose I should go graze a while."* She turned and sauntered out the back of the stall, past a couple of other cows near the door who looked like they were hoping she'd get fed so they would.

"Thanks, Skylar." Del started shoveling out the stall into the wheelbarrow just outside the door. "You know, you really do have a way with cows."

Skylar frowned as he grabbed the wheelbarrow handles. "Did you tell your grandfather that?"

Del paused and a thoughtful line crossed his smooth gray forehead. "I don't think so, but you know

Grandfather. Sometimes if you're thinking the wrong thing, he'll pick up on it and it's all out there."

"Yay." Skylar shrugged. "Life with psychics."

"Life with psychics," Melody echoed as she pushed another wheelbarrow out of the adjoining stall. She seemed to take to the work on the farm area better than any of them—even if she was a corp-brat—although Skylar had stopped lumping her in with the other human kids from well-to-do families after she helped them on Armstrong's Rings. She wasn't nearly as stuck up as the rest of them.

"It's part of the world we live in," Solaria said, carrying another bag past them. "You either learn to live with it, or you live out in the boonies away from everyone." Then she was gone out the door toward the compost pile.

"What is she doing?" Skylar asked as Del filled the wheelbarrow.

Del filled up another shovel full. "Some of the feed went bad. Mrs. Green isn't sure why. She wants the bags dumped in the compost heap. We've already added a general neutralizer to the feed so it hopefully won't infect the compost."

Skylar didn't know much about compost, other than it was supposed to make soil fertile. When Del finished filling the wheelbarrow, Skylar lifted the handles and headed out with it.

"You know, the cows are not happy that their dinner is late." Filzbalm flew down from the rafters and out ahead of Skylar. *"The one with the spots on her face is telling the others that it's your fault they haven't been fed yet."*

If there was one thing Skylar really didn't care about it was how the cows felt about him. "It's not even feeding time."

"I don't think cows can actually tell time. They just judge by the amount of light, and the station controllers are starting to shorten the light cycle as it gets closer to break." Filzbalm landed on a post next to the compost pile. *"Of course, I haven't been able to confirm that's why the light cycle is getting shorter, but I presume if the students aren't going to be around, they'll be lessening the amount of light they let into the station."*

As he upended the wheelbarrow, Skylar shook his head. "I don't think it has anything to do with that, unless they're trying to simulate a yearly growth cycle in the plants and are therefore affecting the cows." He was amazed at some of the ideas Filzbalm could come up with. The little Solar Drake had strange thoughts that were more complex than even Skylar thought about. Sometimes it took him a little bit of thinking to wrap his mind around the ideas.

Instead of trying to figure out what was on everyone's mind, Skylar took up hauling duty and wheeled out the manure and leftover hay as Del and Melody filled the wheelbarrows up.

As normal, Skylar was a bit tired by the time Mrs. Green, the teacher in charge of the farm, called it quits and they scurried off to the cafeteria for dinner. Skylar had found that his appetite increased when he was working, but he was also starting to develop muscles he'd never expected to have. He'd just figured he'd be lanky most of his life, like his mother had been.

Solaria tapped her dermal com, turning on its more advanced functions. During school hours, they were supposed to have the dermal coms set to in-school communications only, so that if a member of faculty needed a student they could get in touch with them, but they weren't bothered by family messages or contacts from friends or social media.

"Hey, I've got a message from Uncle Phil," Solaria said as they made it to the cafeteria. She paused and pulled Skylar to the side of the flow of students going in. "This affects you."

Skylar stumbled a bit as he came to a stop next to her. "What?" He had a sudden hope that maybe Solaria's Uncle Phil, the man who'd brought Skylar to Stars' End after being part of the team who'd rescued him on Hummassa, had word of Skylar's childhood friend, Teir, who'd been missing since the attack. The one time he'd seen Phil since being dropped off at the academy, he'd asked for information, but Phil hadn't heard anything. Even though Phil had left a request with the Intergal Rescue team on Hummassa to be informed if there was any news one way or the other on Teir, nothing had been relayed to Skylar. They hadn't heard from Phil since he'd brought them back to Stars' End from Armstrong's Rings.

"Hold on. I'll put it on broadcast." Solaria tapped her com, and Phil's voice came from her hand.

"Solaria, I've been thinking. School break is about to happen and I'll be coming by to take you home, unless you have other plans. Would you like to bring Skylar with you? I think it might be a good idea to expose him to more different cultures."

Skylar spaced out on the rest of what Phil was saying. He was getting an offer to get off the station for the break! He hadn't expected anything like that. He'd just been planning to spend the time hanging out with Filzbalm. At the thought of the Solar Drake, a worry hit him.

"Well, what do you think?" Solaria asked as she tapped the dermal com.

"Might be fun," Skylar said, trying to hide the mixed emotions that were going through him.

Solaria frowned and crossed her arms. "What's wrong? Did you already have an offer you haven't told any of us about?"

Skylar shook his head. "No, it's not that." He reached up and stroked Filzbalm's head where the little drake rode on his shoulder. "What about Filzbalm? Pantheria is a cold world. Will he be okay?"

For a moment, Solaria pursed her lips. "I hadn't thought about that, and I bet Uncle Phil didn't either. We've got time, I bet we can come up with something, if you want to go." She glanced at Del, who'd, like normal, stopped with them. "What do you think? Can we come up with something?"

Del shoved his hands in his pockets and looked thoughtful. "Probably. I don't think we can make him a coat or anything like that. What season is it right now in your family's settlement?"

"Spring," Solaria replied, then walked toward the line of students getting their dinner.

"So sort of in-between as far as extremes go." Del fell into step with her as Skylar and Melody followed.

"Yeah," Solaria agreed. "Could go either way depending on what's blowing over the mountains at the time."

Del grabbed a tray from the stack at the end of the line. "That means we'll have to be prepared for everything. This might be a bit of a challenge." Del glanced at Filzbalm. "It's also going to have to be size appropriate, unless I can whip up something that can encompass both of you."

"But that would limit my actions to staying with you," Filzbalm complained, finally joining the conversation.

"I might be able to help," Melody said. "I've been working with some micro-tech lately. My mother says that it's the next big trend and my father's company is really interested. I saw some fascinating things when I accessed the company system through the backdoor I set up a few years ago. I like to be able to keep taps on what's going on without them knowing about it."

Del gave his order to the cafeteria worker before responding. "Micro-tech… that could be just what we need." A note of excitement hit his voice, like it always did when there was something new and interesting to be learned. If there was one thing Del loved, it was learning new stuff.

"What are you thinking?" Skylar asked as he ordered his and Filzbalm's meals.

"Something that can be a portable, self-contained heating unit," Del replied. "His size is the big hurdle, but if we can get some micro-tech components, that would help."

"I am sorry I'm small, but it's part of being a young Solar Drake. I will get bigger." Filzbalm leaned forward as Skylar got the cup of raw meat he needed from the woman behind the counter.

Skylar laughed at his comment. "Filzbalm apologizes for being small and says that he will grow." Skylar had met The Mother of All Drakes, and he knew how large Filzbalm could get depending on how long he lived. From what the researchers on Armstrong's Rings told him, Solar Drakes didn't stop growing until they died.

"We can work around his size," Melody assured them.

"I know we can," Skylar said as he carried his tray over to their usual table. "With you and Del working on the problem, I bet we have it fixed within a couple of days."

"I agree." Solaria set her tray on the table first. "So, I'll go ahead and let Uncle Phil know that the three of us will be ready to go when school lets out for break. That way he can get here a little early so he can dock more easily. There's often a big rush of ships coming in to pick up students at the start of break."

"Tell him if it's a problem, I can stay at school." Skylar set Filzbalm's bowl on the table just to the left of his tray and the Solar Drake ran flapping down his arm to get to it. "I hadn't really been expecting to do anything for break anyway."

Solaria shook her head. "He wouldn't have offered if it was going to be a problem." She cut into her raw steak. "This'll be fun. I can't wait to tell the tale of how we rescued Filzbalm from the corp-brats and then journeyed to Armstrong's Rings." She got a faraway look in her eyes. "My family always loves getting new stories to tell. This is so much better than Uncle Rocko's hunting tales."

Skylar suddenly had a new worry—he wasn't sure how he'd feel about being a part of Solaria's tales to her family. The way she sounded, it was like being a minor celebrity. He just wanted a quiet break from school, and this was shaping up to be something entirely different. But at least he was going to get to leave the station for a while and see a world he hadn't set foot on before. That would make any potential embarrassment worth it. He wanted to see as much of the universe as he could, and a great opportunity had just dropped into his lap. There was no way he was going to let this slip through his fingers if he could help it.

3
Technical Glitches

SKYLAR WALKED into the room he shared with Del and their two roommates, Connor Cosmo and Fin Meres. Filzbalm flew over to his perch above Skylar's bed. Del was bent over his desk muttering to himself, and Connor and Fin were nowhere to be seen.

"Hey, you headed back here really quick after dinner," Skylar said, dropping his shoulder bag with his tablet and other supplies on his desk.

"Sorry." Del looked up, frowning as he set down the stylus in his hand. "I just really want to get this design done. We've only got another five days before break starts and you need it." Ever since Skylar had decided to go with Solaria to Pantheria for break, Del and Melody had been working hard on a device that would let Filzbalm visit without risking his health due to the cold. They still hadn't moved beyond the design stage, and both were getting more and more obsessed with it.

"Hey, Skylar." A hologram of Melody waved from the desk next to the table Del had been at.

"Hey, Melody." Skylar waved back. "So why aren't you two in the tech lab banging away on this?"

"All the lab time was booked for the next two days. I was lucky to get a slot on the MTUs about two hours before Phil is supposed to be here for you guys." Del closed his eyes and rubbed his forehead. "I've got no idea why this happens, but it seems like right before breaks, everyone wants to get projects done."

"It's so they can take things home and show their parents," Melody chimed in. "Trust me. I know all about trying to impress your mother and father. Unfortunately, mine don't impress easily."

"Right," Del agreed. "So we're stuck working on this remotely. We just can't get past the thermal transfer problem. So far everything we've come up with either makes the simulations too warm, or not warm enough." He glanced over at Filzbalm. "We really don't want you to end up being a roasted Solar Drake."

"I don't think I could be roasted." Filzbalm flew over to Del's desk and landed above the tablet. *"My kind have evolved for the rigors of heat."*

Skylar laughed as he looked over Del's shoulder at the circuitry schematic on the tablet. "He doesn't think he can be roasted," Skylar relayed between the two of them. Filzbalm could only telepathically speak with fairly high-level readers, although sometimes he could make Solaria hear him if he shouted loud enough to give her a minor headache.

"No?" Del picked up the stylus and tapped a couple of things on the tablet. A video simulation played out. A Solar Drake who looked a lot like Filzbalm had a small gold ring on his foreleg. A tendril of smoke started and the simulation frantically pulled at it, trying to slip it over its claws as its golden skin turned red, then blistered.

"What in the world?" Skylar frowned as he leaned closer to the tablet. "Why is it doing that?" The image of the drake got the ring off, dropped it on the floor and held out its arm, showing the damage.

"I created the simulation of Filzbalm with all the information I could get from him. Remember, we even managed to get Mrs. Knightingale to run him through the medical scanners last week. I put all that into the system so I could make sure I didn't design something that would kill him by accident."

"It's not been pretty." Melody looked down at her hands. "We're trying everything we can think of. With the micro-tech I can program into the MTU, we shouldn't have a problem making the thing small enough; we just have to stop the overheating reaction."

Skylar didn't know a whole lot about the station's Matter Transformation Units, other than they had a set amount of programming for the basic things the students needed, and not much more. He'd never heard of people actually going in and programming them for special items, but it made sense considering how limited storage space was on the station. Almost everything that wasn't in use was recycled down to its base atoms and reconstituted through the MTUs. Each student had so many MTU credits they could use to generate things, but they had to either work or recycle things to get the credits.

Even though their time working in the farm area was punishment, they were still getting extra MTU credits. They'd decided they were going to all go in for the parts needed for Filzbalm's protective device, whatever it ended up being. Skylar just hadn't realized they were actually going to program it into the unit, and not get parts and then put everything together. He was leaving all the techie end of things to Del and Melody.

"I just don't know how to overcome the reaction." Del huffed. "There's got to be a way to put something like a circuit breaker into the design. That would stop it from overheating."

The hologram of Melody perked up. "Hey, that might be the answer. We haven't tried adding any kind of breaker into the system after we added the amplifier." She picked up a tablet and made some notes. The changes showed up on Del's tablet almost instantly.

Skylar looked at the new schematics over Del's shoulder.

Del hummed. "This might work. We've been trying a more complex regulator. Haven't gone simpler." He transferred the new information into the simulator.

Again, the digital duplicate had the ring on its arm. Del zoomed in on the arm with the ring. There wasn't any smoke rolling off it like there had been in the last simulation. The replica drake wasn't acting like it was in pain. Del tapped the screen and a thermometer displayed an easy comfortable temperature around the ring and the Solar Drake's arm.

Pursing his lips, Del nodded. "Looks like this might be the answer." He tapped his chin. "I just wish we could get MTU time with more than just a couple of hours to try it out. Filzbalm's life might rest on this thing we've whipped up working correctly."

"I bet I can get it generated at home, then have it shipped over to us tomorrow," Melody offered, then glanced down at something. "Looks like I've got just enough time to make it out on the mail ship heading this way and get it tomorrow evening at dinner."

"That should give us enough time to test things out, shouldn't it?" Skylar asked. He liked the idea of getting the ring tested out before they left for Pantheria. He and Solaria had discussed the idea that if Del and Melody didn't come up with something, then Filzbalm could spend the whole time they were there with Solaria's folks inside Skylar's clothes, but they agreed that might get uncomfortable for both of them. Solaria was also fairly sure they could heat at least one room of their house to something around Sol Three norm which would be warm enough for Filzbalm without any kind of augmentation. But he didn't want to be separated from Filzbalm when he went on the adventures it sounded like Solaria was planning for them. He wanted the Solar Drake with him all the time. Since they'd finished bonding on

Armstong's Rings they hadn't been more than a few feet apart.

SKYLAR DID his best to hide his enthusiasm as he walked out of the cow barn with his three friends. Ms. Grissom and Professor Aduncus had decided they could have the last two days before break to themselves, to prepare for their final evaluations to wrap up the semester. They got to the main hall when Melody's com beeped. She tapped it, and a message informed her that she had a package waiting for her in the.

She grinned. "That's got to be the ring."

"I thought it was supposed to be here yesterday," Del grumbled as he shifted his bag to his other shoulder.

"I guess the house's replicator didn't get it made in time to make the mail," Melody said, then looked down at her shoes. "Or I might've miscalculated what time it was at home and it might have been too late to get here yesterday."

Skylar didn't care. They had two more days before break started and he wanted to make sure the ring was going to work the way Del and Melody thought it would. "It doesn't matter—let's go get it and try it."

"Have you figured out how we're going to test it?" Solaria asked as they all changed course and headed toward the mailroom.

"We could put it on Filzbalm and let him go with you to your room," Del said. "There's enough of a temperature difference that the ring should become active."

"But the difference isn't as much as it's going to be if he gets caught out in a spring storm." Solaria opened the door to the mailroom and held it for all of them.

"Then what do you want to do?" Del snapped. He'd been really grumpy the past few days. At first Skylar had thought it was because he and Melody were having problems finding out how to protect Filzbalm from the cold, but he had quickly decided it was something else. He wanted to find out what was wrong before they left on break, in case it was something he'd done without realizing it.

Solaria shrugged. "We could take him into the freezers in the kitchen. That should tell us for sure."

"As long as it doesn't cause me to smoke like the simulation did, I don't really care," Filzbalm said.

"I agree," Skylar said, stopping right behind Melody as she approached the mail lady, a large woman of a race he couldn't immediately identify. Her skin was a dark green and her hair was a vivid, verdant hue he'd never seen before.

"You think it would be a good idea to take him to the freezer?" Del shot Skylar an indignant glance.

Skylar rolled his eyes. "Filzbalm just said he doesn't care what we do as long as he doesn't start smoking. We don't need him getting burned by this ring."

"I don't think he will," Melody said as she turned back to them with a small plastic mail carton in her hands. "Now, let's go open this and see if it works. Since I'm a girl, I can go with him and Solaria to her room and see what happens. You two will have to wait out in the hall."

"Sounds good." Skylar was used to the security measures Stars' End had in place to make it difficult for students to have much time alone in non-public places. Girls and boys were not allowed in each other's rooms. A biometric force field stopped people with the wrong genes from entering.

"Okay." Melody stopped at the MRU just inside the mailroom to drop the mailing carton in so it could be recycled. She handed the smaller box to Skylar. It was black and hinged.

Skylar opened the box and saw a small platinum ring lying inside. He picked it up and inspected it. There was a series of extremely tiny lines of circuitry across its surface that sparkled slightly in the light.

"Looks right to me," Del said, peering over his shoulder. "But I'd need to look at it under magnification to make sure everything is correct."

"Do you want to do that before we try it out?" Skylar handed him the ring.

Solaria took it before Del could. "Do you have your tablet with the schematics?"

"Duh." Del glared as he pulled his tablet out of his shoulder bag. He pulled up the diagram of the ring that Melody had sent to have printed and showed it to her.

She wrinkled her brow, causing one of her rosettes on her forehead to nearly close as she looked at the tablet, then at the ring. After a minute of glancing back and forth between the two, she handed the ring to Del. "You can check it if you like, but from what I know of the electronics, it appears to be the same."

"And you can tell that with the unaided eye?" Skylar asked.

"I'm a predator. I've got excellent eyesight." She turned and headed out of the mailroom.

Skylar hurried to keep up with her. "That's your answer to just about everything, isn't it?"

She shrugged. "Sometimes. But it's the truth."

He couldn't doubt her a bit. He'd seen her in action more than once, and she could be downright scary when she wanted to be.

"Yeah, but this is still Filzbalm we're talking about," Del said, stopping in the mail hall. "If it's okay with you, I'd like to check it out with my own eyes."

"Mine too," Melody said. "It should be fine, but I agree with Del."

Solaria kept walking toward the cafeteria. "You two do that. I'm going to get something to eat. You know where to find me when we're ready to test this thing out."

"I'd like to eat now too," Filzbalm said from Skylar's shoulder. *"If it's going to be a few minutes before we're ready to test the ring."*

"Okay." Skylar glanced at Del. "We'll go with her—take your time and make sure everything's good. I'm with you—I don't want anything to happen to him." Skylar had learned from the researchers on Armstrong's Rings that a bonded Solar Drake died when the person they were bonded with did, but they hadn't said what would happen to him if something befell Filzbalm. For both their sakes, he wanted to make sure everything was as close to perfect as possible before they tried something new.

"We'll be back in a few minutes. We should be able to borrow a magnifier without upsetting anyone currently using the lab, as long as we're quick." Del glanced at Melody, who nodded, then they took off down the hall. By the time Skylar looked back toward Solaria, she was stalking through the door to the cafeteria and he had to dash to catch up with her. Like he normally did when Skylar broke from a walk, Filzbalm took to wing and quickly caught up to Solaria.

"You're okay with them double checking things, aren't you?" Skylar asked as he caught up with her at the tray pickup.

"Sure. I'm used to folks not taking everything I see for granted." She started down the line.

There was something in her tone that made Skylar worried she was a little irritated with Del and Melody for doubting her. One of the first things he'd learned about Pantherians in general, and particularly Solaria, was that cat people were moody. He decided to keep quiet until they reached the table.

Since they were the only two at the table, he put his tray across from hers. "You know, we've spent all this time getting Filzbalm ready for the climate, but you haven't said anything about what I'm going to need."

"How cold tolerant are you?" She didn't look at him as she cut into her food.

He set Filzbalm's food off to the side before answering. "Hummassa was a tropical world, so not very."

"Then after we test the ring, we need to spend some of your MTU credits and get you a coat, gloves, hat, heavy pants, boots…unless they happen to have a thermal suit programmed in and you've got enough for it. Then we'll just get you one of those to wear under your regular clothes and you should be fine." She shook her head, then looked up. "Things aren't as bad as everyone claims. Just because all the inhabitants of Pantheria have fur, everyone thinks the climate is really awful. Trust me. Things won't be as miserable as they would if we went in winter. You do realize there are worlds that even we find too cold to deal with."

"And most of them are fairly small with extremely thin atmospheres." Although Skylar wasn't great at Universal Cartography, he had done a bit of research on Pantheria and similar planets. Pantheria was one of the larger cold worlds that could still support life. Most of the other large cold worlds were too far from their sun to sustain life, while many of the other cold worlds were small and had little to no atmosphere.

"And we're lucky we aren't going to any of them," Solaria said as she cut another piece of her meat, then slowly chewed.

For a couple of minutes, silence settled over the table until Del and Melody came back, looking very happy.

Del held the ring out to Filzbalm. "Looks just like what we sent over. Should work just like the simulation did."

Filzbalm took the ring. It looked almost boulder-like in his tiny talons. *"It doesn't feel dangerous."*

Skylar chuckled as he finished his last bite of salad. "He said it doesn't feel dangerous."

"It isn't." Del stood there for a moment as Filzbalm slid the ring on. It was so large that he had to push it up to his upper leg for it to stay on. On his lower leg, it kept sliding down and hitting the top of his claws.

"Are you going to get something to eat?" Solaria asked.

"Can we go test it first?" Del countered. "I'm too nervous right now to eat."

Solaria looked at her empty plate. "I guess so."

"Good," Melody said. "'Cause I'm with Del. I can't eat until we know if this is going to work."

Skylar and Solaria rose, and as a group, they hurried out of the cafeteria to Solaria's room.

"How long are we going to need to be in there before we know something?" Solaria asked as Filzbalm lighted on her shoulder and wrapped his tail around her neck.

"Not long," Melody replied, holding up her tablet. "I'm going in with you and can monitor the ring. I figure it should kick in right after you cross the threshold."

Del nodded. "I agree. We should know something fairly quickly."

A needle of fear lanced through Skylar. He didn't like the unknown, and not having any other way to test the ring beyond Filzbalm going in to try and get it to turn on made him nervous. "If anything goes wrong, you get him out here as fast as you can."

Solaria reached up and stroked Filzbalm's head. "I will."

"I can get myself out if someone leaves the door open," Filzbalm added as he nuzzled Solaria's hand so she'd scratch him behind the tiny orange horns he was growing.

That made Skylar feel a little better. "Yeah, good point. Leave the door open."

"As long as the others don't object," Solaria said, taking a couple of steps toward the door. "Don't forget that I live with three other people, just like you do. They might be in the middle of something they don't want you looking in on."

Skylar sighed and rolled his eyes. Drawing things out like this made it worse. "Okay. Fine. Get in there and let's see if this is going to work."

"Just relax, Skylar," Solaria said. "Everything's going to be all right." She opened the door and put her hand across it so it wouldn't close on Melody before stepping through herself.

The biometric shield flashed, knocking Filzbalm backward as Solaria shrieked and an alarm sounded in the halls.

"What just happened?" Skylar offered his arm to Filzbalm so he could land.

Solaria turned toward them, her hand going to her shoulder where Filzbalm had left several long scratches, so deep that blood was oozing out and discoloring her gray fur.

"This room is for girls only," an electronic voice rang out in the hall. "Boys are not allowed past the doorway."

"Interesting." Del cocked his head and looked from the door to Filzbalm. "I guess Ms. Grissom updated the biometrics to identify Filzbalm as male. Since he's officially a student here, that makes sense. I wasn't expecting the shield to keep him out of Solaria's room."

"I wasn't either," Solaria said as Melody appeared from the bathroom with a towel for her to press over the scratches. "Little guy, you've got some sharp claws. Your predator came out." She didn't sound mad, which made Skylar happy.

"I am sorry," Filzbalm said loud enough that it made Skylar's eyes hurt, but he understood he was probably trying to project enough for Solaria to hear him. *"I didn't know what was happening. Something pushed me off your shoulder and I just tried to stay on."*

She looked at him as she pressed the towel over her wounds. "No worries."

Up and down the hall doors opened and students peered out.

Solaria sighed, then returned the looks. "Nothing to see here!" she roared loudly enough that most everyone ducked back into their rooms.

Ms. Grissom came dashing down the hallway. "What's going on?" In addition to being the school counselor, she was also the monitor for Solaria's hallway.

"We didn't know Filzbalm would set off the biometric shield." Solaria pulled the towel away and frowned. "Nothing major."

Ms. Grissom, a human woman with gray hair and piercing blue eyes, stared at all of them. As usual, she was dressed more like a back-world artist than a school counselor. "And why were you trying to get into her room?" She focused her question on Filzbalm.

Since she was a lower-level reader, Filzbalm addressed her with the same volume he had Solaria. Skylar tried to brace himself, but it didn't help. The mental voice still hurt. *"We're trying to make sure the warm ring Del and Melody made for me works, and Solaria's room is cold enough it should trigger it."* He held out his foreleg so the ring was easily seen. *"We're trying to get ready for break since Skylar and I are going to Pantheria."*

Ms. Grissom nodded and pushed her glasses up on her nose. "I hadn't thought of that when I approved you going off station." She turned her attention to Del as Melody stepped out of Solaria's room. "I will need to see the schematics on this device before I can approve it for use here on the station."

Del held out his tablet to her. He didn't say anything and his gray skin had a dark tinge to it, something that made Skylar wonder if he was embarrassed to be facing Ms. Grissom. He had no idea if Del had ever been in trouble at school before they borrowed the school shuttle.

"I can email them to you if you like, so you can review them at your leisure," Melody said. "It's totally safe. We incorporated some of Dad's micro-tech into it so it would be small enough for Filzbalm."

With a curt nod, Ms. Grissom handed the tablet back to Del. "With a quick scan, it appears safe enough. Ms. Porsche, I'd appreciate that email. I'll forward it to Professor H'lld'l and have him look over it. We should have it cleared by morning."

Skylar's heart sank. If they weren't going to be able to test it until morning, they might not be able to get another one made before they had to leave. Or even if they used the spot Del had reserved at the MTU, they might not have time to test and fix a second one. Then he and Filzbalm would be limited in what they could do on Pantheria.

Ms. Grissom glanced at all of them. "Filzbalm, take off the ring for now. You can test it tomorrow." A thoughtful line crossed her brow as she held out her hand for the ring. "We can probably get permission for you to try it out in the kitchen's freezer. I'll come find you when we're ready to proceed."

Filzbalm flew over to her shoulder, then stretched down her arm to give her the ring. *"Here."* He sounded a little sad as he dropped the platinum trinket in her open palm, then returned to Skylar.

"I'll find all of you in the morning." Ms. Grissom turned and strolled down the hall, back toward her personal room at the end near the main open space.

Silence fell in the hall again until the sound of her door sliding closed reached them, then everyone relaxed.

"Okay, I guess I should've thought of the ring being unapproved tech," Del muttered. "But it's not anything major. It's not going to hurt anyone…well, other than Filzbalm if it malfunctions."

Solaria waved away his concern. "I'll bet Professor Bug wants to talk to both of you as soon as he looks at it. We'll have the ring before lunch and be back on schedule." She pulled the towel away from her shoulder again and grinned. "I've even stopped bleeding. Being a predator who heals easily is awesome."

"Is that why Ms. Grissom didn't seem worried about your scratches?" Skylar asked. There was still a lot he didn't know about his friends, and none of it seemed really important until something like the scrapes came up, and he had to figure out what was going on. Back on Hummassa, any teacher would've had a bigger fit about the scratches than the ring.

"Right. Most Pantherians heal very quickly. We only really worry about wounds that get to the bone." Solaria balled up the towel. "Don't worry about it."

Skylar had never been around anyone who could heal as quickly as he'd just seen her do. He healed fast, but not that fast. It was cool, and a little scary. It made him wonder what other tricks Pantherians had that he didn't know about.

4
Final Preparations

GATHERING THINGS together for the break, Skylar crammed clothes into a duffle bag on his bed. After getting final approval on Filzbalm's ring, he felt a lot better about the trip to Pantheria. He and Del had ended up using Del's scheduled time with the MTU to get Skylar appropriate clothes for the climate. When they were done, they'd all but depleted Skylar's MTU credits. Skylar suddenly found himself wanting to spend another couple of days in the farm area before they went so he wouldn't come back and be unable to replicate anything he needed. Sometimes he really wished he was a corp-brat so his family would provide him with a nearly endless flow of money for the things he wanted.

As Skylar got the last of his stuff shoved into the bag, Del's dermal com beeped. Del stared at his wrist for a moment.

"Well, aren't you going to answer it?" Skylar couldn't remember the last time Del's com had beeped. Like Skylar, he didn't have a lot of friends, either on station or off, and most of Del's family tended to send communications through his grandfather.

"Yeah," Del grumbled as he tapped his wrist to answer the call. Even though the ring worked the way it was supposed to, and Del and Melody had received a lot of praise from Professor H'lld'l, Del had continued to be grouchy.

Skylar turned away from Del so he wouldn't look like he was trying to listen in on his conversation. He was nearly packed, but they still had half a day before Phil was scheduled to arrive. Classes had already let out so the students could finish their plans for departure. Skylar wasn't sure what he was going to do with the time, and was thinking about heading up to the park when Del whooped.

He turned and, for the first time in weeks, Del wore a grin.

"Good news?"

Del nodded. "The best. That was the head curator of the Museum of Time and Space on Nesbit."

Skylar was never going to forget Nesbit or the Museum. It was on the trip back from the museum that Solaria had taken Filzbalm's egg away from Pathal, the corp-brat who'd gotten it from someone there. Nesbit had been the starting point of his life taking a major swing toward the positive.

"They want me to come and do a week-long internship," Del continued. "He was very impressed with the 'thank you' note I sent him after our tour. Apparently, he asked Ms. Grissom about me and liked what he heard. He wants me to see what goes on behind the scenes there." He flopped down on his bed, then immediately got up and started pacing. "This is great. I can't believe this. Who knew a simple thank you could set something like this in motion? It's the type of opportunity I've been wanting for a long time. If I do great there for this, maybe I can get longer internships when we have other breaks. Then when we graduate, I might aleady have a job. It would be so great to actually have something to look forward to as opposed to having to go and farm fish for the rest of my life."

"This is awesome," Skylar agreed. He knew how much Del wanted to get a job using his intelligence, since his feeler skills weren't really strong enough to be in high demand on the job market. He was always worried about having to go back to Tursipia and join the less-gifted members of his family doing aquaculture, although Skylar didn't see anything wrong with that. Before his mother had died, he'd never planned on leaving Hummassa, and since he wasn't artistic in any way, he'd just figured on finding something physical to do with his life.

"Yeah." Del stopped pacing and looked at Skylar. "Hey. I need to say I'm sorry."

Skylar shrugged. "For what?"

Del swallowed. "For being moody these past couple of weeks."

"I barely noticed." Skylar didn't like pointing out flaws in his friends.

"Yes you did." Filzbalm countered, and Skylar was thankful Del was just a low-lever feeler and not a reader. Filzbalm didn't try to communicate with him, and couldn't openly disagree with Skylar.

"But I'm not going to tell him that. That would make things worse."

"Sure you did. But there's been so much going on, you probably just pushed things under the rug as opposed to pointing it out." Del sat on the side of Skylar's bed. "Look. I'm a feeler—just because I'm not real strong doesn't mean I don't perceive things. I know we're trained to be honest so that others don't pick up on things, but sometimes it's really hard to do that. I'll be honest now. I was going to see if you wanted to come to Tursipia with me and Grandpa, but I needed to make sure it was okay with Grandpa first. We've been so busy since Armstrong's Rings that I just never really had the chance. Then when Solaria got the message from Phil, it was like she'd beaten me to the punch and I didn't like that. It felt like she was more important than I was."

Not growing up in a psychic household, Skylar wasn't used to such openness. It caught him by surprise.

He'd known something was wrong with Del, but hadn't been sure what it was until that moment. "Del, man, you're just as important to me as Solaria. More so in a lot of ways. You're my best friend. If I'd known you wanted me to go with you instead, I would've definitely gone. Plus, then we wouldn't have to be worrying about Filzbalm and the temperatures. I bet we'd both love the climate on Tursipia."

"Yeah, you probably would, being from a tropical planet. Next time?" There was a quiet plea in Del's voice that Skylar couldn't ignore. He hadn't realized how much he meant to Del, and didn't know how to express how much having Del around meant to him. Without Del, he probably wouldn't have been on such good terms with Solaria and would still be a constant target for the corp-brats, who had dropped their hostilities to a marginal level. Between Del and Solaria being his friends he was more accepted, and Filzbalm being out in the open gave him an almost revered status with the non-corp-brats. But even Pathal Santos and his crew didn't go out of their way to find and humiliate any of them anymore, which was a great weight off all their shoulders.

"Definitely next time. You know how much I want to see the universe—I can't wait to see Tursipia. It'll be a lot of fun."

"I bet I can fly underwater," Filzbalm piped in as he folded his wings tight against his back and wrapped his tail around his legs, a sure sign he was prepping for a nap.

Skylar relayed the comment to Del.

"There are several species who fly underwater," Del said. "I have no doubt you'll fit right in with them."

Del stood from the bed with a jerk. "I've got to go talk to Grandpa. Let him know I'm heading to Nesbit in a couple of days. At least I've got enough credits to use the MTU to get proper clothes for an internship there. I'd hate to ruin this by looking like a wet-behind-the-fins bumpkin. See you at dinner?"

Skylar nodded. "Sure."

"Thanks for not being mad 'cause I got jealous." Del grinned and stepped toward Skylar, then stepped back as a bit of uncertainty washed off him. "Okay. Later." He turned and headed out the door.

"Why was he uncertain?" Filzbalm asked sleepily.

"I bet he's not sure how I'd handle a hug," Skylar replied as he tossed his duffle bag on the floor at the foot of the bed before stretching out and putting his hands behind his head.

"You're both feelers. He should know that a hug wouldn't upset you."

"He should. But maybe he's worried about us coming from different cultures." He knew from observing the corp-brats that a lot of the humans at the school didn't always act the way he'd been brought up to, but on Hummassa, everyone was very open and friendly. A lot of the corp-brats were closed off and stuck up, or at least that's how they acted when not around others in their peer group. If Melody had taught them all anything, it was that not all corp-brats were brats, but most of them were.

"Hey, where's Del?" Connor, Skylar's human roommate, came bursting into the room. He was a corp-brat who only bordered on brat.

"He went out to see his grandfather and tell him that he'd gotten an internship at the Museum of Time and Space over break." Skylar sat and looked at Connor. "Why? What's up?"

"We're not sure. There's an armada flying past."

"An armada?" Skylar jumped out of bed. "Who are they?"

"Nobody knows." Connor turned back to the door. "They're visible from the central shaft and some of the portals."

"Come on, Filzbalm, we've got to go see this." Skylar had seen some of the Boarisk ships that attacked Hummassa on the night his mother had been killed, and there'd been ships gathered around the docking ports at the Galaxeria when they'd visited the huge shopping space station, but all that was a lot different than an armada flying past the school.

He didn't wait for Filzbalm to land, just followed Connor out the door and into the hall. It was so crowded they could've been getting ready for breakfast. Skylar didn't bother heading to any of the rooms with windows—he knew Solaria and probably Del and Professor Aduncus would be in the central zone where there wasn't any gravity. It was where Z-GBall was played and provided the best view of the stars, if what they were looking at was in the right part of the sky.

The elevator that would take them to the top of the dome had a major line, but Skylar didn't know what else to do, so he stood there waiting for his turn.

"Hey, come on." Solaria grabbed his hand and yanked him out of the line. "We've got a better option."

Skylar did his best to be stable for Filzbalm. He didn't want to end up with scratches like Solaria had received. "Where are we going?" He noticed Melody at her side.

"She's not telling me yet either." Melody didn't sound mad—she sounded excited.

"Where's Del?" Solaria looked around as if surprised to not find him with Skylar.

"Right here." Del appeared beside Skylar, making him jump slightly. "Grandpa had to go into an emergency staff meeting."

"Emergency?" Skylar frowned as they all followed Solaria as she headed away from the students in the elevator line. "Do they think the armada is here for us?" After having one home torn away by invaders, he didn't want to think about it happening again so soon after he had started to get settled into the school.

"Nobody in the galaxy would dare attack Stars' End," Melody said as Solaria led them around the corner and down a short staircase Skylar didn't remember ever having traversed before. "We're one of the safest places around. I'm sure old Fussy Pants and Ms. Grissom have already sent warnings to the armada to keep cruising on by and not try anything. Even if they did, the conflict wouldn't last long. Too many psychics to be easily defeated. They're probably just passing by."

Del shook his head. "Then why aren't they using the stargates? We should just have flybys."

"If they have ships that are too big to fit through the stargates, they'd have to travel directly. For all we know, they've been flying for hundreds of years." Solaria opened a door and gestured for them to slip in.

Del was the last one through the door. "That might explain why Grandpa said it was an unknown armada."

"That's what Connor said when he came to get us," Skylar said. He'd never heard of an unknown armada before, but if Solaria was right and they were having to take the slow route to get somewhere because they couldn't fit in through the stargates, that might explain things. He wasn't sure why the ships hadn't been picked up by a local patrol or something. If they weren't traveling by stargate, they might've been so old they'd launched before there *were* stargates, or come from a society that hadn't been included in the stargate system. Again, it wasn't anything Skylar had heard of before. It sounded very antique.

Solaria started up another flight of stairs. "We're almost there."

"And how did you find out about this route?" Melody asked, keeping close to Solaria.

"I'm a predator. I like to know all routes in and out of places. When I first came to the academy, some of the other Pantherians took the time to show me all the small, seldom-used passages in case I might one day need them. There's a ton of service tunnels and such around. That's why we don't see all the service bots as they travel from floor to floor." Solaria stopped at another door. "Okay, it's a bit of a climb from here." She went through the door and lights came on, running up the wall in front of them. Along the same path as the lights was a series of metal rungs going up a long way.

Filzbalm took off and flew up ahead of them.

"Where does this go?" Del asked as they started up the ladder.

"You'll see." There was an excited edge to Solaria's voice.

Skylar had heard that tone before. Normally it meant adventure, a game, or a fight. Somehow, in that moment, he figured it meant an adventure.

"Wow, there's a great view up here." Filzbalm was almost as excited as Solaria.

Skylar didn't reply. He just kept on going, hoping he wouldn't give out before he got to the top of the ladder. His arms were starting to ache from the climb, even as the gravity around them grew less and less. About the time he was ready to ask for a pause to give himself a bit of a rest, Solaria stepped off the ladder and onto a narrow platform.

When Skylar caught up, he discovered the platform was part of an observation tower on the surface of Stars' End. The tower came up along the edge of the central passageway, and provided an unobstructed view of

Yeldona Three, the gas giant Stars' End orbited, and past its bulk, the rest of the system and beyond.

"Over there." Del pointed away from the planet.

Skylar turned and his breath caught. Several dozen huge ships, most nearly twice the size of Stars' End, flew through the system. Smaller ships darted between the large ones. He could see why they hadn't been able to use the stargate system. They were just too big. That also added to the theory they'd been flying for a long time. Any species that used the stargates knew to make their ships small enough to get through. Stargates were what had helped speed up interstellar travel. Without them, it would take years to get from star to star.

"Look." Solaria pointed a claw toward the closest ship. "See all those gouges and burn marks? These ships have definitely been in space a long time. I wonder why!"

"No idea," Del said. "I'd love to get a closer look at them. They might be antiques, but I bet they have some interesting tales to tell."

There was a crackle of a speaker, then Principal Fuspatula's, Old Fussy Pants, voice rang out. "All students. There's nothing to worry about. We have been unable to reach anyone on the armada, and there are no life signs or brain activity coming off the ships. We're sending probes to follow their path, but do not believe there is anything to worry about at this time. They are not close to the stargate, so they will not impede your departures. Please return to your quarters and continue your preparations for break. Your families will be advised to stick to standard flight paths and avoid the armada as they arrive and depart. We are going to let it continue its journey unmolested."

Solaria frowned. "Well, so much for spending a while watching them go by."

"They remind me of whales," Del said. "Whales like to swim past slowly, never really getting in a hurry for anything."

"We'd better get back to our rooms before the teachers come looking for us," Skylar said, reluctantly starting for the ladder that would take them back to the base of the tower. He didn't want to go. He wanted to stay and watch the huge ships fly by. He wondered, if there was no communications, or life signs and brain activity, why there were smaller ships flying among them. That didn't make much sense.

His friends followed him down.

"I bet everything's automated," Del said as they reached the door leading them back to the main part of the school. "Those smaller ships. They might be repair bots or something similar. You know, if I remember right, some of the first ships to ever leave Sol Three didn't use the stargates. They were huge things that were just trying to leave the planet due to some war or something."

Skylar chuckled. "You know, Del, if you're going to intern in a museum, you might want to brush up on your ancient history." He couldn't wait to hear about all the information Del came up with. He'd probably talk about it for weeks after break was over.

"Hey, maybe I can look up stuff while I'm there," Del said cheerfully as they started down the hall. "I bet they have a lot of information that we don't have in our history classes." It sounded like he had a cause—a subject he could devote himself to. Nothing made Del happier than having something to occupy his mind.

Del went on about the armada and the vast array of knowledge he was going to have access to at the museum as they headed back to their room. The hall slowly filled with students returning from wherever they'd gone to witness the armada, and the noise level increased as everyone speculated what race their crews might be and where they were going.

Right before they split off from Solaria, her com beeped. She motioned for everyone to stop as she answered it. "Sure. We'll be ready…that soon?" She glanced at Skylar. "Uncle Phil's running early. Can you be ready to fly in an hour?"

That was before break was supposed to start. "Will that be a problem with the school?"

Solaria shook her head. "This is Uncle Phil…he's got pull with Ms. Grissom."

The idea of getting out of school before the corp-brats made Skylar grin. "My bag's packed. I'll be ready."

"We're good to go, Uncle Phil. See you soon." Solaria tapped her com off. "Okay, you've got forty-five minutes. Go get your stuff. I'll let the others know and we'll meet you in the docking ring. Uncle Phil said he'd be at airlock five."

"Cool." Skylar glanced at Melody. "Well, I guess we'll see you in a couple weeks. Have a good break."

"You too. I've heard Pantheria is a beautiful planet." She grinned, then her com beeped. "I guess a lot of folks are getting clear of the armada and heading in. See you." She tapped her wrist and headed off as she started talking to whoever had just called.

"Let's go get your stuff, Skylar." Del started toward their hall as Solaria headed toward hers. "Luckily I've got a couple of days before the shuttle from the museum will be here to pick me up. I'll miss the rush out of here."

If he was going to get to head out an hour or so early, Skylar was hoping Del was too. The sooner Del left for the museum, the less time he'd have to sit around and worry about things.

Even as he opened the door, Skylar was thankful they were leaving early—he wasn't sure what he would've done for the extra time himself. They might've spent it trying to start researching the armada, but they didn't really have much time to even get started on that, unless Del was able to get lucky and put in just the right word to get the search going and found what they needed in minutes instead of hours or days. He really hoped Del found out everything about the armada while he was at the museum, and could tell them all about it when they got back to the station after break.

5
Pantheria

WITH HIS duffle bag thrown over his shoulder, Skylar made it to airlock five right behind Solaria, or at least he hoped it was Solaria. After mistaking Mutanio Leapanno, one of the male Pantherians at school, for her on the trip to the museum, Skylar made a point to not call out again unless he was sure the person he was yelling for was the right one. Solaria hadn't said anything about anyone else catching a ride with Phil—but that might've been an oversight on her part. They had all been really busy getting ready for break.

"Skylar!" Solaria shouted from behind him.

He turned and there she was, hurrying down the corridor from the main hall with two of her roommates in tow. "Hey. I'm surprised I beat you here."

"Sorry we're running a little behind." She caught up with him easily, then passed him to get to the airlock.

"Leonada had trouble finding all of her family gifts after the excitement of the armada," Felicianna Palas said.

In the past months, Skylar had met Solaria's roommates, but hadn't had much interaction with them. He kept getting the feeling that they weren't real fond of him, since he was a human and they weren't. It might've been something as simple as they were girls and he was a boy—but then, Mutanio treated him the same way, so he wasn't sure.

"I still think you moved things around on me," Leonada said, running her fingers through her short golden fur.

"And why would I do that?" Felicianna looked slightly offended, but a faint feeling of contrition rolled off her, telling Skylar she probably *had* done something to make things harder for Leonada to find.

A soft chime rang and the airlock opened with a hiss. All conversation stopped as Philaneo Clawson, Solaria's Uncle Phil, walked out.

He scanned the group with his slitted yellow eyes, then a grin split his furry brown face. "Very good. Looks like you're all here. Everyone knows the drill. Go in, stash your bags and get comfortable. I need to go speak to Fiona…ah…Ms. Grissom for a moment, then we'll be on our way." He gave Solaria a quick hug. "Why don't you and Skylar grab seats on the flight deck?" He looked over her shoulder as he released her and gave Skylar a quick wink.

Skylar's heart raced. He'd hoped he would get to fly where he could watch what was going on, particularly with the strange armada floating past, but he wasn't sure. The last time he'd flown with Phil, on the way back from Armstrong's Rings, he'd had to sit in the back with Solaria, Del and Melody. The fact they'd all been in a lot of trouble then might've had something to do with that, though.

Ignoring the looks from the other Pantherians boarding Phil's ship, Skylar and Filzbalm followed Solaria into the cockpit. Where there'd been just three seats the last time Skylar had been there, now a forth had been added.

Solaria walked over to the seat and pushed on it. It didn't move. "Looks like it's maglocked." She tossed her bag in the corner, then plopped down in it. "Sometimes Uncle Phil surprises me."

"What do you mean?" Skylar dropped his bag on top of hers and took the seat he'd ridden in before. Filzbalm hopped off his shoulder and onto the back of the seat, then rested his head on top of Skylar's.

"This chair for one thing." She ran a finger along one of the control panels, then looked at it, frowning slightly. "He's not prone to getting new things. Intergal Rescue doesn't pay great and this chair wasn't cheap. Plus, did you notice it looked like he cleaned up in the back? This ship is normally a mess. It's like he's trying to impress someone."

"Do you think it's Ms. Grissom?" Skylar had been excited enough about getting to ride where he could see out that he hadn't noticed the back area look like Phil had cleaned up.

"Could be." Solaria let out a long breath and tapped a claw against the arm of her chair. "Uncle Phil has always had a soft spot for Ms. Grissom. Makes a point to stop in and see her whenever he picks me up or drops me off."

"Does he normally give the rest of the Pantherians a ride too?" Skylar was still amazed nobody had told him there were going to be others on the flight, but he didn't want to say anything since Pantherians were so easy to upset.

"Sometimes. It depends on if he's free or not. Sometimes we all have to take the community shuttle." She bent over the control panels again as if inspecting them for dirt. "He's definitely been cleaning."

"So you guys don't have your folks come pick you up?" Somehow Skylar thought most of the students had parents that came and picked them up.

Solaria chuckled. "Most of our folks can't afford a ship of their own, or the stargate fees. You know we're not corp-brats. Pantheria has a community shuttle for various off-world trips, including getting us to and from

Stars' End. But since I've been coming here, Uncle Phil normally gives us all a ride, although we're more than a few students now and things are getting a bit cramped."

"And that's not a problem," Phil said as he came through the cabin door. "As long as we've got room to squeeze a couple more seats in, I'll help the community out."

"Thanks for the ride, Phil," Skylar said as Phil settled into the pilot's chair. "I really appreciate the opportunity to see more of the galaxy."

"Glad you could make it, Skylar. I think this is going to be good for you." Phil tapped his com. "This is Philaneo in *Rescue Paw One*, preparing to leave airlock five." He flipped some switches and the control panel came to life. He pushed a button and the ship shook just slightly as it pulled away from the station. "See you in a couple of weeks." Then he took hold of the yoke and steered for space.

Another ship quickly came in and took his place at the airlock.

The unknown armada still floated along toward the side of the solar system opposite the stargate. The ships appeared about half the size they had earlier.

"Do you know anything about those ships?" Skylar asked, hoping to get some interesting information he could take back to Del.

Phil pursed his lips before replying. "I guess I really shouldn't be surprised you kids are interested in them. You're interested in everything, aren't you?"

"Yes," Solaria said before Skylar could. "They look old and battered."

"So they do." Clearing the traffic around the station, Phil turned the ship away from the armada and toward the stargate. "Fiona didn't have much information. Professor Aduncus wasn't able to get more than a bit of mental emptiness from their direction. The station's probe drones didn't do any better. It's not an armada that's shown up on the space charts before. Most of those, particularly ones in well-traveled space, have been plotted and alerts are issued when they fly through populated areas."

"Wait, there are other ships like this out in the galaxy?" Skylar wished he could still see the armada as they flew toward the stargate.

Phil shrugged as he made a minor course correction to avoid a flashy ship that was flying a bit erratically. "Yes and no. There are several fleets of old ships that have been found traveling between solar systems. Most of them are from fairly primitive civilizations, and we leave them alone if they have crews in cryogenic suspension. Depending on which race they are, the Galactic Council might decide to wake them up or not. The more dangerous ones we keep an eye on, but let them float away in hopes they never become a problem. But in the cases of cryo, there's still brain activity. Aduncus was amazed that there isn't. The school's not equipped to dispatch a survey mission over to the ships, so they've put in a request with the Council to send one out. There's a possibility that since we're so far out on the edge of everything here, it may have come from another galaxy and have technology we don't understand."

"That's cool." Skylar suddenly wished he could have the option to go explore the strange ships. To be the first human to encounter something new and interesting would be great. But even if they weren't about to take the stargate halfway across the galaxy to Pantheria, he doubted the school would give the students the opportunity to volunteer to go somewhere potentially dangerous. They'd just finished up their punishment for stealing the school ship and going to Armstrong's Rings.

He didn't think it would be a good idea to do anything like that anytime soon.

He wasn't sure how much trouble he could get into before he'd get kicked out of school, and if that happened, he didn't have anywhere to go. He and Filzbalm would probably end up back on Armstrong's Rings, never to leave the planet again. Solar Drakes weren't supposed to be out in the universe, and it had taken renegotiating an old treaty with them to let Skylar and Filzbalm leave the first time.

"Maybe, maybe not." Phil looked like he was going to say something else, then he glanced over at Solaria. "So, what all do you have planned for Skylar? Anything I should be worried about?"

"Why would you be worried about something I did?" Skylar asked. The sudden change of subject bothered him, but he was going to let it go.

"Ms. Grissom has put me in charge of your safety," Phil said. "If anything happens to you, she's going to skin me alive." Then he smiled. "Even orphans need someone to watch out for them."

His statement made a warm spot in Skylar's chest. He often felt like he and Filzbalm were alone in the universe. Sure, he had Del, Solaria, and Melody, but knowing that Phil felt like he should watch over him made him feel better than he had in a long time. He wasn't ready to take on the universe on his own, and it was good knowing he wasn't going to have to. A happy smile spread across his face. "Thanks, Phil."

"If it's okay, I was planning on taking him on a Belesk hunt and showing him some of more scenic places, like the ice falls and fire plains," Solaria said, drawing attention away from Skylar.

"Sounds like a good idea. The ice falls are just starting to melt, so it's the perfect time of year to see them," Phil said with a thoughtful nod. "The fire plains should be breaking out in flowers in the next week or so—if you're lucky, you'll get to see that. Your mother and I will be happy to go out on the hunt with you. It sounds like you're going to try to make Skylar into an honorary Pantherian."

Solaria chuckled and shook her head. "I think it's going to take more time than we have on this break for that to happen. But he's a predator too, so he should get more in touch with his inner hunter."

Phil laughed, then turned to Skylar. "Just remember Skylar, you don't have to run around a strange planet naked if you don't want to."

Although the Hummassans he'd grown up with weren't as stuck on clothes as most humans, their planet was tropical. He couldn't imagine running around naked on an ice world like Pantheria. "I don't think I'm going to this time."

"If you're going to be an explorer, you might have to think about going native from time to time." Phil turned back to the instrument panels. "It's a good way to make friends. But I can definitely say that things can get awkward when you do."

Solaria went back to tapping the arm of her chair with her claws. "I'm not going to have to stay dressed the whole time, am I?"

"I guess that's between you and Skylar," Phil said. "If he's okay with you being naked, then it should be fine. However, I'd also suggest you take it up with your mother. She might have something to say on the subject."

"Yeah." Solaria rolled her eyes. "Mom normally has something to say on most subjects."

Skylar repressed a laugh. His mother had been the same way, and at the time, it got old fast, but now he wondered how she'd react to him going to spend a couple of weeks on an ice planet with cat people who preferred to not wear clothes. She'd probably throw a complete fit and decide it wasn't something he was going to do. But then, she'd been so terrified of psychics, she wouldn't have let him go to Stars' End either. When he'd left Hummassa, his life had changed dramatically, and he wasn't sure his mother would recognize him anymore. He reached up and stroked Filzbalm's muzzle. He would give almost anything to have his mother back, anything but Filzbalm. The little Solar Drake filled his soul in ways he could never begin to explain, and he never wanted to do anything that would hurt their bond.

PANTHERIA WAS a huge, light gray ball floating in the dark sea of space. There were two small moons that moved in a perfectly synchronized orbit. The moons glowed with a bright silver light that seemed to come from their surfaces as opposed to the yellow sun the planet circled. Clouds played across the planet's topography, giving it the appearance of some snow storms Skylar had seen in video games. It was an incredible sight. Goose bumps rolled over his skin as he shivered. It was surreal, so incredibly different than anything he'd seen in real life before.

"This is Philaneo Clawson in *Rescue Paw One*, requesting landing at the main space port." Phil angled the ship down before he continued speaking. "Roger that. I'll be at the port in ten minutes."

Phil kept his focus on the descent, but flipped a switch on the control panel to his left. "Students, we'll be landing in nine minutes. Please make sure you're buckled in. I've been informed that your families are already waiting for us at the space port." His voice echoed through the ship.

He'd never used his intercom when Skylar had been on the ship before, just yelled into the main cabin. Skylar wondered if he was being a bit more formal due to the other students onboard.

Phil flipped a switch and the front view screen darkened as it started to show the glow from the reentry flare the atmosphere caused on the nose of the ship. Even though he knew he wouldn't be able to see much due to the flare, Skylar wished the screen was still active so he could watch their descent as soon as the flare dissipated.

As if reading his mind, Phil flipped the switch back to its original position and the screen cleared, showing a mountainous, snowy landscape. Several oceans covered a good portion of the world, with large land masses spotting the planet. Phil banked the ship as they flew over one of the oceans, heading toward the biggest land mass Skylar could see. What looked like a massive city occupied part of a large peninsula near the ocean.

Phil banked again, and their flight leveled out, heading straight for a building with a number of other ships parked around it. From the looks of it, the structure was simply a landing pad. There were passageways spreading out from it to other, larger buildings.

Seconds later, Phil set down between two huge ships. As soon as they landed, the power cycled down, and there was the soft click of a walkway attaching to the airlock.

Phil flipped a few switches and stood. "Okay folks, we're on the ground. Get your bags and head on out. I think everyone knows where to go."

There was a hearty round of thanks, and the other passengers began grabbing their bags and running for the airlock.

"You guys also know when to be back here if you want a ride back to school," Phil said as he leaned against the passageway threshold. "If you aren't here, I'm not waiting. If anything happens to my schedule, I'll let you know."

Everyone shouted, "We'll remember."

Skylar glanced at Solaria, still seated in her chair. "Are we leaving or not?" He wanted to go out and see what the spaceport was like.

"Give them a minute," Solaria said. "Uncle Phil's got to do a couple of things to lock down the ship before he leaves. He's probably already arranged for his hover car to be ready for us."

The mention of a hover car sent a chill through Skylar. He and his mother had been riding in a hover car when the Boarisk attacked, and she'd been killed. He'd somehow survived, but he still had nightmares of his mother's arm sticking through the vehicle's windshield before the car exploded. He wasn't sure what he'd expected on Pantheria, but he hadn't thought it would be a hover car, although they were the most popular form of land transport in the galaxy.

"We'll be okay." Filzbalm said as he hopped from the back of Skylar's chair to his shoulder. *"There aren't any Boarisk attacking today."*

The way Filzbalm was always in his head, listening to his thoughts and reacting to his fears had taken Skylar a little while to get used to, but it was becoming very comforting and reassuring. *"Thanks."* He ran his fingers along Filzbalm's wing, finding the spot near where it joined to his back that Filzbalm loved to have scratched.

Phil looked back onto the flight deck. "Okay, you three, let's get her locked up and head to the house. Solaria's mom is probably already working on dinner."

"What can we do?" Skylar asked, eager to help out in any way he could. Like everything else with space travel, he wanted to learn it all, even the little things that some people might find tedious.

"Well, since most of the shut down and refuel are automated and I've already sent the power down commands to the central computer, all we need to do is grab our stuff and get out. I can lock the door from the outside." He waved them out of the flight deck. On the way through the main cabin, he stopped and grabbed a medium-sized bag from a cupboard.

Skylar followed Solaria to the airlock, and they stepped out and into a gray hallway. The first thing that hit Skylar was the dramatic temperature drop. He suddenly wondered if Phil made the climate in his ship closer to what Skylar found comfortable when Skylar was aboard. He shivered.

"My ring's working just fine," Filzbalm announced, even as he crouched down in Skylar's shoulder like he might be cold himself.

"Good," Skylar said as he and Solaria waited for Phil to clear the airlock.

"Is his ring working the way it's supposed to?" Solaria asked, obviously having guessed what Skylar was replying to.

"Yeah. That's a good thing. I just hope it holds out the whole trip." Skylar was still a little nervous about what would happen if the ring failed at the wrong time and Filzbalm got too cold. He was already wishing he'd thought to put on his heavier clothes before they left Stars' End.

"I trust Del and Melody to have gotten it right," Solaria said as Phil emerged. "It'll hold out."

"What will hold out?" Phil tapped a series of numbers on the airlock's keypad. "Oh, I bet you're worried about that warm ring Del and Melody worked up. I'm with Solaria, I bet everything's going to be fine. Now let's get down to the parking area so we can head out."

Skylar and Solaria followed Phil across the access tunnel to an escalator that went down several stories. The escalator made Skylar stumble to a stop as its steps rolled out below him. The entire conveyance was done in light grays and whites, like most everything Skylar had seen on the planet to that point. On the sides of the escalator, some artist had gone in and made it looked like a rocky waterfall—even the moving steps looked more like flowing water than metal. It was surreal and for a moment, it looked like if Skylar stepped onto it, he was going to be swept down the side of a snowy cliff. It was only after he saw Solaria and Phil standing there gently going down that his mind accepted he wasn't going to die, and he stepped on.

The whole thing made him wonder—if the Pantherians had taken so much time to make the escalator at the space port look like it was part of their natural world, what more they had done? He couldn't wait to see it all.

6
Aunt Blizza

THE RIDE from the spaceport to Indruias, the outlying settlement where Solaria's parents lived, took several hours. The entire time, it felt like she pointed out every possible landmark she thought Skylar might be interested in. Things like the Norvashan Icefalls, which was where the Cordoran River splashed over the last rocks of the Holcashan Mountains and onto the Lasholoran Plain, would be forever etched in his memory.

Since he loved experiencing new things, Skylar welcomed all of Solaria's commentary. He wanted to know and see everything. It was all so different from Hummassa, which was basically a tropical, swampy planet. He knew what ice and snow were, but he'd never seen them in the vast quantities he was faced with while riding in Phil's hover car.

"Hey, there are the Pillars of Folica." Solaria pointed to a trio of towering stone spires that reached several hundred feet into the air. They were covered in cascading ice runoff that made them so round they nearly touched, yet the ice was clear enough to show the brown stones beneath.

"They never completely thaw," she explained. "There's a legend that says if the Pillars of Folica ever completely thaw that our people will be forced to leave the planet and never come back. I hope that never happens. I love my home."

Phil chuckled as he turned the wheel. "The odds of that happening are astronomical. That's why it's a legend. Pantheria never gets warm enough, especially in this area, for something with so much built-up ice to thaw."

"But we'll have a ringside seat for it, if it does." Solaria gestured in the direction they were driving and her ears twitched in a sure sign that she was getting excited. "We're almost home."

On the horizon, a series of domed buildings dotted the landscape. They were all gray and white, looking more like huge boulders than any houses Skylar had seen before. Similar to parts of the spaceport, it looked as if the settlement was designed to fit in with the environment.

"This place has grown since the last time I was here," Phil said, steering the hover car to the right.

"Several new families had moved in when I was here in the fall," Solaria said. "Mother told me they were trying to get as many new folks as possible, in hopes of getting enough people for more government money for civic improvements."

"Good luck with that," Phil muttered. "The Galactic Council is tightening the purse strings on a lot of things. We're even seeing that in Intergal Rescue. We've had to cut back on the amount of time we spend at the scene of tragedies."

"Is that why no one ever found Teir?" Skylar asked after his best friend from Hummassa every chance he got, and there was never any word of finding him, alive or dead. It was like Teir had just vanished.

Phil pursed his lips and sighed. "I hate to admit it, but probably. I know most of us would've liked to have at least another month on Hummassa, but the head office didn't have the funds for it, and there were other worlds crying for help."

Skylar knew that Phil and the rest of the Intergal Rescue team went from planet to planet helping find people after disasters, but beyond that, he wasn't sure how they operated. Were there certain criteria they had to follow for what constituted a disaster, or did they just get dispatched to poorer areas that couldn't afford to fund the rescue efforts, or places that didn't have the raw manpower or resources? He took the opportunity to ask, "What kind of help were the other worlds needing?"

Phil got a faraway, thoughtful look and started counting off on his stubby, claw-tipped fingers. "There was a massive asteroid strike on Yutalan—if we hadn't shown up in time, it could've been an extinction level event. The asteroid was so solid, their planetary defense system couldn't break it up in time to save them. As it was, all of their continents were moved by the resulting planetquakes and we had to employ atmospheric scrubbers to clean the dust out. It took a couple of weeks to get things where the locals could handle it. Then there was a strange attack on the Tulica system, where the sun was hit by an energy weapon and pushed to supernova. We had five inhabited planets to evacuate in two days. Then we had to disperse them to other systems that needed people."

"Wait a minute." Skylar turned in his seat and stared at Phil. "How did somebody get an energy weapon close enough to a star when there were five inhabited planets in the system? Shouldn't someone have spotted them and stopped them?" It didn't make sense, just like the strange armada back at Stars' End hadn't made sense. He thought everything in the galaxy had been tracked and identified.

"These are strange times in the systems of the Galactic Council," Phil said, turning again and pointing toward a large dome with several smaller domes around it. There was fencing around the larger building that appeared to have been designed to hold animals. "We're not sure exactly what's going on, but things like exploding suns, Boarisk raids, ancient armadas, an increase in the number of rogue comets and other events are occurring more frequently. Planets on the rims are getting scared, and those in the central habitable systems seem to be waiting for things to start happening to them." He pulled up in front of the main dome, parking in the midst of three other hover cars and a couple of utility vehicles. "Unless they ask, don't let your folks know I told you guys about the unrest."

Solaria patted him on the shoulder. "We'll keep our mouths shut, won't we, Skylar?"

Skylar nodded. "They won't hear it from me."

"Me, either," Filzbalm chimed in. Skylar didn't bother relaying it.

Two female Pantherians came out of the large door that looked like the main door to the dome. One of them looked a lot like Phil, but had a feminine grace to her. The other moved slower, and had fur marked like Solaria's, mottled gray and white. She looked older, but Skylar couldn't say exactly why. There was just something about her jerky movement, and the slightly slumped way she held herself. If she wasn't older, she'd had a rough life, or something wrong with her.

Solaria pushed open her door and jumped out of the hover car. "Mother!" She ran and threw her arms around the brown-furred woman who resembled Phil.

"Solaria!" Her mother picked her up and spun her around, then put her down and looked at her. "You've grown again. An inch and five pounds. All muscle from what I can tell."

Solaria nodded. "If there is a positive result from us having to work in the farm area, it's putting on muscle. Mucking out stalls is hard work."

"And hard work is good for you." Her mother turned and put her arm around Solaria's waist. "And this must be Skylar Mars."

Skylar offered his hand. "Yes, ma'am. Pleased to meet you."

She ignored his hand and gave him a warm hug. It was the first time anyone had hugged him since his mother had died. Emotions flashed through him. He realized how much he missed his mother, and he felt a genuine happiness from Solaria's mother.

"Now Felonia, let the boy breathe," Phil said, touching her arm. "I'm not sure how much of that he's used to, plus you just met him. He might be worried you're going to eat him."

"Sorry." Felonia stepped back, then pulled Phil into a hug. "We're a very affectionate people, brother, you know that."

Phil laughed and patted her back. "Sometimes a little too well."

Seeing how normal their family appeared made Skylar happy he'd come with Solaria and Phil. In the past months, he hadn't had anyone around to make him feel like part of a family. Solaria and Del were the closest things he had to it.

"Don't forget about me," Filzbalm added.

"I couldn't if I tried." Skylar reached up for him, then realized he wasn't on his shoulder, but hovering above it.

"And this must be Filzbalm," Felonia said, holding out her hand to him. "Solaria has told me a lot about you too."

Filzbalm landed on her hand and gave her a short bow. *"She's very kind."*

He hadn't spoken loud like he did when he was trying to get Solaria to hear him, so Skylar relayed what he said.

Felonia laughed. "I do my best, although I'm sure there are people who would disagree with you." She addressed Filzbalm, and not Skylar, telling Skylar that she viewed him as sentient, and that raised his opinion of her even higher.

"And when you don't introduce everyone, it doesn't exactly look good on you," the older woman said.

Solaria laughed. "Oh, Aunt Blizza, sorry. You know how things are. Skylar, this is my Aunt Blizza. Aunt Blizza, this is my good friend Skylar Mars, and his Solar Drake Filzbalm."

Aunt Blizza cocked her head and looked at Filzbalm. "I thought that was what you were when I heard you. Never thought I'd actually see a Solar Drake. Your kind are very elusive."

Felonia took Blizza's arm. "They are very unique and he's quite lovely. Now let's head into the house. Aniu will be home shortly and we should have everything ready." She glanced back at Phil. "Sorry, he's not here to greet you all, but there are some interesting developments at the site. If you all hadn't been coming in, I'd still be there myself."

Skylar wondered what she was talking about. Solaria hadn't told him much about her parents, or what they did.

As if hearing his internal questions, Solaria glanced at him as they all started toward the door. "Mom and Dad are archeologists. They've been working a dig site not far from here. Mom thinks it predates the settlement of Pantheria."

"The settlement of Pantheria?" Skylar thought the Pantherians were the original inhabitants of the planet, but that made it sound like they weren't.

Felonia glanced around, and a nervousness that hadn't been there a few seconds before rolled off her. "Let's get inside." She gestured and the door swung open.

Skylar was happy with the idea of getting inside. He still hadn't had time to change into the warmer clothes he'd brought along, and the springtime cool was starting to make his teeth chatter. He wished he had a ring or something similar to Filzbalm's that would help generate heat around him.

While the inside of the dome wasn't that much warmer than outside had been, it was enough to take the bite of the temperature away.

"Solaria, why don't you show Skylar where he can put his bag? And I bet he would like to change into something a bit warmer. Unless he didn't bring anything because you didn't warn him about our temperatures."

She frowned. "Mom. He's my friend. I wouldn't do that to a friend."

"Good." She let go of Blizza's arm. "I've got the room across from yours set up for him."

"Come on Skylar." Solaria shifted her bag higher on her shoulder. "Let's get you two settled, then Dad should be home and we can eat. I don't know about you, but I'm hungry and I'm sure Filzbalm is."

As he followed her across the wide hall that ran across the top of what appeared to be a communal space, Skylar laughed. "You know he's always hungry."

"I am not." Filzbalm sounded indignant. *"After I eat, I am not hungry for at least two hours."* His words were loud enough that Skylar knew Solaria had heard him.

Blizza drew in a quick breath, causing Skylar to turn toward her. The old woman's eyes were large and she stared at Filzbalm.

"I think she can hear me," he said. *"I didn't think most people could."*

"I'm not most people." Blizza's mental voice was a lot stronger than her physical one had been.

Solaria sighed. "Aunt Blizza, you know it's not polite to listen in on other people's conversations, even if Filzbalm is a bit loud occasionally." She touched

Skylar's elbow and continued into the hallway that spiraled down, below ground level. "You'll have to learn to ignore her most of the time. She's not all there. Something happened to her way back when, before I was born. Nobody likes to talk about it, but it impacted her reader abilities. She frequently can't control them, but luckily, she's not very powerful anymore. If she was as strong as Professor Aduncus, we'd all have major problems."

"Then how was she able to hear Filzbalm?" Skylar asked as the stairway came to a landing where there were two doors.

"I don't know, other than he is rather loud." Solaria didn't pause on the landing, continuing down.

"He's loud so you can hear him, but that shouldn't carry very far, unless this is somehow tied to her gifts not working right anymore." Skylar wasn't sure if he wanted to talk to the old woman and find out what had happened to affect her mind so badly, or if he wanted to avoid her and her out-of-control reader powers.

"Hard to say." Solaria kept going past another landing and another two doors. The stairs continued to spiral down, and things grew a touch warmer. "My folks have always been fairly quiet about her. She's dad's sister—that's why they take care of her, and for the most part she's harmless."

"It must be nice to have extended family nearby," Skylar said as Solaria finally stopped at a set of doors on the third landing. "It was always just me and my mom." It suddenly hit him that he'd missed out on a lot. Sure, he'd had Teir, and Teir's family had always treated him like one of their own, as it had been the Hummassan way to take everyone in and make them part of the clan, but he'd never had anyone more than his mother to be close with. It didn't feel fair.

She opened the door on the left. "This one's yours. Sometimes family can get to be a bit much, but neither Blizza nor Phil have kids of their own, and my folks were limited to just me after that order from the Galactic Council a few years ago to restrict family size on most developed worlds. So this is all the family I know, but with us all being psychic to one extreme or the other, it can get fairly crowded around here with just us."

"I know a lot of people on Hummassa were happy they weren't considered a completely developed world when that decree came down. The natives there like large families." Skylar walked into the room and carried his duffle over to the mid-sized bed with the thick blue comforter on it. There was also a small desk made from some dark stone, and a matching chair of a similarly dark wood.

"Looks like Mom gave you three blankets. If you need more, let either one of us know and we'll get you some."

"Three blankets?" Skylar stared at the bed for a moment. He wasn't sure if he'd ever slept under three blankets. There were times in Hummassa he'd never used a sheet because it was too hot to get comfortable with one over him.

Solaria nodded. "We're not really set up for lots of heat, but if something happens to Filzbalm's ring, we'll make sure it's warm enough in here for him, even if we have to bring in a wood stove or something."

"Oh." Skylar was suddenly at a loss for words. He'd known it was going to be cold, but he really hadn't been prepared for the reality. He realized the cold he'd felt when he'd gotten out of Phil's hover car could get a lot worse if he wasn't properly equipped.

"Tell you what, why don't you change into the thermal suit you generated?" Solaria slunk toward the doorway. "I'm going to stash my bag and go see if Mom needs some help. Just follow the stairs up when you're ready. If you go down the stairs, you'll just end up in storerooms."

"Okay." Skylar went to his duffle bag. "You think I should hang anything up?"

Solaria paused and shrugged. "Guess that's up to you. I don't normally. I just live out of the bag until I'm ready to go." She pointed to the door near the bed. "There's a closet and a bathroom through there."

"Thanks." He waited until she closed the door behind her to unzip his bag. As he dug out the thermal suit he'd generated for the trip, Skylar wondered why all the Pantherians he'd seen so far had been clothed. Both Solaria and Del had warned him that Pantherians preferred to go unclothed even in their frigid weather.

"Maybe they're being polite," Filzbalm suggested as he fluttered from Skylar's shoulder to land on the bed next to the bag.

"Could be." Skylar found the thermal suit and pulled it out. "I'm not sure how I'd feel about seeing Solaria or her mother naked."

"I really do think most humanoids spend too much time worrying about their clothes." Filzbalm stretched out on the bed and looked very content as Skylar started to change. *"I've observed how a lot of the students at Stars' End spend much time primping and making sure everything's just perfect with their appearance."*

"I think that's because the boys want to look good for the girls and the girls want to look nice for the boys." Skylar wasn't sure he wanted to have that kind of discussion with Filzbalm at that very moment. Years earlier, when his mother had spoken to him about sex, he'd simply nodded and did his best to figure out what she was talking about. Apparently she thought she should be explaining things, but he'd never really had any stirrings, as she called them, about any of the kids in school. Faced with the possibility of having to explain things to Filzbalm, Skylar found the prospect unsettling.

"But you, Del, and Solaria don't' seem to worry that much about your appearance. Melody worries more about it than you three do, as does Connor, but Fin doesn't. Come to think of it, a fair number of the non-humans don't worry as much, although I noticed that Felicianana kept trying to wave her hair at someone I couldn't see through the door on the flight here. Since there were several people across the main compartment from her, I am unsure who it would've been."

Skylar hadn't been aware Filzbalm had been watching the others through the cabin door, although the Solar Drake often seemed fascinated by the actions of the people around them. "She was probably flirting with Mutanio. Solaria says that even though he's a butthead, he's one of the more desirable male Pantherians at school. And since she's one of the more desirable females, he can't understand why she puts him off the way she does."

"Maybe I should ask her. Maybe if she knew Felicianana was interested in him, Solaria might also take an interest."

"I doubt it." Skylar slipped into the thermal suit. It was tighter than he had expected, fitting him like a second skin. But as he pressed the auto-close seam shut, he was instantly several degrees warmer. He wasn't sure he wanted to take it off until he was off Pantheria.

"But I wouldn't offend her if I asked, would I?"

One of the other things Filzbalm was constantly worried about was offending people. Skylar didn't know where that came from, other than the need Solar Drakes had to please and revere The Mother of All Drakes. That might have made him more sensitive to offending others. "Probably not. But I'd keep your voice down around

Aunt Blizza. If she can hear us talking, she might say things you don't want her to say."

"You might be right."

Skylar dug out the brown heavy leather jacket he'd generated at Solaria's suggestion. He put it on and looked at himself in the mirror. He'd done that at school too. There was something about the way the leather felt that he liked. He couldn't really explain it. It was just better than the synthesized fabrics he was always wearing at school. Maybe it was closer to organic, like he was used to on Hummassa. He wasn't sure, but he didn't want to recycle it when he got back to school. He wanted to keep it for occasions when he might need it.

"Okay, Filzbalm." He sat to pull on his boots, also leather, and better suited for an unusual environment than the simple shoes he wore at school. "You ready to go get something to eat?"

"Always." Filzbalm gave a final stretch, then flew up to Skylar's shoulder. The leather was so thick Skylar didn't need the quilted pad he normally wore for Filzbalm to land on.

He looked for a light switch as he opened the door, but didn't see one. When he stepped into the hall, the lights went out. He closed the door and headed up the steps, retracing the path they'd taken to come down.

7
Dinner With Predators

WHEN SKYLAR reached the main floor again, there was another man there. He was larger than Phil, and his fur markings were the same as Solaria's and Blizza's.

"Ah, you must be Skylar." He came over and offered Skylar his hand.

Skylar was glad he wasn't the hugging type like Solaria's mother. He would've felt awkward hugging the big man. "Yes, sir."

He looked at Filzbalm. "And you'd be Filzbalm. Smaller than I figured, but then we don't know much about Solar Drakes, do we?" He grinned. "I'm Solaria's dad, but you can call me Aniu. I think that's easier than Mr. Unica."

"Thanks, Aniu." Skylar felt odd addressing the father of a friend by his first name, but figured if that was what Aniu wanted, that's what he'd do.

"Everything okay down there?" Felonia asked. "I tried to make sure you'd be warm. If you need more blankets, I can get them."

"I should be fine," Skylar said. "If I need more, I'll let you know."

"See, Felonia, the boy's going to be fine." Aniu went over and hugged his wife. "You've been worrying for days, but look at him. He's a fine strapping boy for a baseline human. He'll be okay. He's also got good taste in clothes."

Solaria laughed. "Dad, you hate clothes. The only reason you're wearing them is to not embarrass Skylar. I do appreciate the effort, too."

"We always try to make guests feel welcome," he said with a wide grin that, if Skylar wasn't used to Solaria's facial expressions, would've unnerved him. Pantherians couldn't help but show a lot of teeth when they grinned.

"Then let's get this meal going." Felonia carried a platter of meat in from the kitchen. "Skylar, Solaria said that you're used to her eating habits, so I only grilled enough for you."

"That's fine, ma'am."

"Felonia," she corrected. "If you're going to use Aniu's name, you'll use mine too. I'm sure by the time you go back to school, we'll all be family."

He gave her a short nod. "Thank you, Felonia."

"Anyway. I figured Filzbalm could eat what we do, so I didn't make anything special for him." She looked at the little Solar Drake. "I hope that's okay."

"It looks delicious," Filzbalm said.

Before Skylar could relay that, Aunt Blizza said. "He's such a polite little guy."

Neither of Solaria's parents seemed to notice, so Skylar told Felonia what he'd said and she smiled at Filzbalm.

"So, Solaria was saying you're both archeologists," Skylar said as he reached for his first serving of meat, then put some of the raw meat on a plate for Filzbalm.

Aniu nodded as he stabbed some meat with a fork. "That's right." He glanced at Phil. "Did Felo tell you the current dig might be pre-settlement era? It's got a lot of things in it that are way too big to be Pantherian, and some of the writing is stuff I've never seen."

Skylar welcomed the conversation going back to what it had gone to when they were out in the front of the house. He wanted to know what they meant by pre-settlement.

"She did." Phil took his own plate full of meat. "That must be very exciting for you both, but don't you have to be careful? The Galactic Council is very touchy about revealing any proof that some of the worlds were settled and not native populations. They've spent hundreds of years covering up that fact."

"Wait," Skylar blurted out, nearly spitting a piece of meat across the table. He closed his mouth, quickly chewed, then swallowed. "What do you mean 'settled and not native'? I thought Pantheria was your native planet."

Felonia and Aniu shook their heads.

"If we were to all be honest, our home planet is Sol Three, just like the humans." Aniu set his fork down and explained. "When an advanced DNA analysis is done of a majority of races, you'll find that there's a mingling of human DNA with various other species from that planet. We were all genetically engineered for the climates of our worlds. We made perfect early colonists, and have been able to make the most of the natural resources of the planets. It's a growing belief that the Galactic Council had expunged the knowledge that some of the worlds had other sentient life on them when we all arrived, and that they removed the native life and all evidence of them. What we've run across in our dig is evidence of that life, and we might even find evidence of what the humans did to them to remove them from the planet."

"But we have to make sure we've got all our evidence before we can publish anything," Felonia said. "The odds are the Galactic Council won't be happy if we expose this massive coverup. I would love to find hard evidence on other worlds too, but I don't know if we can get other scientists across the galaxy to work on this with us. We might end up with just our evidence here to start things off. But we need you all to stay quiet about this until we're ready to go public with what we find."

The whole idea that there was a multi-thousand-year coverup that they were getting evidence of was interesting, and Skylar wanted to know as much as possible. "I'll keep my mouth shut."

"Me too," Solaria agreed. "But you already knew that."

Her mother grinned at her. "We did, but it's nice to hear you say it."

"If you get hard proof, I might be able to get some of my contacts working with you," Phil offered. "With the universe in upheaval right now, something like this could cause a lot of trouble for the Galactic Council."

Aniu shook his head. "I'm not sure we want to do that. But it would be nice for the truth to come out."

"But Aniu, you know how the truth can have a way of causing problems, even when you don't want it to," Phil said.

"I know." Aniu sounded grim as he picked up his fork. "That's one of the reasons we're taking this slow and making sure we've got everything in order before we start talking about it beyond the dig site." He looked over at Solaria. "We probably shouldn't be talking about it now, but we don't get to see the two of you that often and we wanted to let you know what we've been doing."

"We appreciate that," Phil said, taking another bite.

"So much of the past is dark," Aunt Blizza said, sounding far away.

Skylar glanced her direction and saw that her eyes had a glazed look.

"Light needs to be shined in the nooks and crannies," she continued in her strange, far-away voice. "But the Light will chase out the truth that shadows our world. Beware the things that Light will bring to life. We might not be ready for everything that is exposed."

Aniu and Felonia's coms buzzed at the same time, interrupting the dinner.

8
Out Of The Darkness

AS ANIU and Felonia tapped their coms to answer, Phil grab-bed his head. "Anger. Pain. Fear." He closed his eye and let out a long breath.

Something stabbed through Skylar's head. Someone was screaming.

Filzbalm wrapped his tail around Skylar's neck and everything backed off. *"Someone very powerful is very angry."*

"Are you blocking for me?" Skylar stood so he could do the exercises Professor Aduncus had him doing for shielding. It felt off to do that in the Unica family dining room, but they were psychics too and probably had their own methods of shielding.

"I am trying to," Filzbalm said as Aunt Blizza screamed and collapsed.

Skylar and Solaria moved together to Blizza's crumpled form.

"Help me get her to the couch," Solaria said as she positioned herself on Blizza's right side. Solaria's breath was tight and ragged. "I don't know what's going on, but it hurts."

It felt like the attack was growing—more of the anger was getting through Filzbalm's shields. As Skylar helped lift Blizza's limp form, he wanted to scream at everyone. He wanted to pound the old woman as opposed to help her. He gritted his teeth and pushed back the feelings, knowing they weren't his.

"I'm trying to block," Filzbalm said, sounding very upset. *"But it's so powerful."*

"Too strong," Blizza mumbled as they managed to get her onto a couch that appeared to be made from the pelts of several animals.

Once she was free of her aunt's weight, Solaria straightened. Her expression was tight, and when she spoke, it sounded like she was spitting the words out. "This shouldn't be happening."

"What is it?" Skylar balled up his hands and shoved them into the pockets of his jacket. He hoped by putting them there, he wouldn't have the urge to hit people. He had no doubt that if he got into a physical fight with Solaria, she'd knock him out quickly, particularly with the way she was flexing her hands, flashing her sharp, gray claws each time she extended her fingers.

"Psychic attack," Aniu exclaimed through gritted teeth. "Strongest I've ever felt. It's like a team of readers all hitting us at once."

"Feelers," Phil said. "This is too emotional." His face was set in a hard mask as he pushed himself straight out from the table. "We have to find the source and shut it down."

"We've got people dropping all over the settlement," Felonia said as she tapped off her com. "We don't know who's doing this." Her brow was creased in concentration, but not like Solaria's was. Anger, pain and struggle wrinkled Solaria's forehead, making her look hurt and dangerous. Knowing her the way he did, Skylar didn't want to say anything to interrupt her for fear she would lash out at him with her claws.

The information didn't help Skylar not want to hit anyone. He took a centering breath and stepped to the middle of the living room so he could begin his katas. The movements helped him focus and create a shield stronger than what Filzbalm had put around him. As the shield strengthened with each repetition of the motions, his anger backed off and he could think of something other than hurting people.

"That's better," Filzbalm said, sounding less stressed than he had moments earlier.

Skylar went through the motions three more times before he felt like things had backed off enough for him to concentrate.

As he stopped his katas and looked at Phil, the powerful feeler gave him a tight smile. "Very good, Skylar. I'd heard you were coming along now that your teachers have found a way for you to focus. It gets a lot quieter when you're not stumbling around trying to block things, doesn't it?"

Skylar glanced at Aunt Blizza, who was sprawled on the couch, looking like she was in agony. "Is there anything we can do for her?"

"Felonia will have a dampener on her in a moment." Aniu rubbed his forehead and frowned. "We keep them on hand in case her powers get out of control. I never expected to have to use them because of an attack on all of us." He let out a long breath. "That was the worst attack I've felt since I was in school and we were practicing attack and defense. Too many holes in my shields now."

"I think we can all say that." Felonia returned from the curving stairs. Skylar hadn't even realized she'd left. She had a leather bracelet that looked a lot like the one Skylar had worn until Filzbalm started helping him block things and control his powers. She slipped the bracelet on Blizza's wrist, and the older woman instantly stilled. After a deep breath, she lay motionless. For a moment, Skylar worried she might've just died, before he noticed her narrow chest rising slowly under her lightweight blouse.

"Okay, we've got the family taken care of," Aniu said as he started for the front door. "Phil, if you can keep an eye on things here, we need to get to the dig site. The call was from there. Something happened. I couldn't get a straight answer—it sounded like everyone there was suffering from the same attack we experienced."

"So what do we do?" Solaria asked. "We can't just stay here and wait for something to happen. If it affected the settlement, they might need help."

"She's got a point," Phil said. He ran a shaking hand through his sweat-rumpled hair. "I work for Intergal Rescue. If this was some kind of attack, I need to see what I can do to help people, not just sit here and babysit two kids who are old enough to be out there helping if there are others in need."

Skylar nearly cheered for Phil taking up for them. He wanted to be out making sure everyone was safe.

"We can stay with Uncle Phil as he checks the settlement out, while you guys go make sure everything's okay at the dig site," Solaria said. "If we activate the home security system, Aunt Blizza will be okay."

Her mother looked like she was about to argue, then her com buzzed again. She frowned. "Okay. Just be careful. We're only a call away if anything goes wrong." She tapped her com and headed out the door in Aniu's wake.

"What do we need to do, Phil?" Skylar asked before the door closed behind them. He'd known from when he'd been found on Hummassa that Intergal agents used their gifts to find people trapped or lost, as he'd been. Doing something physical would help him keep his mind off the little bit of anger that was still seeping through his protections.

Phil pursed his lips. "Let's get a few more dampeners from my hover car. I don't know how many higher-level psychics are in the nearby area. If any of them are being hit as hard as we were, they might need help to pull themselves back together."

He started toward the door, then stopped. "Now, you three follow my instructions. If I tell you something, you do it without question. Got it?"

"Got it," Skylar and Solaria said in unison. Filzbalm echoed them.

When Phil nodded, they all hurried outside. Solaria took time to set the security system. A soft hum filled the entryway for a moment, and then they were beyond the door.

Outside, the sun had gone down and the wind had picked up. The cold lashed at Skylar, and Filzbalm moved so he was between Skylar's neck and the collar of his leather coat.

"Cold?" Skylar asked as he pulled up the collar to offer both of them a little more protection from the wind.

"A little, but my ring continues to function as it is supposed to." Filzbalm laid his head in the hollow of Skylar's neck, and his warmth helped Skylar a little bit.

"It's not supposed to be like this," Phil mumbled as he opened the door to the hover car. "The weather was for a clear, cold night."

"Is it connected to the attack?" Solaria asked.

Skylar had only seen a few references in his school books of psychics disrupting weather patterns when they used their powers, and that was restricted to movers. What they had experienced was a feeler attack. It shouldn't have impacted anything other than the emotions of the people around the area.

"Don't know." Phil straightened and looked at them. "Tell you what, let's take the hover car. It'll keep us out of the weather, at least a little bit. Unfortunately, we're going to have to do physical checks of buildings until the attack backs off. We can't risk dropping our shields long enough to scan the buildings from the car."

Happy to get out of the wind tearing at his clothes, Skylar scrambled into the back seat where he'd ridden from the spaceport to the house.

As the doors shut, Phil's com beeped. Without hesitation, he tapped it. "Are you sure?" He started the vehicle. "Do you know where it's gone? Yes, I know it's still out there somewhere." He started to sound short, then took a deep breath. "Okay. We're searching the settlement for people."

Phil pulled the hover car away from the dome and headed toward the next one over. "The attack sounds like it's worse at the dig site." He drove down the road. "Your folks say they haven't gotten all the way in yet, but have already encountered several unconscious people. It's even hitting non-psychics. We're going to have to be careful."

Skylar had heard about psychic attacks affecting non-psychics before. When his powers had lashed out a few months earlier, he'd affected some of the non-psychic students. Like he'd done then, he wondered exactly how powerful something had to be to be able to do that. "How far is the dig site?"

"About three miles," Phil said as they pulled into the first drive. "To hit us as hard as it is, we're dealing either with a group of people, or one whose power is off the charts."

"Why would anyone attack the dig site?" Solaria asked as Phil brought the hover car to a stop.

"Might be someone got wind of your parent's finds." He shook his head. "Although it's a badly kept secret, the Galactic Council is willing to do anything to keep our origins hidden. This could be them trying to silence your parents."

Solaria reached for her door handle. "I hope not. We'll all be in a lot of trouble if that's the case. Skylar and I might not make it back to school."

"What are you talking about?" Skylar didn't understand where she was going with her line of thought. She got out of the car and he rushed to follow.

"Skylar, the government isn't always our friend." Her voice was low and grim as she walked up the short path to the front door of the dome that looked a lot like her parents' home. "They want to stop their secrets from getting out and are willing to do anything to accomplish that."

"Now hush," Phil said as Solaria reached the door.

"We will," she replied as she knocked. They waited several seconds before she touched the door and it opened.

"Mrs. Tig, are you here?" Solaria called out as she walked inside.

"Solaria, is that you?" a pained voice replied.

"Right here." Solaria turned in the direction it had come. "Are you okay?"

They entered a kitchen that resembled the one at the Unica house. There was a man lying on the floor with a woman crouched over him. They both had orange fur with thick black stripes. As the woman straightened and it registered with him that she didn't have any clothes on, Skylar looked away. When Solaria frowned at him, he realized he was being rude and forced himself to turn back, doing his best to limit where he looked. He wasn't used to seeing naked people, even if they were perfectly fine with being naked around strangers.

"What's happening?" Mrs. Tig asked. "He started saying something about the anger, then he collapsed. I have a headache, but nothing else."

Phil knelt down and appraised Mr. Tig. "Looks like some feeler overload."

Mrs. Tig frowned. "Overload? But he's only a level three. He's not that sensitive."

"Something's happened out at the dig site," Phil said as he pulled out a dampening bracelet and slipped it on the unconscious man. "We're not sure exactly what. When he wakes up, he's going to be disoriented, but the bracelet is going to block everything. We'll call when it's safe for him to take it off."

She nodded and stroked her husband's forehead. "Thank you, Phil. It's been too long since you've been around."

"Staying busy with Intergal Rescue." Phil stood. "We should keep checking and make sure everybody's okay. Aniu and Felonia are trying to find out what started this. We'll let everyone know as soon as we have it figured out."

Without rising, she held her hand out to Phil. "I understand. Be careful out there, particularly with the young ones in tow."

"I'll do my best." Phil released her hand, and gestured for Skylar and Solaria to head back out to the hover car.

Happy to get out of the house with the naked people, Skylar followed Solaria.

"You need to relax around these people," Filzbalm said. *"This is their way of life."*

"I know, but it's just not who I am," Skylar whispered as they made it out of the front door and he relaxed.

Solaria laughed as she got into the hover car. "Skylar, it's not that bad. These are just our bodies. There's not much we can do about them. It's not your fault that you aren't used to seeing naked humanoids, you know. How would you feel knowing that Q'uT'omael at school is always naked?"

"Yeah, but he's in an envirobubble," Skylar countered. "He's a sentient ooze. Or I *think* it's a he. But anyway, there's not much in him that's like me.

Pantherians are humanoids, and from what you're saying, engineered from humans. Doesn't that make a difference?"

"No," Phil said as he got in and closed the door. "We're all from the same stock. There's no reason we should be ashamed of our bodies and exposing them. I think those who don't have those restrictions are a lot healthier, both physically and mentally."

Skylar tried to understand what everyone was telling him, and he didn't want to be rude to any of the Pantherians he ran into, but he'd been raised to wear clothes and wasn't sure how people could go around and not wear them. It didn't make sense to him. He'd shaken off a lot of what his mother had told him, like that psychics were evil and not to be trusted, but he realized there was still a lot for him to get over. He sighed. "I guess I need to think about things."

Phil chuckled as he drove down the drive. "That's all I can ask of you. Think about things and come up with your own answers."

9
Chasing Light

SKYLAR YAWNED and shuddered as he got back into the hover car. The sky was still dark. Solaria had told him the night wasn't even half over, but he was bone tired. The Tigs had been the start of their efforts to make sure the folks in the settlement were okay. Everyone had been affected to one degree or another. It seemed to be dependent on the person's sensitivity. The more power psychics had, the more they were affected, and the closer to the dig site, the greater the effect was. Before they were even halfway through the settlement, they all knew something had happened at the dig.

Solaria's parents kept telling them they were investigating, but until they were sure the site was safe, they didn't want anyone else out there. They did say everyone at the site was unconscious, and medical staff were coming.

"All right, you three." Phil settled into the hover car and hit the button to start it up. "Other than the dig site, we've accounted for everyone in the settlement. We're lucky nobody is really hurt."

"Except for poor Mrs. Splotz," Solaria noted as she strapped herself in. "She was in really bad shape after tumbling down her stairs."

"But she'll recover." Phil pulled on the yoke to get the hover car moving. "She didn't even need anything beyond what we had in the first aid kit. If she hadn't been going down her stairs when the attack hit, she'd be okay." He rubbed his head.

Skylar sighed and settled back in his seat. The attack had stopped nearly two hours earlier, but his brain still throbbed from the intensity of the mental onslaught. He wondered if his head would ever feel normal again.

"Where to now?" he asked as Filzbalm yawned and snuggled tighter around his neck.

"Home," Phil replied, pulling out into the street. "We can get some sleep until Felonia and Aniu come home, and maybe then we can get some answers."

"Can't we go to the dig site?" Solaria objected. "The attack is over. We should be safe." She crossed her arms. "Besides, I had my initiation into the women's warrior circle last year. They're treating me like I'm a kid."

Phil tsked as he drove toward the Unica house. "Or maybe they're thinking of Skylar. He's not a warrior and might need someone to protect him."

"We can give him a blaster," she muttered.

All night she'd seemed very upset that her parents were being overprotective. But as long as they were out helping people, she was keeping it mostly to herself. With them heading home, it sounded like she was ready to voice some of her unhappiness. Skylar understood. He wanted to be treated more like an adult too, but he wasn't about to say anything that would get folks upset. Their best bet for getting a little respect was to stay quiet and do as they were told. Eventually adults would start treating them as equals, or at least that was what worked on Hummassa.

"Since we're not sure what we're up against, we don't know if a blaster would work or not," Phil said as they turned the corner and Skylar realized their headlights were the only unnatural light he could see.

It was strange with just moonlight, starlight and a slight green luminescence dancing across the horizon. Even on Hummassa there had been lights from the neighbors, and a soft glow that indicated where the city was. He couldn't recall being anywhere except Armstrong's Rings where there were no lights, but where they'd been on the Rings, it hadn't ever grown truly dark. Heavy twilight was the closest it got.

"What's that?" He pointed toward the green glow.

Phil stopped the hover car and tapped the steering wheel. "Now, that's a very good question. If we weren't on Pantheria, I'd say it's an aurora borealis, but we don't have those here." He turned on the communications console in the middle of the dashboard. There was just static. He tapped his wrist com. "Aniu, we've got a green atmospheric glow to the east of the settlement. Any ideas? No, Skylar spotted it…we were headed back to the house. Okay. It might take a little bit of time…oh, it appears local coms are still working, but worldwide coms are down. Right, we'll check in as soon as we know something…you two be careful too." He tapped the wrist com again, then turned the steering wheel. "Okay gang, we're going to go find out what that glow is. Per Aniu, it shouldn't be happening."

When he reached the end of the street, he just kept going. One of the big advantages of hovercraft over wheeled transport was that hovers didn't need a hard surface to make the best time. Most areas that were settlements or larger had roads just to keep the citizens from driving all over the place. Skylar wasn't sure what the landscape was beyond the glow of the headlights, but he doubted it was tame in any way. From what he'd seen on the drive in from the spaceport, the area was mostly rocks, snow, and ice.

Something moved in the darkness.

Phil swerved. "Damned ice bears."

"They're diurnal," Solaria said. "They shouldn't be out in the middle of the night."

"I know," Phil mumbled. "Something is not right at the moment, and we need to figure out what it is." He hit a button on the dash and the headlights grew brighter. With the reflection off the snow and ice, it almost looked like daylight.

Skylar wished there was more he could do, but he stayed in his seat and stared out the windshield as they sped along, heading toward the glow that never seemed to get any closer. He was out of his element, although since he'd left Hummassa, he hadn't figured out what his element was. Sure, he was starting to fit in at Stars' End, but he no longer had a real home to go back to. He loved it when he was in space. More than anything he wanted to find a way to get a ship, and when he graduated, take to the stars. Beyond that, he had no idea what he wanted to do.

Spending the night helping Phil make sure the people of the settlement were safe had been interesting. It reminded him of a time he and his mother went to the coast after a tidal wave had hit hard and left people dead or homeless. They'd been part of the massive cleanup that had taken weeks. He'd always liked helping people, but even as a feeler and a reader, he wasn't sure how it all worked together.

"We have time." Filzbalm yawned again, his words sounding like he was going to sleep. *"You don't have to have it all figured out today."*

"I know," Skylar replied mentally, since he didn't want to distract Phil or let Solaria in on his conversation with Filzbalm. *"But I'd just like to figure out where I'm going."*

"Toward the green light. Isn't that all that's important right now?"

"But I want to be more than just in the now. Being in the now doesn't get us very far."

"But it gets us through the moment." Filzbalm suddenly felt heavier where he curled across Skylar's shoulders and neck. Skylar didn't need to probe his mind

to know he'd fallen asleep as the hover car floated along on the snow and ice.

Skylar decided it was time for him to start doing some research and find out what kinds of things he could use his psychic powers for that would give him the opportunity to be out in space. Even though it was taking him some adjusting to get used to life at the Academy, there was a subtle difference he could feel when he was there that he hadn't felt in school on Hummassa. Del often told him he was crazy. Despite his friends' insistence, Skylar knew there were differences and he could tell when he was on a space station, a ship, or a planet. He just felt more alive in space. He often dreamed of being in his own ship and flying out to discover new worlds and species. But he wasn't sure what it would take for him to live that life. Phil's work with Intergal Rescue was the closest thing he'd found to what he dreamed of, but he didn't think that was exactly what he was supposed to be doing.

Phil brought the hover car to a stop in a cloud of snow. "Weather's turning." The words came out with a soft growl. "Not sure we can get anywhere."

"Ah, come on, Uncle Phil," Solaria said, sounding sleepy, because she never whined unless she was really tired. "We've got to be able to do something."

"We're an hour out from the settlement." Phil scanned the horizon, then tried his com again. "We're no closer to the source of the glow. It really is acting like an honest aurora borealis. Just some magnetic ionization in the atmosphere that is causing the lights, but the atmosphere here doesn't have the right proportion of certain elements to react with charged solar particles to make this happen. There aren't any settlements in this direction that would be causing this. I don't get it."

Skylar perked up, suddenly feeling useful. ""You know, if the planetary coms are down, I wonder if the interplanetary ones are down or not. I've got my interstellar communicator back at the house. If the interplanetary system is up, we should be able to get a call out."

"Wait." Solaria straightened in her seat. "You said the lights are caused by ions and magnetism. Could the lights be what took out the planetary system?"

"Maybe." Phil leaned back in his seat. "But that doesn't explain why the local coms work."

"Because if the source of the attack was centered on the dig site, and is also causing the lights, the local coms should be down too," Skylar added. It made him smile a little—he liked being helpful.

"Right." Phil drummed on the steering wheel. "There's got to be something we're all missing."

"Yeah, but does this mean we're giving up?" Solaria yawned, then quickly covered her mouth.

Phil nodded and turned the hover car around. "I think we're all dead on our feet, or in this case, in our seats. We need to head back, see what your folks have to say, see if Skylar's communicator can get out to someone who might be able to lend a hand, and get some rest so we can think clearly."

Skylar settled into his seat, not having realized he was all but leaning over the back of the front seat as he'd talked to Phil and Solaria. Normally Filzbalm would've complained about him doing that, but the Solar Drake was sound asleep. That didn't help Skylar to stay awake as they headed back to the settlement, and he didn't remember much after Phil turned around.

10
Grim News For Breakfast

THE TASTE of blood filled Skylar's dreams, and he jerked awake. Staring at the darkness above him, he wiped his mouth, expecting it to come away with blood. There was nothing.

As he adjusted to the dark room, he remembered he was in Solaria's home. He'd fallen asleep soon after getting back from chasing the lights they could never reach. They'd beaten Solaria's folks home, and even though everyone had wanted to wait up and see what had been found when they went to the dig site, they'd all been too tired. Using their psi skills to try to locate people in the settlement, while trying to keep their shields at the ready in case of another attack, had worn them all out. Filzbalm had fallen asleep before making it home.

At the thought of Filzbalm, Skylar sat up. The Solar Drake wasn't on his pillow the way he normally was. *"Filzbalm!"* he called through their mental link.

"I'm in the kitchen," came a contented reply.

"How did you get in the kitchen?" Skylar swung his legs out from under the covers and instantly jerked them back underneath. It was a lot colder than he'd anticipated. His thermal suit was across the room. He wished he was a mover and could make the clothes float across the room so he didn't have to get out from under the blankets to get dressed.

"I heard Solaria come out of her room and called to her to let me out so I could find some food. I was very hungry." The taste of blood increased with his mental

contact. *"She's been feeding me. I'm not sure I've ever eaten so much. But I was hungry."* Given how much of Filzbalm's eating was bleeding through their connection, Skylar knew he was hungry, tired or both. Normally the Solar Drake filtered the baser feeling and sensations out of their communication.

"Oh," Skylar replied as he forced himself out of the bed and toward his thermal suit, shedding his sleeping clothes. *"I'll be there in a couple of minutes."*

"I'll probably be done by then, but Felonia has made sure to set aside some food for you."

"Okay." Skylar put on his thermal suit as fast as he could. The change from the chilly air of his room was nearly instant as the suit adjusted itself to warm him. He'd known Filzbalm could speak to Solaria when he wanted to, but Skylar had never been left out of their connection before. For a moment, he worried about Filzbalm bonding to her and leaving him, but then he remembered the information he'd gotten from the researchers. A Solar Drake could only bond with one person, although the strong ones could mentally speak to other readers, if the reader was strong enough to hear them. He, Solaria, and Del debated why Filzbalm had bonded to him—and not Solaria—since they had all been there when he hatched. The only thing they'd been able to come up with was the amount of time Skylar had spent with him while he'd still been in his egg. Although Solaria had spent time with him every day as well, it had been too cold in her room for him, so he'd stayed with Skylar and Del.

By the time he left his room, he'd managed to push aside the fear of Filzbalm bonding to Solaria. He was still a little fuzzy-brained, but chalked that up to the long night they'd all had and how tired he'd been. He yawned as he started up the stairs, and had to admit that he was still more than a little bit tired, but wanted to know what was going on.

He reached the kitchen and found everyone except Phil and Aniu around the table. Filzbalm was curled up around a medium-sized earthen bowl that was empty except for a little bit of blood pooled in the bottom. His yellow-scaled stomach was slightly distended like it normally was after he'd eaten a large meal. And, as after most large meals, Filzbalm looked sleepy.

"I was beginning to worry you'd sleep all day," Felonia said as Skylar walked up to the table.

"Sorry." Skylar covered another yawn with his hand. "I guess last night took a lot out of me."

"Don't worry about it," Solaria said, pushing her plate toward the center of the table. "We're just now getting going."

"Not all of us," her mother said. "Your father and uncle have been gone for a couple of hours." She pulled a plate from a warmer on the wall near the sink and carried it over to the table for Skylar. "Here you go. I knew if I didn't set something aside, Solaria would eat it all."

"And you're always telling me to eat all I want." Solaria pouted slightly. "What with me being a growing girl and everything."

"Well, when's there's company we try to leave enough for them."

"Thank you." Skylar picked up his fork and started cutting the meat. It was cooked, so he doubted it would've been Solaria's first choice, but he knew the amounts she could eat and was thankful for everything that could be rescued from her.

Solaria looked at her mother. "So, you haven't explained why Dad and Uncle Phil are out and about so early. Does it have to do with last night?"

"Maybe," Felonia said as she settled at the table next to Solaria. "We aren't sure what's going on. There was an emergency signal sent out from Glacier City right before dawn this morning. It was cut short. As the only Intergal Rescue agent currently in the area, Phil's been asked to go and see if he can determine what's going on."

It sounded more exciting than spending the night checking houses in the local settlement. "How far is Glacier City?" Skylar asked as he finished chewing the bite of meat.

"It's the closest large city," Solaria said. "What, four to five hours by hover car?"

Her mother nodded. "Yes, but Phil was able to request a gyrojumper from the spaceport. They should've already reached Glacier City." She glanced at the large clock hanging over her kitchen sink. "I keep thinking we'll hear something at any time."

"I'm sure they'll call when they find out something," Solaria said as she stood and carried her plate to the sink. "So, what did you guys find at the dig site last night?"

Felonia frowned. "We're not sure. I need to go over there as soon as you three are ready. I just didn't want to leave you alone here. Some of the things I want to check on in the daylight and see if they make more sense."

"Are we sure the psychic attack came from there?" Skylar asked as he took a fork full of what looked like eggs. At least they had the right consistency for them, even if they were blue and not yellow.

"We think so." She rubbed the bridge of her nose and looked tired. "We're still not sure what caused it. But most of the dig staff still there were knocked out by the attack. It was strong enough to take out non-psychics as well as psychics. The only person who was still awake was Romalda—she's got the strongest shields of anyone I've ever met, and even she said it felt like she'd been hit in the head by an ice ox."

"Ice oxen are going to be the least of our problems." Aunt Blizza spoke up for the first time that morning. She looked and sounded a lot better than she had the night before. "Changes are blowing on the wind. There are bad things…powerful things going on." She held up her arm that still had the bracelet on. "When we have to blind ourselves to survive."

"Blizza, don't scare the kids." Felonia stood and collected the old woman's plate. "Sure, something happened last night—we just don't know what it is yet. We'll get it figured out, and everyone will be fine."

Her com beeped and she tapped it, almost dropping the plate and spilling some of the blood that had been on it. "Aniu, do you know what the problem is yet?" She frowned and pointed from Solaria to the spill. "Are you sure? What could've caused that? …Of course. We were about to head to the dig site—do you think it's safe? Oh, good point. I'll let you know if we find anything…Okay. Keep in touch. If we can do anything from here, let us know." As she tapped off the com, she put the plate in the sink.

"So, what's up?" Solaria asked as she finished wiping the blood up. "Sounds grim."

"Glacier City is in ruins." Her mother leaned against the counter. "The search for survivors has already started. Phil has put in a call for Intergal Rescue to get ships here to help find the injured. Also, something is making the coms spotty. He said we might have to reroute things."

Solaria dropped to the floor, looking scared. "What do you mean, in ruins?"

Her mother spread her hands questioningly. "I don't know for sure. I doubt it's like an archeology ruin—it's probably more like a war zone. But either way, we're going to stay here and see what we can find from last night that might be helpful."

"Does Aniu think the two things are tied together?" Skylar asked, suddenly not sure if he could finish his breakfast. If Glacier City had been left in ruins, that sounded a lot like what had happened on Hummassa. But there they'd known what had caused the destruction. It had been Boarisk raiders. They'd come as slavers to get as many of the survivors as they could.

But Boarisks weren't psychic. They were one of the few species in the universe that didn't possess any mental powers. They couldn't use a psychic attack on a planet.

"He doesn't know yet." Felonia knelt next to Solaria and gave her a big hug. "We're all going to do what we can to find out what did both things and make sure they don't happen again."

Solaria nodded into her mother's shoulder.

Seeing Solaria need comforting from her mother sent a shiver of fear through Skylar. He wasn't used to Solaria being scared of anything. She was always going on about being the strong, powerful predator. She was the strongest of his friends. If she was scared, there was something for him to be afraid of.

Aunt Blizza laughed. "Boy, there is always something to be afraid of. Only the stupid aren't afraid of things. Solaria isn't stupid, and I don't think you are either."

"Blizza!" Felonia snapped. "You know it's not polite to read other people without their permission."

Skylar stared at the older Pantherian. He hadn't sensed her reading his mind. In all his training sessions with Professor Aduncus, he'd always felt when the professor read him. There was a slight push to it, and once he'd figured out what it felt like, it was easy for him to spot. He didn't doubt that Aunt Blizza had just read his mind, but he was amazed he hadn't felt anything from her doing it.

Aunt Blizza looked from Felonia to Skylar. "I am sorry, young human." She touched her chest and Skylar noticed the dampening bracelet still on her delicate forearm. "Sometimes I don't seem to have much control of my mind, or my mouth for that matter." The words sounded a little different from some of the things she'd said previously—they were more coherent.

Skylar nodded to her. "No problem, ma'am." His mind reeled at the idea she could still pick up his thoughts even with a dampener on. The obvious answer was the bracelet was defective in some way, because if it wasn't, then she was scary powerful—stronger than even Professor Aduncus.

She flashed him a smile that said she knew what he was thinking, and she *was* scary powerful. "I think I'll go lie down. Is it okay that I stay here while you all go to the dig site? I'll be fine by myself."

Felonia frowned, then sighed. "I guess we don't really have much of a choice. With Aniu trying to figure out what happened in Glacier City, if I don't leave you here by yourself, I have to take you with me, or leave the kids with you."

"What about that alarm you and Dad got for her a few months ago?" Solaria asked and she and her mother stood. "You haven't mentioned it in a while."

Her mother kissed her forehead. "That's a very good idea. Blizza, when we leave, I'm going to set the alarm. If you need us, use it. Will that be okay?"

"Of course." Blizza stood. "With any luck, I won't even know you're gone." Without another word, she hobbled out of the kitchen and into the living room.

Skylar let out a long breath. Less than a year earlier, meeting a psychic as powerful and uncontrolled as Blizza would've sent him running for the hills. He was still worried about being around her, but she wasn't completely terrifying. He'd learned a lot about psychics and himself, although he was constantly being reminded of how much he still had to learn.

"Okay. If we're all done with breakfast, let's get to the dig site before we lose too much daylight." Felonia took Filzbalm's bowl and put it in the sink with the other dishes.

Filzbalm had been curled up around the base of the bowl. He unwound and stretched. *"I'm still sleepy."* He looked up at Skylar, then launched himself up to his shoulder. His little leather wings blew a bit of Skylar's hair up as he landed. *"I can sleep here until I'm needed."*

"That's fine." Skylar welcomed the added warmth on his neck as Filzbalm curled up. "You might have to move a bit when I put on my coat."

Filzbalm yawned. *"I can do that."*

"Let me go get my coat and boots and I'll be ready." Skylar stood from the table and headed down the hall to his room. He promised himself that he was going to start putting on his heavier clothes even if he was just around the house, since it seemed they were going to be running in and out, doing things with little preparation.

On the first landing, Blizza leaned against her door.

Skylar stopped, although he really wanted to stay as far away from the old woman as he could. "Do you need a hand?"

She turned and her eyes were unfocused. "Be careful, young Skylar. There are many dangerous things in the darkness. But you could be the Light." She reached toward his face and it was all he could do to not jerk backwards as her cold fingers brushed his check. "Yes, you could be the Light."

"Skylar, hurry up!" Solaria called from above. "We need to get moving."

He stepped away from Blizza. "I need to get my stuff."

She nodded, and turned into her room.

"She's a little creepy," Filzbalm muttered from Skylar's shoulder.

"More than a little," Skylar agreed, then dashed down the stairs to get his stuff. He had no idea what Blizza was going on about. He wasn't the Light. He wasn't anything more than simple Skylar Mars, student at Stars' End Academy. He wasn't even sure what he wanted to be when he graduated, except he wanted to be out in space exploring. How was he supposed to do that if he was someone's light?

11
The Past Is A Frozen
Hole In The Ground

"FROZON PLANETS like Pantheria present archeologists with extra problems," Felonia explained as she drove the family hover car toward the dig site. "Luckily, we've dealt with ice for a couple thousand years and know how to handle it."

Skylar shivered even though he had on his thermal suit. He wasn't sure he'd be able to deal with living on a frozen world. He might've complained about the heat on Hummassa every summer, but at least he hadn't had to bundle up every time he wanted to go outside.

"Yeah," Solaria said from the seat next to her mother. "We've had tons of time to evolve to the point where the cold doesn't bother us anymore. Well, unless it gets really, really cold."

"I don't want to deal with really, really cold," Skylar said. "Springtime is enough for me."

"We were talking about archeology," Felonia said. "Not the cold. Skylar, the biggest thing you'll need to learn about the cold is to not dwell on it. If you dwell on it, it gets worse."

"Yes ma'am." He wasn't sure how he was supposed to *not* dwell on it, when it was ever-present and just waiting for something to go wrong before it froze him and Filzbalm solid.

"But in the dig site, we've been having some amazing discoveries." She angled the hover car toward a low building. "There are runes we never expected to find, proof of a civilization that was here thousands of years or more before we were. I don't know what's more exciting, the evidence of a previous society, or going back to the start of our own time on the planet."

"You've always told me that the universe is old enough, and none of us are the original inhabitants of our worlds." Solaria sounded a lot more like Del than herself, and Skylar wondered if she was trying to show off for him or her mother.

As they neared the building, a debris field came into view. It seemed to originate somewhere behind the place, and extend over the horizon.

"Right." Felonia pulled up in front of the building and cut the engine. "There's a fair amount of evidence in the dig site that the Pantherians were planted here. The problem is, even with evidence—hard, frozen evidence— most species aren't going to believe they didn't evolve on their world. There are too many similarities in most of the upright bipeds in the universe to think we might've generated from separate species. A five-fingered hand is not exactly the best way things should work."

"I guess so," Skylar mumbled. On Hummasssa the natives had three fingers, but he'd never stopped to think that the rest of them, beyond their hands, had looked a lot like him. And Solaria and her people did too: even if they were furry, they were about the same size and build as humans, and had five digits on their hands—he'd never seen Solaria's bare feet, so he couldn't say there. He hadn't expected to come on a break from school and end up thinking about scientific things.

Felonia got out of the hover car. "Okay. Let's go see if they found out anything since we left last night."

Skylar followed toward the closed door. The amount of damage was worse than he'd seen on the drive over. It reinforced the idea that the attack was more than just a single feeler. There had to be someone with mover abilities involved. Considering the debris trail outside, the inside of the building was in good order.

A tall, slender Pantherian with gold fur, who looked a bit like Felonia and Phil, was working at a computer terminal. She looked up as they came in. "Oh, Felonia. I think we may have found something interesting, I just can't make it out."

"What is it, Chillarni?" Felonia went over and stared over her shoulder. "It's definitely a language of some kind. I just don't recognize it. Have you run it through a translator?"

Chillarni nodded. "Right before you came in. There are a few repeated symbols, but nothing that really stands out. I don't think there's enough of it for the translator to work properly."

Skylar peered over her shoulder. It was a group of hieroglyphics. They were strange symbol-letters that didn't make any sense to him. "I wonder if Del could sort this out."

"Who's Del?" Felonia asked as she straightened to look at Skylar.

"He's a Tursiops we go to school with," Solaria said before Skylar could. "He's our best friend. He's really good with languages and riddles."

Again, Skylar was taken a bit aback. He'd never heard Solaria refer to Del as one of her best friends. He was, but she wasn't big into telling folks about that back at school.

Chillarni frowned. "We're still uncovering the wall where the writing is. Once we get it done, we might have enough to get the translator to work."

"Or we might not," Felonia said as she crossed her arms. "We need to try and get this sorted out as quickly as possible. You saw the damage that thing did last night. We need to know what it is and how to stop it as soon as possible. If Del can help, then let's send him pictures of the glyphs and see if he has any idea what they are."

"Okay." Skylar held his communicator over the small markings on the screen and snapped a couple of pictures. "Let me send them, and I'll inform you of what he has to say." As he sent the pictures, he hoped Del was awake and could help. Time flowed differently on each planet and he couldn't figure out if it was currently day or night on Stars' End, or if Del was even still on the station or had already gone on to the museum where he so wanted to be.

"I doubt he'll be able to do anything with it if the translator can't." Chillarni went back to her computer screen. "If we can get more of the permafrost chipped off the wall down there, we can have more of it exposed. Of course, we have a lot more exposed now than we did this time yesterday."

"Have we been able to determine what came out of the site?" Felonia asked.

"Not yet. It was big, that much we know." Chillarni pulled up a series of static-filled video feeds. "Whatever it was, it impacted electronics that were in close proximity. It was like it used a telekinetic burst as well as a telepathic blast. We're all lucky to be alive."

"Tell that to all the people in Glacier City," Felonia grumbled. "Come on kids, let's go take a look at things down in the site. It was a disaster last night by floodlight. It probably doesn't look any better now." She turned and walked out the door behind the desk, then down a long flight of wooden stairs.

"Wow, so we're going deep underground," Skylar said as the stairs led to a tunnel that continued down. Here and there, along the steeper parts of the tunnel, stairs had been carved, apparently to make the going easier. He started wondering why Felonia thought things would be different in the daylight than they had been under floodlight.

In the hood of his coat, Filzbalm stirred for the first time since they had taken off from Solaria's house. *"It feels strange down here."*

"Yeah it does." Skylar had thought it was just the act of going underground, but there was a strange prickling along his mental senses. The farther they went down, the more antsy he became. He wanted to run back up into the small building.

"What does?" Solaria asked from a few feet in front of him.

"Filzbalm was just saying that it feels strange down here," Skylar relayed, wishing the Solar Drake had included Solaria in his thoughts.

"Everyone says that," Felonia said. "I've been to a lot of archeological dig sites over the years and they all have an odd presence: old. I've never really been able to put my finger on it, but this one—this is different. Even the people like Chillarni who aren't very psychic can feel something unusual. So far, we haven't discovered anything to account for the sensation. It might be years before we do. At least it doesn't appear to be harmful."

That news didn't make it any easier for Skylar to keep walking down the stairs.

Before they reached the end of the stairs, natural light filled the tunnel, overriding the bright LEDs strung along the ceiling.

"What's causing this?" Solaria asked as they stepped into a huge chamber at the base of the stairs.

Her mother gestured up toward the ceiling, which had a huge hole in it. The ice along the edge of the hole was rough and jagged. "Until last night, the light was just from the ice here being unusually pure, crystal clear. I've never seen ice like it, particularly at the temperatures things get around here. Last night, whatever it was that attacked us and Glacier City blasted out of here. The hole made the light that much brighter. Any worse and we'd need protective eyewear."

"I hate snow blindness," Solaria said, moving away from the stairs.

"Luckily we're far enough down, we don't have to worry about it," Felonia said as she walked across the chamber. On the far side was the wall with the hieroglyphics. One man with thick black stripes on his orange fur was working with a chisel, knocking chunks of ice off the wall into a growing pile at his feet.

He turned and looked at them. "Felonia, did Chillarni show you the pictures? This is incredible. We've never had hard proof of a pre-settlement civilization before. This writing is primitive, nothing a spacefaring race would use. But we've been told for hundreds of years that if a planet was inhabited it wouldn't be intruded upon. This proves otherwise."

Felonia walked up next to him and put her hand on the wall. "It is amazing. And this wall literally hums with power."

"Even more than before." The man knocked another chunk off. "I think Romalda is down in the chamber we found last night when everything went crazy." He pointed with his hammer toward a new-looking rope ladder that went over the edge of the crater. It was such a large hole that Skylar wondered where all the ice that should've come out of it had gone. The area looked way too clean for the broken ice to be new, but the edges weren't worn in anyway.

"We couldn't get down there last night." Felonia looked down the ladder. "Thanks for bringing this."

"Thank Romalda—she was the one who showed up with it." He struck the chisel with his hammer again and more ice cascaded to the floor. "I figured we were going to need to go hire a couple of movers to float us down."

"If there are any strong movers in any shape to do anything today." Felonia walked to the edge of the hole and started down the ladder. "If you three want to come down you can—otherwise stay out of Clytin's way."

Solaria looked at Skylar. "I'm going. It's up to you."

Although Skylar didn't like the idea of climbing down a rope ladder into an icy pit, he nodded. "Sure. Let's go."

"I'll protect you," Filzbalm said.

Skylar resisted laughing. He really doubted the little Solar Drake could lift him up if he started to fall. The odd feeling grew stronger still as he knelt down to put his hands on the ice and lowered himself down to the first rung of the ladder. Everything swayed a little bit as either Solaria or Felonia did something below him to make his passage down less stable. He glanced at the heavy metal spikes in the ice where the ladder was anchored. They looked strong enough to support them all. He just hoped the cold wouldn't cause the rope to fray or anything before they got down, then back up.

The further down he went, the more he wished he was a mover like Solaria, since he'd have felt better if he could at least slow his fall if he slipped.

"You're almost there," Solaria called out as the ladder stopped moving with other people's motions.

"She's right below us," Filzbalm announced.

Skylar didn't want to look down. He stayed focused on the wall of ice a few inches from his nose. If he kept his gaze there, he wouldn't have a problem. He remembered why he hated climbing trees back on Hummassa. He'd always been afraid he was going to slip and fall, particularly after he'd done exactly that and broken his arm. His mother had fussed over him for days.

Suddenly there wasn't a rung under Skylar's foot. His heart pounded as he tried to find it.

"Skylar, you can drop from there," Solaria said in a familiar, somewhat haughty tone. "It's just a couple more feet."

He suddenly felt really stupid. It was all he could do to let go of the ladder and fall the couple of extra feet to the ground.

Solaria smiled broadly, then shook her head. "Sometimes you humans are so cautious. If you'd just embrace your predator side, things would come a lot easier." She turned and stalked across the open area to where her mother was talking with a woman covered in dark black fur. Or at least it looked dark black in the weaker light of the deep pit.

The strange pricking feeling was stronger than ever. Skylar wanted to scurry up the ladder and run up the stairs. Something deep in his brain wanted him to flee. He didn't feel like he was safe.

"It was huge," the dark female said. "I've never heard of anything on this planet so large."

"Do you think it might've been alien of some sort?" Felonia asked as she knelt down, running her hands along a shallow impression in the ice.

The dark female shrugged. "I honestly don't know. What I do know is when the laser drill hit the ice, something happened. It was like something was draining the light from the drill. Everything glowed bright, then exploded upward." She gestured through the hole they'd just climbed down. "I wish we had vid. But there was something—I don't know if it was telekinetic, an EMP, or what. It knocked everything out."

"Yeah, Chillarni showed us the static feeds." Felonia rose and walked around to the other side of the depression. "Glacier City is destroyed. Whatever got free from here is on a rampage."

"Glacier City?" The dark female frowned. "But the force wave didn't extend that far."

"Right, but whatever we let out traveled that far and is destroying everything in its path," Felonia said as she stood. "At this point, I think the two priorities are getting a translation of the wall upstairs, and cataloging this area. It doesn't look like there's anything down here other than this depression, which is too smooth to be natural ice. Someone left something buried down here, and we woke it up. Now we have to figure out what it is and stop it before it destroys Pantheria."

Skylar wanted to go find Phil and ask for a ride back to Stars' End. He'd been expecting a nice quiet break with Solaria showing him how to hunt and what her world was like. He didn't know what he was going to be able to do to help save the world, even if Aunt Blizza called him the Light—whatever that meant.

12
Lost Signal

WHEN THEY reached the office area again, Skylar's communicator beeped. He tapped it quickly, hoping for a message from Del saying he'd managed to decipher the glyphs. But it was just a system indicator saying his transmission couldn't reach the interplanetary net.

"Hey, does this mean everything's down?" He glanced at Solaria. "Try your com."

She did, then frowned when it beeped at her. "Mine's down too. I wonder if that strange pulse took it out."

"Local coms are working." Chillarni looked up from her computer terminal. "I've been uploading things to the main storage bank at your folk's house all day. But I can't reach off planet. And the closest interplanetary relay is in Glacier City."

Skylar sat on the edge of a desk. "Which has been destroyed."

"Right." Chillarni tapped something on her terminal and a 3D projection popped up next to Skylar, making him jump off the desk. "At this point, we're not getting any signals from Glacier City. Until we hear back from Aniu and Philaneo, we're not going to know how bad things are there. We could try bouncing a signal off the space port, but that might or might not work the way we need it to." The projection showed what looked like the communications grid for Pantheria. There was a dark spot near where Skylar thought they were. Lines from all the surrounding area turned black. The other lines appeared to be intact.

"Then we should at least try." Solaria made an adjustment to her com. When she tapped it, it gave her a normal beep. "If we force the signal to the spaceport we should be okay. Mom said something earlier about coms being spotty. I'm not Del, but I think the only thing that could really mess with the coms would be an EM pulse of some kind."

Skylar had had a brief class on how the coms worked when he got to Stars' End, but he didn't remember much of it. He tapped his com to bring up the projected display, then did what he thought should work. He got a high-pitched whine in his ear. Frowning, he put it back the way it had been, then made a different adjustment. It was a louder screeching noise.

Solaria shook her head. "Here." She took his hand and made small adjustments on the display. "Coms aren't that hard." When she was done, she tapped it and the display registered sending the images to Del. "That should work fine."

"Thanks," Skylar said.

"I paid close attention to what she did," Filzbalm announced. *"I'll be able to help you replicate the fix should the need arise."*

"Let's hope it doesn't," Skylar said. He didn't know how often communications networks went down, but as they were the heartbeat of the universe, he didn't think it would be broken for long. "I wonder if that interstellar com I have would be affected." Skylar suddenly wished he hadn't left it in his room back at school.

"Probably not," Solaria said. "That thing worked from Armstrong's Ring—it'll work anywhere."

Chillarni straightened and turned from her terminal. "You two have been on Armstrong's Ring? Your folks didn't say anything about that. It's one of the most secure systems in the galaxy."

"I think we're supposed to keep all that quiet," Solaria said. "Mom and Dad know, and Uncle Phil came to rescue us after our ship got blown up by Boarisk raiders. But beyond that, we aren't supposed to talk about what happened there."

"And the Mother of All Drakes greatly appreciates that," Filzbalm said, sounding like the leader of the Solar Drakes had just spoken to him. He did things like that from time to time, and it made Skylar wonder if she was somehow linked to Filzbalm even over the vast distances of space. There was so much about the Solar Drakes they didn't know, or at least, wasn't available on the public networks, or even the dark web. Del had been trying to find out more information for months with only minimal success, and if Del couldn't find it, it was either well-hidden, or wasn't out there.

Chillarni frowned. "I understand. We try to keep closemouthed over what we're finding here. Your mother said she'd told you a little about how we're discovering more and more evidence of pre-Pantherian society here. If there are things like this on other worlds with humanoid inhabitants, it could blow the lid off the ancient theory we all evolved on our own planets, no matter how much like humans we are."

"Right," Felonia said, coming through the door. "Kids, I just got a message from Aniu. He'll meet us just outside of Glacier City. The entire town isn't destroyed—there are survivors and they need us."

"Hey, before you go," Chillarni interrupted as she picked up something off the desk, "how do you want me to categorize this?" She held up a huge blue crystal that was nearly as long and thick as her forearm. The end of it looked like it had been carved to resemble a cat's paw with the claws extended. The paw motif was also carved into the central pad, where the digits connected. There was something about it that looked like the glyphs on the wall.

"Oh, so that survived the blast last night?" Felonia walked over and took it from her. "It's so delicate, it shouldn't have."

"I'm surprised the building is still standing." Chillarni ran her fingers over the hologram still projecting from the desk. "This telekinetic blast radius is one of the largest ever seen. I wouldn't doubt that the mover who did this is off our scale."

Felonia seemed to study the crystal for a moment before handing it back to Chillarni. "Go ahead and put it in the trunks with the other artifacts we've unearthed the past month. Keeping them all together is probably a good idea. Also, since the blast did some damage to the building, if you could take everything to the house, I'd appreciate that."

"Sure." Chillarni put the crystal back on the desk. "I'll run some drones down the new shafts and see if I can get some mapping done. Since the blast came from the dig site, maybe we can find something useful."

"I hope so," Felonia said as she gestured for Skylar, Solaria, and Filzbalm to follow her out the door that lead to the parking area. "We need to have something to tell the officials when they realize where the blast originated. I'm really surprised they haven't come knocking on our door already."

"Me too. They're most likely too busy with Glacier City."

Felonia opened the door. "You're probably right. I'll stay in touch. I'm routing communications through the main system at the space port, so unless something happens there, we should be fine."

"I hope nothing happens," Solaria muttered as they stepped through the door her mother was holding open.

"Me too," Skylar agreed. He didn't want to end up cut off from the universe, even if he was with Solaria and her family. There weren't many species in the galaxy that could go toe-to-toe with Pantherians, but something they'd released from the ice had managed to take out one of their cities. That was going to be a major problem. Skylar didn't want to come face-to-face with whatever that thing was.

13
Glacier City

A COLUMN of smoke rose up from the horizon as Felonia drove the hover car across the sheer ice plain. The wind had whipped up great piles of snow.

"You've got to be careful," Solaria said as they continued. "It's easy to get stuck in one of the snow drifts if you aren't paying attention to what you're doing. Since they're constantly moving in the wind, there's no way to map them."

Skylar said. "With any luck, I won't get caught out here without either one of your folks or Phil driving." He knew how to pilot a hover car—his mother had been teaching him right before the attack on Hummassa. He just didn't have a lot of experience doing it, let alone in a frozen, constantly changing environment.

Felonia said. "She's giving good advice—you don't know when you might be alone, or one of us might be injured. If you aren't careful out here you could get stuck and freeze to death, even with an envirosuit on. Their passive power systems only last so long."

"Right." Skylar shuddered. "I'll remember that."

"If that happened, I might be able to find a way to share the warmth from my ring with you," Filzbalm added. *"We really don't want to die out here."*

"No, we don't."

"That's looking really bad." Solaria pointed to the rising smoke, growing darker with each second they flew toward the destroyed city.

"I've never seen anything like it," Felonia said.

"Hummassa looked like this after the Boarisk attack," Skylar said. "Or at least Cordnisar, the city where I lived, did. It was horrible."

"Any kind of attack is horrible," Felonia said. "We have to be strong and see what we can do to save the survivors." Her com beeped and she tapped it to answer.

A hologram of Aniu hovered above her wrist. "We're on the south side of the city. Phil managed to get hold of the Intergal Rescue team a couple of systems over. They'll be here shortly. They were close to their stargate. More are coming soon. We've got the initial tents set up."

"Right," Felonia said, and turned the wheel. For a second the hologram stretched across the hover car, then went back to normal as her hand returned to a flat position.

"Over there." Solaria pointed toward something Skylar couldn't see.

"I've got you," Felonia said. "We'll be there shortly."

"See you soon." Aniu's image looked grim, then vanished.

"With the local coms down, some of the scanners might not be getting good readings," Felonia said. "So we're going to be relying more on our own minds and our observational skills than technology. Skylar, don't push yourself too hard. Solaria said you're a little behind most kids your age as far as using your psychic gifts."

He glared at Solaria, but kept his tone level. "I've learned a lot."

"Well, this'll be a major learning experience for you. A bit like what you were doing last night with Phil, but this time we know there are dead, and we also know there are survivors. The goal is finding the survivors and getting them to medical help." Felonia drove the hover car to the small cluster of tents and vehicles that sat on the ice flats just beyond the first of the shattered buildings.

Before she had the hover car stopped, Aniu came out of the closest tent. He rushed up and gave her a big hug as soon as she got out of the vehicle. "It's the worst thing I've ever seen. I wish you all didn't have to be here for it."

She hugged him back. "I'm sure all the people who didn't survive would wish we didn't have to be here too." She released him. "Now, let's get busy."

Skylar got out of the hover car, and Filzbalm snuggled deeper in the hood of his coat. The wind felt like it was worse than it had been at the dig site. It made the bit of exposed skin on Skylar's hands and nose instantly cold. He shivered.

"Catch." Solaria threw something at him.

He barely managed to get his hand up in time to snatch the gloves and face mask she'd tossed.

"We always carry spares. They'll work with your thermal suit to help keep you warm." She took out a knit mask like the one she'd thrown him and rolled it down over her face, even covering her ears with the thin fabric. It was the first time he'd ever seen her with anything, other than an envirosuit, on over her head. It looked like a gray blob on her shoulders. "The winds here are horrible."

"Yes, they are." Her mother waved them all toward the tent her father had appeared from.

As they walked, Skylar put on the mask Solaria had given him, then pulled the gloves over his hands. The change was almost instantaneous. There wasn't a lot of warmth in the small tent—that tent reminded him of the ones Intergal Rescue had used on Hummassa. But there, the wind hadn't been so bad and whipped things around so dramatically.

Aniu handed Solaria a holomap. "We're trying to mark the areas we've already been through, but we have to keep coming back to basecamp to synchronize the holomaps. With the com network down, we can't rely on the maps to stay up-to-date." He paused and smiled at them. "I also want to make sure the three of you are okay from time to time. If you don't check in every two standard hours, either I or your mother—" he stared at Solaria for a moment before continuing "—will come looking for you, starting at your last known location."

Solaria sighed and Skylar was pretty sure she'd rolled her eyes, even though the mask hid her expressions. "I was born here, Dad. I know the drill for a snow-blind situation. I'll keep Skylar close so he doesn't get lost, although I'm sure Filzbalm will let me know if there's anything wrong."

"She's right." Filzbalm shifted slightly in Skylar's hood, spreading the warmth against Skylar's neck out farther.

"Okay." Aniu popped up his holomap. There was the vague delineation of streets and neighborhoods, but it looked like everything else had been wiped out, blown apart and fallen over like a model city in a windstorm. "I want the two of…sorry, three of you—" he glanced at Skylar's hood, as if he'd momentarily forgotten about Filzbalm "—to start over here. Do a house by house search like you did last night with Phil. If you find anyone, see if you can get to them without moving anything. If you can't, try your coms. We're hoping routing them through the spaceport network will continue to be stable. If for some reason you can't get through on the coms, then let the person know help is on the way and come back to camp. Phil says there're going to be several movers coming in with the Intergal ships. They'll be able to help us get to people." He looked at Solaria again. "I don't want you to overtax yourself, young lady. If you think it's too big to move, it probably is."

She nodded. "I understand." Her tone was quiet and a little dangerous. Solaria didn't like being told what she could and couldn't do. It was one of the things Skylar had learned early on about her.

Felonia gave her a quick hug. "We're going to be working near your zone, so we can get to you quickly."

Watching such exchanges still made Skylar miss his mother. He turned away as Phil came up, with a large Pantherian over his shoulder. "You kids be careful out there," he said without stopping as he carried the man to a cot and laid him down. "This is some of the worst destruction I've seen in thirty years with Intergal. If we didn't need the help, we wouldn't have called you two in."

"I like being helpful," Skylar said as he watched Phil get the man settled.

Phil straightened and looked at Skylar. "You're a fairly remarkable kid, Skylar, even if you don't look like much at first glance. I guess that's one of the reasons you and Filzbalm get to explore the galaxy."

"Come on, Skylar." Solaria tapped him on the shoulder. "We've got people to find."

"Be careful," Phil repeated as he bent back over the man he'd brought in. "Some of the buildings are ready to fall with the next strong wind."

"We will, Uncle Phil." Solaria waved and headed out the door. Skylar hurried after her.

"We'll be fine," Solaria muttered as they started out away from the tents, heading around the edge of the ruined city.

"I know." Skylar hurried along with her, which was a bit of work since she was stalking across the frozen ground fairly quickly. "But at least you still have your family."

"And thanks to Uncle Phil, we're kinda your family too." She stopped and looked at him. Her eyes were the only part of her face visible in the gray woven mask. "Uncle Phil thinks you're important. But you're also a lot cooler than most of the other kids at school. Mom wouldn't let just anyone come home with me."

Skylar had figured they'd issued the invite simply because they didn't want him to be alone. Combined with Aunt Blizza's ramblings, he was beginning to wonder what was going on and what people were expecting out of him. He didn't like the idea that he was special. Sure, he had psychic powers he'd never suspected, but they were treating him like something more and that made him nervous.

Solaria turned down the start of one of the streets. "This is the edge of our sector. Wake Filzbalm up and see if he can help with the scanning. It might make this go faster if we don't have to go into every building looking for people."

Filzbalm yawned. *"I can help. I'm not asleep."* His mental voice was loud enough Skylar was fairly sure he wasn't going to have to relay the thought to Solaria. *"But we might want to check each building even if none of us can get a reading of life. There are some heavy shields that are still intact."*

"Shields?" Solaria frowned and then looked at her holomap. She shook her head. "Okay, so we ended up in Psy-town."

"What?" Skylar asked, looking at the buildings that appeared to be made of ice rather than the traditional wood or brick buildings he was used to.

"Glacier City and some of the other larger cities on Pantheria have special sections of town for psychics," Solaria explained as she continued walking toward the first dwelling. "The non-psis think it keeps them safer from us. Helps prevent minor telekinetic bursts from hurting them, or restrains the nightmares of strong readers so they don't impact their sleep. Mom and Dad never said much about it, but since attending Stars' End, I realize it's just a way for scared people to feel safer."

Skylar knew his own mother had been terrified of psychics, and he'd had to overcome that fear to learn to accept his own gifts. At school, the teachers and other students made it sound like most planets accepted their psychic population. This made it sound like, at least on Pantheria, psychics were feared.

"You bipeds fear a lot of things," Filzbalm said, softer than when he'd been loud enough for Solaria to hear. *"If you let fear control you, you can never really prosper as a species."*

Solaria stopped at the first house. When Skylar thought about the spaceport and how so much of it had been designed to look like it was part of the environment, he wondered if that was what they had been trying in Glacier City as well—to make their city look like something built of ice and snow, and now that it was crumbling, it looked like crushed ice.

"I don't feel anything," she said, but continued to stare at the building.

Skylar carefully lowered his personal shields and reached out with his mind. It didn't feel like there was anything, or anyone there. "Me neither."

"I agree," Filzbalm announced loudly. *"And there are no shields in place around this dwelling. I believe we are safe continuing on."*

Solaria turned and walked across the lane. "Then let's keep moving. We don't want to stay out past dark. A storm could come up. It's spring—storms can brew quickly and hit hard."

"Okay. I'm following you." Skylar figured it was probably for the best to just follow along and do anything

Solaria suggested. She was the native and the more experienced psychic.

"Good." She walked up the three steps to the door. Neither the steps or the door seemed overly damaged, but the windows were all broken out, and the roof was sagging. Solaria sighed. "I think there's a shield here."

"You're right," Filzbalm said before Skylar could comment.

There was a feeling of emptiness in the structure. But that was slightly different from the feeling of not having anyone there. It was like there was a void between him and the next building. Skylar had never stopped to wonder what Professor Aduncus' shielded workroom must feel like from the outside. He just knew what it felt like from the inside. Sometimes he needed to slow down in his constantly hectic life and notice more so he was better prepared for the things he ran across.

"Alright, so we go inside." Solaria pushed against the door. It didn't open. She pulled her arm back, and something tingled along Skylar's senses right before she slammed her fist into the door. It shook slightly, then creaked open.

"Movers gotta move," she said lightly as she pushed the door open. "Hello?" She called with both her voice and her mind.

They waited on the threshold for almost a minute, listening for a response. An uneasy silence filled the air around them.

"Okay." Solaria stepped into the battered home. "Let's see who we can find."

Without a word, Skylar followed her in. An easy, peaceful feeling existed in the house. The shield was still in place, but Skylar felt like it was probably just an empathic shield. There was too much physical damage for it to have been a field to keep a mover's powers contained. The shelves and bookcases were tossed around and lay on the floor, their contents broken and scattered.

Solaria hissed and stepped back from the first room she'd looked into. "We don't need to go in there." She hurried to the next room. "I don't think there's anyone here."

Skylar paused and looked into the room. A leg with orange and black fur stretched out from under large chunks of icy ceiling pieces. It was too still to be alive. Skylar turned and hurried after Solaria. He'd seen enough death in the past year—he didn't want to dwell on any more.

SKYLAR'S FEET were sore. He pulled his glove down slightly so he could see his com. Based on the time, they'd been searching Psy-town for three hours. The cold had permeated the place and him. Although Filzbalm kept assuring him he was warm enough, Skylar wasn't sure *he* was ever going to be warm enough again. He and Solaria hadn't encountered anyone alive. They were marking the houses where they found bodies on the holomap, so once Intergal Rescue had accounted for all the living, they could go back and take care of the dead.

Solaria paused at a door. "What do you think— should we just bust it down and go on in? Doesn't seem to be much point right now with being polite."

Skylar pursed his lips. He had to agree with her, but it still felt wrong barging into a place when they didn't know for sure if there was anyone there or not. With what they'd seen to that point, the odds weren't in their favor of finding anyone, but he didn't want to take that for granted.

"Just in case—let's do it the way we have been."

She sighed wearily. "Okay." She tried the door first. It swung open. All the others had been locked. She stared for a moment before calling out.

In the distance, a soft voice hollered for help.

Skylar's heart raced. He'd been hoping for someone to be alive.

Solaria moved before he could. "We're coming!"

"She's over to the right!" Filzbalm sounded as excited as Skylar felt.

They went down a short hallway, climbing over the remains of crumbled walls and ceilings. A shattered door frame had enough strength left in it to keep some of the debris from hitting the floor and provided a space for them to get through.

The ice-like building material let a lot of light through, making it almost day-bright inside, even in the spots where the roof was intact. A sleek black-furred arm stuck out of some of the rubble, but it was still twitching.

Solaria touched the hand. "We're here. Are you in a debris pocket, and is there anything else on you? Can you move your hand?"

The fingers curled around hers. "I managed to block most of the wreckage, but my arm is stuck and I've got something heavy on my legs." The voice sounded vaguely familiar, but it shook and she was obviously near tears.

"I'm a mover," Solaria said. "I'm going to try and shift this off you so we can get you out."

"I've been trying, but I'm only a level two and it's too heavy for me. She was so angry. She shattered the shields. She's too powerful." The girl was rambling.

Skylar wondered who *she* was, but they needed to get her free, then they could concern themselves with that mystery.

"Don't worry—if I can't get this, we'll go get someone stronger who can." Solaria gave her hand a final squeeze and straightened.

"What do we do?" Skylar asked. He really wished he was a mover and could help out.

"I want to try something," Solaria said, and let out a long breath. "Remember how we joined minds when Filzbalm hatched?"

They'd worked together with Del to help the little Solar Drake out of his egg and into the world. It had been the first time Skylar had used his new gifts in unison with other people. "Yeah. But that was telepathic, not telekinetic. I'm not a mover."

"But I am," Solaria countered. "I read somewhere a while back that movers could augment their powers with the help of other psychics. If you and Filzbalm link with me and send me power, I should be strong enough to get her free. We don't know how long it'll be before Mom and Dad can get someone here."

Skylar didn't like the idea of leaving the first person they'd found alive stranded until they could get someone else to help. He was willing to give it a try.

"I'll help, too." Filzbalm uncurled himself from the back of Skylar's neck and walked out onto his shoulder. *"I'll touch both of you, it will make this easier."* He spread his wings so the tip of the one nearest Solaria brushed her gray mask.

The fabric wasn't enough to keep a connection from forming. As Filzbalm joined them, Skylar was acutely aware of Solaria's thoughts. She was terrified she wasn't going to be strong enough to save the woman, or worse, that she wouldn't have the stamina to hold the load once she had it high enough to get her out.

"We can do this," Skylar said, doing his best to sound reassuring. "You're really strong, mentally and physically."

"Thanks," she whispered, then closed her eyes.

A slight sucking feeling encompassed Skylar, like he had just opened himself to the vastness of space and was being pulled out. Everything flowed toward Solaria.

He felt a little light-headed before Filzbalm did something to regulate the flow between them.

Through their link, Skylar was well aware of the force Solaria put behind her thoughts as she reached out with her mind. He could almost see the woman—actually she was more the size of a teenager, like them. Solaria felt around her to get a mental grip on the pieces of roof, wall, and shelf that lay across her legs and formed the air pocket around her. With a huge surge of power that dropped both of them to their knees, Solaria forced the debris upward.

"Skylar, grab her hand and pull her out!" she shouted through their link.

She was pulling so much power that Skylar had trouble focusing. He grabbed the dark hand Solaria had held minutes earlier. "Come on!" He pulled her through the opening Solaria had created.

Skylar rocked backward with the effort of yanking the girl through while he was on his knees. The motion broke the physical connection Filzbalm was maintaining. A backlash of psychic energy hit them. Something crashed not far away, and a bubble of energy sprung up around them.

"Are you all okay?" Solaria asked, sounding weak and wobbly.

"I think so." Skylar rubbed his throbbing head. "Let's not do that again any time soon."

"I am fine," Filzbalm announced, then slipped back into Skylar's hood.

"She's very angry," said the girl they'd rescued. In the pale light they finally got their first real look at her. She was covered in dust, dirt and crystalline debris, but he recognized her.

Solaria flung herself at the girl and hugged her. "Leonada, oh my gods."

Leonada hugged her back. "Solaria, is that really you? I didn't know you were so strong." She blinked, then jerked back. "She will destroy our world to reclaim hers." Then she collapsed.

Skylar stared at Solaria's roommate from school. He couldn't figure out what it was about Pantherians who were suddenly spouting strangeness. He didn't know Leonada very well, but she was a fairly stable girl. Smart, and almost as good at Z-GBall as Solaria. Why she was babbling, he had no idea. Like Solaria, she wasn't prone to rambling on about nothing. It made Skylar wonder what she'd endured when Glacier City was destroyed.

14
Pantherian Council

SKYLAR DID his best to stay out of the way after they got Leonada to the rescue tents. While they'd been out, at least one of the Intergal ships had arrived. There were more people, most of them from other worlds, around the basecamp. The two who'd spotted him and Solaria carrying Leonada between them hadn't recognized them and had been worried they were also survivors. Phil showed up with another survivor about the same time and smoothed things over for them.

"Here." Solaria handed Skylar a warm drink. "This will help with the fatigue."

He glanced in the steaming mug. "What is it?"

"An herbal brew Uncle Phil uses to get his strength back when he's been rescuing people for too long." She'd already pulled her mask off. When she took a sip of the liquid, she curled her lips, flashing her fangs. "Man, this stuff is vile. But it does help. I keep some at school so I don't have to crash so hard after a touch Z-GBall game, or a rough day of mover training."

Pursing his lips, Skylar braced himself for something that tasted like medicine, but when he sipped it, it reminded him of one of the holiday drinks Teir's family used to make on Hummassa. He wondered what was in it and if it might be the same things the Hummassans used, although he doubted it. Herbs from different planets could taste similar, but have completely different effects. "Not too bad."

Solaria downed the rest of hers in one gulp, then shook her head. "You have strange taste buds, Skylar."

Filzbalm crawled out of Skylar's hood and down his arm to take a quick lap of the stuff. *"Not bad, but I think it is more suited for someone who is either omnivorous or herbivorous. Carnivores wouldn't like it."* He took a longer drink, then climbed back up to his spot in the hood. *"Definitely rejuvenating."*

Uncle Phil came over after conversing with the medic looking after Leonada. "She's like the others we've found. A little worse since she's a psi. They're all going on about anger, or she's angry, or she's going to take back her planet. The sad thing is, they keep jumping back and forth between being fine and ranting. It's almost like whatever attacked them has imprinted something on their minds. Like it's a warning."

Solaria frowned as she put her cup down on the small bedside table next to the unused cot with a pillow and folded utility blanket they all stood next to. "A warning of what, that we have to leave the planet? This has been our home for nearly a thousand years, more if we're to believe what we're told by the people who think we evolved here."

"If we're dealing with a force that can destroy a city in a few hours, we might not have much of a choice," Phil said. "Right before I found my latest survivor, I was informed that the Pantherian Council is convening at the spaceport. Since I'm the liaison between our people and Intergal Rescue, they want me there. They're also requesting your parents be there since the trail of destruction starts at their dig site." Phil sighed and finished off his own mug of brew. "I'd rather not go. We haven't finished going through the whole city, but I don't have much choice and we've got another ship of rescuers that cleared the inner stargate an hour ago. It'll be in orbit in a few hours. It's a hospital ship and we'll be able to get the survivors out. I won't be needed as much for that."

Felonia stalked over, looking cold and tired. "You explaining things to the kids?"

Phil nodded. "About to get to the good part."

"Let me." She rubbed the back of her neck. "We've got a couple of options for you kids. Either you can go with us to the spaceport, or you can go home and stay with Blizza."

The less time Skylar had to spend with the old Pantherian, the better he liked it. Before he could voice his opinion, Solaria spoke up. "I think we should head to the spaceport. I've seen all the reports on how the council works, but I've never seen then in action. I'm actually amazed this managed to get them doing something."

"Are you okay with that, Skylar?" Felonia asked.

Skylar nodded. "Sure. But why does your planetary council meet at the spaceport? Don't you have a capital city or something?"

"In case you haven't figured it out, we're a fairly clan-based society. Even as we grew into a spacefaring species, we maintained our clan, or village, way of life," Phil explained. "Until we built the spaceport, we didn't actually have permanent neutral ground to discuss things. Every time something major came up, we had to declare neutral ground to resolve it."

"And when they built the spaceport, all the clan leaders declared it neutral so if fighting broke out, we wouldn't lose contact with the rest of the universe," Solaria interrupted.

Phil glared at her, but didn't reprimand her for rudeness. "She's right." He glanced at Felonia. "Is Aniu back? It might save a little time if we could all ride together."

Felonia got a faraway look, then sighed. "He's coming in. His team located another survivor. We're finding them, but not in large numbers. Glacier City might never be rebuilt if this is all we've got to populate it."

"She was fairly devastating, whoever she happens to be." Phil set his cup down next to Solaria's.

Skylar added his cup to the growing collection. He was already feeling better, although his head still pounded slightly. At least his thoughts were his own and he wasn't having trouble putting them together.

THE MINUTE Skylar walked into the council room at the spaceport, he could tell it had a dampening field around it. In the hall, the chaotic thoughts and emotions rolled over him like a rough ocean wave, but inside the room, everything was quiet in his mind. Even Filzbalm seemed far away. The link with the Solar Drake was weaker than it had been since it finished forming on Armstrong's Ring. A stab of fear went through Skylar.

"Don't worry, I'm still with you." Filzbalm rubbed his head against Skylar's ear. *"They really don't want people reading each other's minds in here."*

"Feels like it," Skylar replied silently.

A sleek Pantherian with orange fur offset with large dark rosettes approached them. "Philaneo, Felonia, and Aniu, thank you for making it so quickly."

Phil bowed slightly. "Zhetallia, I wish this could've waited a little while. We were still going through Glacier City looking for survivors."

Zhetallia frowned and cocked her head. "We were informed more Intergal ships had cleared the inner stargate, with one of the larger ships soon to go through the outer gate. We figured there were enough feet on the ground to cover for you while we met to discuss the situation."

"That's correct." Phil frowned as he took the woman's arm and stepped out of the doorway. "But

Glacier City is a complete disaster. We need everybody we can spare to finish the rescue mission. With our extreme climate, it's more important than on temperate planets to find any survivors as quickly as possible."

"Then we'll do our best to not keep you overly long." Zhetallia jerked her arm out of Phil's grasp and snapped, "We're only waiting on two more village elders to arrive, then we can begin. Unless you can report Hezpulana from Glacier City is among the survivors you've found."

"No." Phil sighed and put his hands together over his stomach. "Unfortunately, the mayor of Glacier City has been identified among the dead."

"Then we don't need to wait for her." Zhetallia moved to the head of the table.

Skylar wished he could mentally ask Solaria what was going on, but the room's defenses prevented him from touching her mind.

"Over here." Felonia led them to a small group of chairs set back from the table. "Since we're not chiefs, elders, or mayors, we sit back here."

Solaria leaned close to her mother. "So, I guess we should stay quiet and just watch?"

Felonia cocked her head and sighed before hugging Solaria. "You are so very much your father's daughter." Her voice was soft and gentle. "Yes, please. I'm sure if there's a spot where your input would be appreciated, you'll know."

"I hope this is more interesting than a history lesson at school." Solaria plopped down in a chair, then looked up at Skylar and patted the one next to her.

Skylar sat, but the room was so cool he kept his coat on and hood up, hoping he wouldn't insult anyone by doing so. It also helped keep Filzbalm out of sight, since he was again curled up around the base of Skylar's neck.

Things grew fairly quiet as they waited for the last couple of people to show up. There were brief, whispered discussions. At one point, the biggest Pantherian Skylar had ever seen came over to where they were sitting and waiting patiently.

The man was a good seven feet tall with tawny fur marked by scattered rosettes. His shoulders were easily twice the width of Skylar's. "Aniu Unica, I believe you are responsible for the human in our midst."

Standing, Solaria's father nodded. "I am. He's here as part of our family and was on Pantheria before the incident happened."

"And you have brought him to the council chamber—why?" The big man looked between Skylar and Solaria. "This is not likely to be a discussion children should be exposed to."

Phil rose and stood at Aniu's side. "Under normal circumstances we would agree with you, Sabeto, but these are hardly normal circumstances. As a father yourself, I'm sure you can understand wanting to keep a family together in uncertain times. We also felt it would be a good idea to expose Solaria to the working of government. Skylar came along rather than having us leave him at home, wondering what was going on."

Sabeto frowned, but didn't bare his teeth. His look made Skylar shiver. The big Pantherian obviously had something against humans, but Skylar doubted he'd get to find out what it was, and as long as it didn't get him killed, he really didn't care. Skylar looked away first, remembering what Solaria had told him months earlier about dominance and how if you wanted someone to overlook you, you shouldn't look at them.

"We expect you to keep them quiet." Sabeto turned and stomped back to the table where two new Pantherians had just arrived.

Zhetallia stood at the table. "I want to thank everyone for coming on such short notice. I think we all understand that we can't schedule catastrophes, and what we are dealing with here is definitely a catastrophe."

One of men who'd showed up at the last raised a hand. "Do we know what happened to Glacier City?"

"Other than the utter destruction of the city and most of the people therein, no," Zhetallia said. "But maybe Philaneo Clawson, who was present when the disruption began and has been at Glacier City working on rescue efforts, can explain what they've found so far." She pointed at Phil.

Phil stood and approached the table. "Esteemed council members." He bowed slightly. "It saddens me to be here under such dire circumstances." For several minutes, he related the past day, from the time the first attack happened until he was called to council.

When he was finished a strained silence filled the room. Then a heavy-set woman with nearly pure white fur raised her hand. "Philaneo, do we have any theory on why the Indruias settlement and the smaller encampments between there and Glacier City were spared, if the attack did indeed begin at the dig site in Indruias?"

That was one of the big questions Skylar hadn't been able to figure out. It didn't make much sense that something would nearly destroy one city while leaving a smaller settlement untouched, unless you counted knocking most everyone there out or giving them raging headaches. He wasn't overly surprised the council knew where the destruction started—all they would've had to do was look at satellite images to see the trail of destruction that seemed to grow the farther the force got along its path.

"Until we know exactly what we are dealing with, we'll not be able to answer that question," Phil replied, leaning heavily on the table.

"And do we have any idea what we are dealing with? Other than a very powerful psychic force?" The woman pushed on with her questions.

Aniu stood and walked up beside Phil. "I may be more qualified to answer that than Philaneo is."

Zhetallia inclined her head toward him. "The council recognizes Aniu Unica, chief archeologist. What has your team found?"

"As has already been stated, it has a very power psychic force—beyond that, we aren't sure. We believe it may be one of the originals."

The room erupted into shouts and accusations. Zhetallia pounded on the table with her fists but the chaos continued. She roared at the top of her lungs, and everyone stopped talking or shouting and stared at her.

"Council members, we need to hear Professor Unica out. He's well thought of in our academic circles. He's not prone to flights of fancy."

"But we don't need to hear fantasies about long established myths," Sabeto shouted nearly as loud as Zhetallia had roared.

"But all myths have a basis in fact," Aniu countered. "Please, council members, if you would give me a moment. I know some of our beliefs are a bit outside established thinking, but we are discovering facts to back us up."

"It is easy to misinterpret the facts when you already have a mold you wish them to fit into," Sabeto snapped as he glared at Aniu.

"That is very true," Aniu countered. "But let me assure you that what we are discovering at the dig site outside Indruias has taken us by surprise and only helped confirm what we have suspected for some time." He glanced toward the seats where Skylar, Solaria and Felonia were seated. At his nod, Felonia rose and strolled over to him.

"If you would, please allow us to show you what we've found so far." She pressed the back of her hand onto the table so she could link her com with the table. Seconds later a hologram rose from the table.

Skylar recognized the dig site. The representation floated there for a moment, until she reached into it and spread her fingers apart to cause the hologram to zoom in. It was just part of the pictures Skylar had sent to Del and still hadn't received a response on.

"We believe this is a language from before the colonization of Pantheria," Felonia explained, slowly panning through the primitive writing.

"Don't you mean before our species evolved?" Zhatalla said.

Aniu shook his head as he took over the narrative from his wife. "No, we do not. There's growing evidence that our species, like many others in the galaxy, was genetically engineered—most likely by humans since theirs are the genes we all have in common."

"That's preposterous." Sabeto stood and glared at Aniu.

Skylar's heart pounded as it looked like the larger man might attack Solaria's father.

"No. It's science," Aniu said, his voice level and unemotional. "Science often proposes preposterous things, only to have them proven over the years. I believe that is what will happen with this. But I don't think it is going to take years."

"I tend to agree with you," said a man who appeared in the doorway.

Everyone turned to stare at him. He was the first human, other than himself, Skylar had seen since leaving Stars' End.

15
Cafpar O'Byrne

THE MAN was dressed in an impeccable dark blue coat that matched his eyes and briskly walked up to the table. Like Skylar, he was dressed for the cold, but he didn't have on gloves. Skylar wondered how the man's fingers weren't freezing, even with the slight heating the spaceport had.

"Is there something wrong?" Filzbalm asked, but didn't move. *"Something has changed."*

"Can you see the man who just walked in?" Skylar didn't want to stare. He wanted to stay as close to invisible as possible.

"The human. He's fairly unremarkable, but he moves like he's a professor at school."

It was more than that. With the weakness of their link while in the room, Skylar didn't want to try to explain complicated things to Filzbalm.

"I don't think you belong here, *human*." Sabeto stressed the last word like it was something foul.

Zhetallia stood. "Sabeto, sit down." She pointed hard at his chair. "Please excuse my colleague, Cafpar O'Byrne, these are troubling times."

Skylar's breath caught. Although he hadn't recognized the man, he knew the name Cafpar O'Byrne. Nearly all humans, and individuals who did any travel between planets, knew the name. He was the CEO of O'Byrne Corporation, the most powerful company in the galaxy. They controlled the production of the majority of human starships, and most of the ships used by the other bipedal races. It was rumored they were trying to get control of the other races' transports too. They had helped establish the stargate system nearly a thousand years earlier. They were also rumored to have control of most of the Central Galactic Council, either through money, blood, or manipulation.

O'Byrne inclined his head toward her. "Indeed it is." He walked over to one of the several empty chairs around the table and sat across from Zhetallia. "I was near a stargate when I heard of the crisis here and came to offer whatever aid O'Byrne Corporation and the Central Galactic Council can provide. I have President Cranby's assureance that we will do everything we can to rebuild Glacier City."

"What about all the lives lost there?" Sabeto grumbled. "Do you have the ability to bring them back?"

"Unfortunately not." O'Byrne put his hands on the table. His dermal com glistened gold on the back of his right wrist. "But we can get the city ready for new settlers."

Sabeto shot to his feet and glared. "No!" he roared. "The Galactic Council will not resettle one of our cities that has been destroyed. We will not allow it."

O'Byrne waved the idea away. "That's not what I meant. Pantheria is still a developing planet. There is plenty of room for your people to grow and expand. Glacier City was one of the largest here. Its loss will hinder your people. I simply meant that we could prepare the city for when your people are ready to resettle it. The only offworlders we'd suggest are builders, and then only as long as they're needed. We would suggest that you consider more interaction with the Central Galactic Council in return for our help. There are a lot of advantages to being more active in the council."

Zhetallia again motioned for Sabeto to be seated.

He glared but did it.

"We can consider your proposal, Mr. O'Byrne, but right now we're trying to determine what happened and how to prevent it from occurring again. As you pointed out, Glacier City is one of our largest cities, but it's not the largest, or the most important. We need to acquire more information if we're to determine how to keep our people safe."

O'Byrne nodded. "Of course you do. I believe your Mr. Unica was giving us his theory on an original inhabitant arising to smite the invaders down." He gestured at Aniu. "Please, Mr. Unica, continue."

Skylar tried to understand how one man could walk into a meeting of a group who weren't even the same species and suddenly take over. He knew how arrogant a lot of the corp-brats he'd dealt with both on Stars' End and on Hummassa had been, but this was more than arrogance. This was a man who wielded power and was used to people doing what he wanted. Skylar wondered how long it had taken for him to get so powerful, and what he would do if the people around the table decided they didn't want to listen to him.

Aniu glanced at Zhetallia, who nodded. "As we were explaining, we are finding evidence that humans created a good number of the bipedal races in the galaxy."

O'Byrne shrugged. "I'm sure you can understand why I can't confirm that at this time."

The way he phrased it was all but a confession of humans playing with the other races. The idea hit Skylar hard. He'd always believed that each species evolved on their own home world. A good number of systems had planets that were capable of supporting carbon-based lifeforms, and on those places beings had mostly developed either as bipeds or quadrupeds. Even with what he'd heard around the Unica household since he arrived on Pantheria, to actually have one of the most powerful humans in the galaxy admit it made him stop and think.

"Not exactly surprising," Filzbalm said from Skylar's hood.

"But why is he admitting it now?" Skylar wondered to the Solar Drake. He wished he could ask Solaria, but knew they dared not even whisper. He didn't want any attention on him. The stress level in the room was rising with each word, and he didn't want to be the one to cause it to boil over.

"What?" Zhetallia roared. "How can you sit there and calmly all but admit this? This…this…this is outrage. How dare you come to our planet and say this!"

Others turned to each other, expressing their displeasure more quietly, but no less adamantly if the waving of hands and throwing of papers and cups was any indication. In just a few seconds, they'd damaged the table well beyond easy repair—it was going to need to be replaced due to scratches and chunks taken out of it.

Several members of the council stood, glaring at O'Byrne, looking like they were about to take him down before their neighbor put a calming hand on their shoulders, or one of the security guards leveled hard looks that resigned them back to their chairs.

"This is going to turn the Galactic Council on its ear," Phil said with more anger than Skylar had ever heard.

He was right—the news would to upend things on a level the Council hadn't seen in hundreds, if not a thousand, years.

Even as he wanted to fade away into the woodwork, O'Byrne's gaze fell on him. He seemed to study Skylar for a moment as he continued talking. There was a searching intensity in his gaze that told Skylar he could tell Skylar and Filzbalm were speaking telepathically, but that shouldn't have been possible in the dampened room.

"If I were to confirm your suspisions, I'm sure you understand that the original human explorers didn't find all enviroments to our liking, and in most cases it was just easier to find other mammals which had traits that would allow them to survive on a hostile planet…like Pantheria. Unfortunately, those other mammals needed pushing to get to the point they could be our equals. So we made the genetic sacrifice and found ways to control the new planets we found."

"At the expense of other species?" Felonia sounded furious. "What gave you the right to do that?"

O'Byrne sighed dramatically. "People have been debating conquerors' rights for many thousands of years. Let's just say, for the most part, we had the bigger guns. But that doesn't resolve your problem on Pantheria. We need to find whatever it was you let loose and stop it before it lays waste to more of your cities."

"What? You don't know what was here before us?" Felonia's claws left groves in the table surface.

"I have researchers working on it. But sometimes, even highly classified information can be lost. For now, let's just say that I believe your theories are correct and we need to find it and stop it. To that end, I will assist you in locating your attacker."

"So this is the humans' fault," Sabeto grumbled.

"I didn't say that," O'Byrne objected.

Skylar projected a feeling of calm to Filzbalm, hoping the Solar Drake would get the idea to stay quiet until they could get out of the room and away from Cafpar O'Bryne. With the level of agitation coming off Filzbalm, he could come bursting out at any moment, and some gut instinct told Skylar that would be very bad.

Several coms beeped at once. Phil's was one of them. He stepped back away from the table as he answered it. "What? You're sure? I'm on my way."

"Zhetallia." One of the other Pantherians stood. "It is attacking my city. I must go."

"If I could get a ride with you, Lusino," Phil said. "I believe it might be faster than my hover car, and my ship won't be ready to leave the space port for several hours."

"I might be of some help too," Aniu announced. "If it's like the last attack, we'll need every hand we can get.

"I have a long range shuttle we can use," O'Byrne said. "I can have us there in minutes."

Without much discussion, the ones whose coms had gone off followed him out of the room, all of them moving as quickly as possible.

Skylar stayed in his seat as some of the remaining adults conferred around Zhetallia.

Solaria leaned over. "I still think you look like an O'Byrne."

He rolled his eyes. "I really am starting to believe you just think all humans look alike." Other than the color of their hair and eyes, he didn't see much resemblance.

With a soft chuckle, Solaria tapped near the corner of her right eye. "Predator."

There were times that her fallback answer to things like that really irritated him, but he stayed quiet. Although Skylar's mother had never given him a name for his father, he couldn't see any way it could be Cafpar O'Byrne. He was the CEO of a major corporation, and she'd hated everything to do with corps. She also hated psychics and he was sure O'Byrne was a fairly strong one. There was no way Solaria was right.

16
Scattered Words

SKYLAR STAYED quiet as the council meeting hastily wrapped up and then followed Solaria and Felonia out to their hover car. He waited until they were on the way back to Indruias before he started asking questions.

"If the bipedal races being gene-engineered by humans is such a secret, why did O'Byrne tell us just now, and why didn't he make all of us sign nondisclosure agreements or something?"

"I'm betting he had the agreements ready and the new attack distracted him," Felonia said as she turned on the hover car's lights. She tapped the autopilot icon on the control screen, then turned in her seat.

"Can we look forward to him showing up with them soon?" Solaria asked. "And didn't you think O'Byrne looks a lot like Skylar?"

A thoughtful line crossed Felonia's brow. "Maybe." She hummed. "Yes, I can see some resemblance, but as diverse as humans have become, it's hard to say. They've been playing with their own DNA as much as ours. It is nice getting a confirmation from him about our findings. Now I'd like to see hard data. We don't just deal in one man's words. We believe in science. We need to see the proof."

Her words confused Skylar. He understood how the scientific method worked, but if he had an idea that went against common belief and had just had one of the most powerful men in the galaxy confirm it, he'd be thrilled. It sounded like Felonia wasn't as happy as he thought she should be.

"But it's a start," Solaria said.

Felonia nodded. "It *is* a start. But right now, we need to figure out what's happening on Pantheria. Who have we awakened and what can we do to stop her from destroying our world?"

"Are we sure it's a her?" Skylar asked.

"Almost positive. Nearly every survivor from Glacier City kept going on about 'She's angry,' or some derivation of that." Felonia turned slightly like she was trying to find a position where she could see out *and* see Skylar and Solaria. "If it's not actually female, it's coming across that way in the waves of psychic anger it's projecting."

Skylar's com beeped. He glanced at the display that appeared over his wrist. "It's Del." He tapped the com twice so a hologram of Del projected where the display had been. "Del, do you have anything for us?"

"Just a second." Del tapped his wrist and Melody's hologram appeared next to him. "Okay, unless you need to link Solaria in on this, I think we're all here."

"I'm right here," Solaria said. "So's my mom."

Del bowed respectively. "Greetings, Mrs. Unica."

"Greetings, Del," Felonia replied. "I've heard a lot about you from Solaria."

"Good, I hope." Del's gray forehead darkened slightly.

Felonia looked at Solaria and then grinned. "Very."

"Okay, so do you have anything for us?" Skylar asked. He really hoped Del had been able to dig up some good information on the writing they'd found.

"Yes. It's actually a combination of different primitive scripts." He pulled up a display of the glyphs they'd found. "We have figured out some of it."

Felonia looked doubtful. "Some of it?"

"Right," Melody spoke up. "When Del sent this to me, I checked it against some of the data my mother has access to—she's got human files going back ten thousand years, as far as recorded human history. Or at least the parts that weren't lost to one disaster or another."

"And that's where we found two of the symbols." Del touched an image that looked like a strange bird. "This one is from some ancient human tombs, but there are also similar drawings in Alpha Centari, the Globulan System, and even on Tursipia. Once we figured that out, we went digging further." He gestured and several more of the pictures lit up.

"All of these also appear in primitive writing on multiple worlds," Melody said. "At this point we are trying to decide which meaning is appropriate depending on the context of the sentences. It would help if we had more of the writing."

Felonia pursed her lips and looked closely at the lit-up symbols. "We hadn't thought to look at the individual symbols. Our translation programs look for repeats and try to put them into some known pattern. You two really are geniuses. If you want to be part of an archeological puzzle-solving team when you get out of school, let me know and I'll make sure there's a spot for you here, or in any other dig site you want. I've got contacts all over the universe."

"Thanks." Del blushed again. "I'm hoping the museum offers me something beyond this short internship."

"I've got some friends there. If it's what you want, I'll put in a good word for you." Felonia rubbed her chin. "I'm presuming you haven't been able to match up the other symbols yet."

Del nodded. "Correct. There are so many languages in the universe—it may take a while. I've got an image match program running in the background while I handle the things the director wants me to be working on. It's really exciting stuff. So much to learn."

"Sounds like you're having a lot of fun," Skylar said, feeling a bit left out of the conversation.

"Even if I get a full-time position, I could never learn everything I have access to. It's great." Del gushed in a way only he could. Skylar knew other kids who loved learning things, but none of them would geek out over just about any new knowledge the way Del did.

"Glad you're enjoying yourself," Solaria said. "We're dealing with some kind of ancient mega-psychic who's determined to wipe everyone off the planet." She grinned. "It's better than hunting."

"A mega-psychic?" Melody looked pale. She tapped one of the unlit symbols. "This glyph is the most repeated on the images we received. I think it may represent someone, or something. Del's not sure. He thinks it could just be a preposition of some kind."

Felonia nodded. "It could be either. We'll be back to the dig site shortly. I'll check with the crew there and see how much more of the writing has been uncovered. When I put it through our translator program, I'll also send copies to the two of you. You've made more progress than we have since we uncovered it two weeks ago. I have to ask you to be very careful about showing anyone else this. It could be a very important archeological find."

Del and Melody both nodded.

"We'll keep it quiet,' Del said.

"Right," Melody agreed. "You guys keep us posted on your ancient mega-psychic."

"Will do." Skylar gave them a thumb's up with the hand that didn't have the hologram coming out of it. Then the image faded away.

Felonia frowned at them again. "Although I appreciate the headway they made in deciphering the writing, I need you both to understand that we can't be just spreading this information across the net. We have to be very careful about who knows what."

"Sorry, Mom." Solaria looked at her lap. "We'll keep it just between us."

"I promise," Skylar added. He hadn't stopped to think that the Unicas might want to keep what they had discovered quiet until they had all the data. It made sense.

"Hey, do we know anyone living in Wegascu?" Skylar asked, wanting to change the subject. He never liked dwelling on things he'd screwed up, even if they had been with good intentions.

Solaria pursed her lips and hummed for a second. Then her shoulders slumped. "Mutanio. The Leapanno family is fairly high in their local hierarchy."

After finding Leonada in Glacier City, Skylar was worried the other people he knew from school might also be in trouble. Mutanio might've had some major anger issues, but he was still a student of Stars' End. Skylar didn't like the idea of anyone else dying because of the thing rampaging across the planet.

"Don't you three even think about going out there to find him. Aniu and Phil are there, and that's enough members of this family in the line of fire," Felonia said sharply. "When we get home, I want the three of you in bed. The odds are we'll be part of the search and rescue team again tomorrow. We all need our sleep."

Felonia's com beeped. She tapped it. "Aniu. What do you have?"

"Not much," Aniu replied. In the background, it sounded like things were exploding. "I'm not even sure how I'm getting this signal through—there's a lot of EM radiation coming off that thing. So far, we haven't even gotten a clear look. It's dark and she seems to blend in. O'Byrne has some portable psy-scramblers that are keeping the worst of the effects away from us, but only just. They're giving Phil a major headache. They don't work well with feelers."

"Both of you be careful." Felonia reached for the hologram as if to touch his head.

"Doing our best. The damage is worse than Glacier City." The signal broke up and the hologram flickered. "O'Byrne's pushing us to get closer. He thinks a psychic attack might be the answer. I just wanted to see you before we do that. I love you and Solaria."

"We love you too," they said in unison.

There was a strange squawk and something exploded on the other end. The connection was lost.

Felonia closed her eyes.

Solaria took her mother's hand. "He'll be okay, Mom. I just know it."

Skylar turned away. He felt like he was intruding in a private family moment. Out the window the frozen night landscape zoomed past.

"There is a major psychic disturbance to the northeast," Filzbalm said, speaking for the first time since they left the council meeting. *"I'm unsure what is causing it, but it is stronger than anything I've felt outside of the Mother's presence."*

"You know the Mother of Drakes could be fairly scary to some of us," Skylar replied. Having Filzbalm talking to him gave him something else to focus on instead of feeling like he was eavesdropping on Solaria and her mother's grief and worry.

"Is it strange that I want to go see what's causing it?" Filzbalm seemed to ignore Skylar's comment about the leader of his people.

"No. I want to too. We're out here to explore the universe. That's part of what the Mother of Drakes tasked us with. Finding what is doing this falls into that category...I think." Skylar wasn't sure how they could go about doing that without really upsetting Felonia.

"I agree. But we must honor Felonia's wishes." Filzbalm rubbed his head on Skylar's neck. *"Is this what caring about others is all about?"*

"Yes, it is." Skylar found it interesting how Filzbalm understood some things and had to have others spelled out for him. Emotions were the hardest things to grasp. The Solar Drake operated on hard logic and sometimes failed to understand why Skylar did some of the things he did.

"It is odd to put someone else's wants and desires ahead of your own. Although we Solar Drakes can work together, it is unusual for us to reach out to anyone beyond our mates and children. We are not Felonia's children. Yet, she is putting us in her thoughts, trying to keep us safe. It feels like she is worried about us as us, and not just Solaria's friends. She is treating us like family."

"That she is." The idea that they were being accepted as part of the Unica family spread a warmth through Skylar, something that had been missing since his mother had died.

Felonia's com chimed again as they pulled up to the house. She tapped it, but didn't activate the hologram. "Yes. Okay. I'll be there shortly." She tapped it off. "Solaria, go in and make sure your Aunt Blizza is all right. I've got to run to the dig site. They've uncovered more of the writing. I'll get images and send them to you and to Del. Maybe with more data, we can get this figured out and stop her."

"That would be good." Solaria opened the door and slipped from the hover car. "See you later."

Skylar followed her example. He so wanted to head out to Wegascu and help before it was just a rescue mission, but he knew he wasn't as trained as Phil or Aniu were. There were probably a lot more highly adept psychics than him there to defend the city, if defense was even possible.

They managed to get the front door closed before Aunt Blizza descended on them.

"What's going on?" the older Pantherian demanded.

"We're not sure yet, Aunt Blizza," Solaria said. "Have you eaten?"

"Of course I've eaten." She put her hands on her hips and glared at them. "What do you and your parents think I am, an imbecile? I know how to feed myself. If I wanted to I could probably go hunting for myself, not that your father or mother would let me do any such thing."

She paused for a breath and gave Solaria an opening. "Good. Mom was worried that you might not have eaten. Mom said we all need to get a lot of sleep." She yawned and Skylar was sure it was more for effect than out of need. "We might have to go to Wegascu and help out tomorrow."

Blizza frowned. "I can feel it getting worse." She held up her wrist with the dampener on it. "Even with this, I can hear their screams. Every night people are dying and there's little we can do. Only a source of light can help us right now." Her gaze fell on Skylar.

Fear that she was about to repeat what she'd said that morning went through him, but she stayed silent.

"Then we should hope this light shows up soon," Solaria said, then turned her aunt toward the stairs. "Okay. Let me get you tucked in, then Skylar, Filzbalm, and I are going to eat something before we turn in."

She shook off Solaria's hands. "I know my own way to my room." She continued walking down the stairs, moving with an awkwardness that was unlike any Pantherian he'd met to that point. She moved even slower than she had earlier. It was like the things she was feeling through her muddled state were draining her. He wondered how bad she would be if she didn't have the dampener on. He hoped he never got that powerful. It was scary.

Solaria stood there on at the top of the curved hall until Blizza disappeared down below, then she sighed and turned. "Okay, let's go find something to eat."

Skylar hadn't realized he was hungry until she'd mentioned food. His stomach growled.

"Food sounds really good." Filzbalm crawled out of Skylar's hood and flew ahead of them. It was just warm enough in the house and he'd been a little antsy most of the way home. Since he hadn't flown all day, Skylar figured that was the biggest part of the problem.

In the kitchen, Solaria went the cold storage cabinet. "Warm meat for all of us?"

"It's better than cold meat." Filzbalm lighted on the counter next to her.

"Filzbalm says it's better than cold meat, and I have to agree." Skylar hopped up on the island across from her. "So what are we going to do?"

"I don't know." Solaria pulled out a platter of meat and put it in the warmer. "It feels like a hunt I'm being left out of. I want to be out there helping. I want to do more than just search for survivors."

"Me too," Skylar agreed. "But I don't know exactly what else we can do. Until we know what we're up against, we don't know how to fight it."

"Right. Maybe Del and Melody will have something more for us when Mom sends them the new pictures." Solaria pulled the platter out of the warmer, then frowned. "I guess I need to actually cook yours and not just warm it." She pulled off some for herself and Filzbalm, then put the rest back in the warmer.

"Sorry I'm just human," Skylar said, even though he wasn't actually sorry about his species. "You know, we don't have any kind of pictures of what it is that's attacking. Its EM manipulation makes that impossible, but is it because she's disrupting electronics, or is she disrupting the storage devices?"

"What do you mean?" Solaria asked around chewing her warm, raw meat.

"What if there are images being captured, but because they're being stored locally, the storage media is being affected by the EM field? Maybe if some cameras could be rigged up to multiple storage locations around the planet, we could get an image, and with an image we might be able to figure out what she is." He wasn't sure if he was reaching for an idea or not. He was trying to think of what Del would be doing, or saying about then.

Solaria chewed thoughtfully. "Okay, so let's say we could get some long-range cameras set up to send pictures to a distant storage location, something outside her area of effect—then you're right, we might be able to get an image. This is a good idea. We just don't know where she goes after she attacks a city. It was if she completely disappeared during the day. It's like she's allergic to light or something."

"So you think she might only be active at night? Like a Corelinian Vampire?" Skylar slid off the island and the warmer beeped, indicating his food was ready.

"Corelinian Vampires only exist in that game you and Del play. They aren't real, but that was what I thought of when she disappeared after hitting Glacier City and then hit Wegascu right after dark. Even through the officals searching for her didn't find anything in the ice and snow during the day, it doesn't mean she wasn't somehow hiding somewhere."

Skylar picked up a knife and fork to start cutting up his meat. "Exactly. She's hiding somewhere during the day." He thought of Blizza mentioning light and wondered how that played into everything. If they were dealing with some kind of vampire creature, light would be its nemesis, or at least it was in all the legends.

"So we need to figure out a way to track her in the ice and snow." Solaria finished off her first piece of meat.

"Maybe we could get Del to hack into Pantherian satellites and have them scan for a heat source in the ice," Skylar suggested. As they brainstormed the situation, his thoughts got to churning. Even if they weren't actually out fighting the thing, they were doing something constructive. Maybe if they could come up with a few good ideas, they could get the adults to act on them.

"The Pantherian communication system is open to the public." Solaria chewed slowly, and the mouthful of food distorted her voice slightly. "We wouldn't have to hack into it." She got up and walked over to a desk sitting at the end of the counter. She started tapping things, then a hologram popped up above it. "If we ask the system to get a thermal reading from the area near Wegascu we might be able to track what's happening." The view shifted, and there were just a few red dots in the area of the city.

A chill went through Skylar as some of them slowly faded away. Those were the bodies who were quickly cooling in the frigid climate. A bright red glow radiated out from the center of the city. It was too bright to be a person's heat signature.

"What's that?" He pointed to the glow.

"I bet that's the geothermal shaft that powers the city." Solaria zoomed in on that section of the city. "Most of our cities are powered by geothermal energy."

An idea hit him. "Was Glacier City?"

She nodded. "Yeah."

"How about Indruias?"

"No. We're too small. We're strictly wind and solar." Her voice trailed off. "Wait a minute." She waved her hand through the projection of Wegascu and the hologram scrolled across the planet. "There's no geothermal signature in Glacier City."

As a thrill of discovery went through him, Skylar pointed at the hologram. "I think we might be on to something. If there was a geothermal source there previously and there isn't now, she might not be after the people at all, but the power. The people are just in the way."

Solaria stood and stalked a few feet from the desk, then turned back. "But if that's what's going on, she may be trying to get more powerful."

"And that would be very bad." Filzbalm finished off his cup of meat and carried it over to the sink. *"She's powerful enough already."*

Skylar shuddered again. "She's so powerful, Aunt Blizza can hear her even through the dampening bracelet. If she can absorb all the power from a geothermal source—"

"Then she's something more than just a psychic," Solaria butted in, finishing his thought. "We need to figure out where she's sleeping and take her out before she gets strong enough to kill us all."

As he stared at the dark spot where a massive energy source had been, Skylar wondered if she wasn't that strong already.

17
Thoughts And Prints

"IS THERE any way to get the cities built over geothermal power sources evacuated?" Skylar asked as soon as Felonia shuffled into the house carrying a large gray plastic box like the ones they'd seen at the dig site earlier. Solaria's mother looked exhausted. Her eyes were half closed and her ears drooped. She set the box down on top of several more just like it.

She blinked at him, and then Solaria. "What?"

"She's going after the geothermal power," Solaria said as she hopped off the desk she'd been sitting on. "There's no heat signature left in Glacier City, and while looking at the satellite feed, we watched Wegascu go dark."

"Wait a minute." The information seemed to enliven her. "You two think you've found what she's after?"

"Maybe," Skylar said. He tapped the screen and played back the loop of the heat signature of Wegascu disappearing. "It's just speculation, but it's all we have at the moment."

"But, Mom, if she is somehow destroying the geothermal power sources, that means she's super-powerful," Solaria added. "We need to figure out a way to stop her."

Felonia let out a long breath and closed her eyes. "And save as many people as possible in the process. I'll call Zhetallia and let her know what you two have found. Skylar, send me that vid you just showed me, so I can send it to her. It'll take time, even with Intergal already here—evacuating cities isn't something that happens quickly."

As he sent the file to her, a warm, happy feeling filled Skylar. He loved being able to help, and finding a clue as to what was happening and hopefully taking a step toward stopping the destruction made him feel like he was helping.

Solaria paced around the living room. "Have you heard from Dad since we got home?"

"No." Felonia rubbed the bridge of her nose. "But they haven't been there too long. I figure Wegascu will be very similar to Glacier City."

"Are we going to go help again?" Skylar didn't want to just go comb through the wreckage of another city; he wanted to help find whatever the being was who was doing the damage. There had to be more he could do.

"Probably. Right now, why don't you three get some sleep? Tomorrow is most likely going to be another long day." Felonia dropped onto one of the couches. She tapped her com, and waited.

Skylar scooped Filzbalm up from the desk where he'd fallen asleep right before Felonia returned.

"I'm not really asleep," Filzbalm muttered groggily.

"Sure you are," Skylar said as he started toward the stairs.

"He's trying to tell you he's not sleepy, isn't he?" Solaria rubbed Filzbalm's head with the back of her hand. She always said her fur there was softer than the pads on her hands.

"I'm not. I don't need as much sleep as you do." Filzbalm sounded slightly more awake.

"But we're all going to get some sleep." Skylar continued down the curving stairs. He didn't bother trying to explain to Filzbalm that the Solar Drake slept more than most humans.

"Yeah." Solaria yawned. "We've got to be ready to go as soon as Mom says we need to."

Skylar remembered getting to his room, and Filzbalm flying onto the bed, but he fell asleep almost as fast as he lay down.

"THANKS FOR the tip on using the thermal cameras," Felonia said as they sped across the icy landscape heading north. "We haven't been able to get a lock on her position, but we think she's traveling via subterranean passageways, or possibly moving through the planet's crust on her own." She shuddered. "I've never heard of anything powerful enough to do that. It takes massive equipment to tunnel through a planet."

"What if she's using some kind of psychic power to do it?" Skylar asked. After their discussion the previous night, he'd begun to wonder if some unknown psychic ability was letting the unknown being move about without being spotted. The basic psychic skills were well documented, but what if there were others that weren't? Would that give someone the power they needed to pull off what they were suggesting?

"It's possible there are gifts we haven't discovered," Felonia said as she made a course correction.

"Or something that's been forgotten," Solaria added. "Mom, we have to ask what the government has been hiding from us. I doubt it stops with the fact that a lot of us are from engineered human stock."

Felonia nodded. "I agree, and we have to be very careful how we let that information out. To tell the truth, I was amazed O'Byrne was so forthcoming with his confirmation last night. That's not how his kind normally operate, unless that's the root of our problem."

"What do you mean?" Skylar leaned slightly over the seat, but his seatbelt prevented him from going too far.

"Maybe what we're facing is one of the original inhabitants of either Pantheria or some nearby planet," Felonia suggested. "We've got at least two other planets in this system that show signs of previous civilizations. We've been assuming they died out before we evolved, but maybe they didn't. Maybe when the humans came, they weren't able to find a peaceful way to co-exist with the natives and just killed them."

"Then why isn't she dead?" It didn't make sense to Skylar that the humans would keep one representative of a species alive when they were slaughtering the rest of them.

Felonia sighed. "I don't know. Maybe when we catch up to her, we'll have the opportunity to ask."

"If she isn't killed first," Solaria said.

"Our tech hasn't changed much in the last thousand or so years," Felonia said. "We've been so busy expanding the empire…sorry, the Galactic Council's reach, we haven't worried much about improving tech. If they couldn't kill her then, it's doubtful we could kill her now."

"But they appeared to have imprisoned her," Skylar said. "We have no idea how that would work, do we?"

"No." Felonia rubbed her chin. "We have no idea what really happened. For all we know she went into some kind of hibernation and the symbols on the wall are mean to be a warning to not disturb—"

Skylar's com beeped before Felonia could finish what she was going to say. He glanced at his wrist. Del's info was on the holoscreen there. "It's Del." He tapped the com to connect. "Hey, Del. What have you got for me?"

Del's image popped up for a second, then the image of a cat's paw print replaced it. "Does this mean anything to anyone?"

Solaria laughed. "Del, we're on a planet of cats. It's all over the place."

"Yeah, Del. We need something more than that." Skylar added. No matter how smart Del was, there were times he was good at asking obvious questions.

"Okay." Del sighed like they were missing something very obvious. "This symbol—which if you look closely—is a bit more than a cat's paw, is repeated several times in the last round of images Solaria's mother sent last night. It's not in any database I can search. Melody's digging into some of those ancient records her mother has. I think it might be important, particularly the way there's a bit of a starburst and lines going out from the paw."

Felonia turned from the landscape and stared at the image rotating in the hologram just above Skylar's wrist. "I've seen something else with that on it recently, but it's slipping my mind right now."

"If you find it, it might be a key to something. Let me know what it is." Del sounded impatient, which wasn't like him when he was getting to dig up new information.

"We will," Skylar promised.

"Anything else, Del?" Felonia asked.

The paw print disappeared and Del reappeared. "Not at the moment. I just hoped you might know something about that."

"Okay. Well, we're approaching Wegascu. It doesn't look good." Felonia pointed out the hover car's windshield.

Across the horizon, smoke rose from the ice. Somehow the damage looked more raw and brutal than Glacier City had been.

"Del, we need to go. Call back when you've got something more." Skylar hated rushing Del off like that, but he figured they were going to be needed quickly.

"Will do. If you find out anything, let me know." He tapped his wrist and broke the connection.

Skylar's heart sank as they zipped closer to the damage. Where the worst destruction in Glacier City had seemed confined to the city center, in Wegascu it looked like the whole town had been razed to the ground. He wondered if there would be any survivors at all.

18
Cave-in

INTERGAL RESCUE seemed to be on top of things again. They already had their white tents set up, and Felonia pulled the hover car over by them. Once they were parked and glanced around, it was obvious nobody was there.

"This is odd," Felonia said as she opened her door and got out. "Even if they have parties out searching for survivors, Phil says there's always personnel at a base camp."

"Maybe with everything that's going on, they're stretched really thin," Solaria suggested as she and Skylar followed her mother toward the closest tent.

A strange mental buzzing nagged at Skylar as they walked the short distance. It made him nervous. He felt jumpy, ready to run at the least little thing.

"This is coming from somewhere close by," Filzbalm said, sounding like he was trying to explain the feeling Skylar had.

"But what is it?" Skylar muttered.

"What's what?" Solaria asked.

"That buzzing," Skylar said. "Filzbalm says it's coming from somewhere nearby."

Felonia paused just feet from the closest tent. "You're right. I can't put my finger on it, but it's like some kind of psychic static."

"Right." Skylar nodded. "Have you ever felt anything like it before?" He was new enough to being psychic that there was a lot he didn't know about.

"No. It's like something's trying to reach out to us, but it's not on the right frequency." She sighed. "This is making me wish I'd left you three at home."

Solaria rolled her eyes. "Ah, come on, Mom. Now is not the time to get all motherly on us. You said it yourself before we left: we need every viable sense on this hunt. We'll be fine. Having us along gives you three extra sets of senses. If there's anything to be found, we'll find it."

"That's part of what I'm afraid of," Felonia said as she turned and resumed closing the distance to the tent. "We need to help the survivors. What we don't need to do is actually find what's doing this. We need to leave that to the people who are more powerful. Like Phil or O'Byrne."

"Do we even know how powerful O'Byrne is?" Skylar asked as they entered the tent.

"No." Felonia shook her head. "The O'Byrne family is very hush-hush about what they can do, but the fact they control most of the Galactic Council tells us a lot about them. I'd just watch yourself around him, or anyone else from that family."

"They've probably got their genes hacked to the max," Solaria said.

"But that's not legal." As soon as he spoke, Skylar knew he was sounding stupid.

Solaria shot him a glance over her shoulder. "And when someone has money, what does legal have to do with anything? Come on, Skylar, you should know better than that."

He hung his head. "Yeah."

Felonia held up her hand, signaling them to stop. The tent was empty of life. It looked like it had been set up to receive people, but there was no one there. The cots still had unused pillows and blankets on them. There was a small desk right next to the tent flap and an unlit stove midway down the tent.

"This isn't right." Solaria started to walk past her mother, but Felonia stopped her.

"Wait."

A weak telepathic probe brushed Skylar's mind, then went on. Felonia's eyes were closed as she searched.

Skylar stayed still. In class, they always said to do as little as possible if someone nearby was doing a psychic probe. It was considered polite, and helped prevent their scan from failing.

Felonia shook her head as she opened her eyes. "Nothing. Nothing except the buzzing."

Solaria gasped. "Then what happened to Dad and Uncle Phil?"

"I don't know," Felonia said. "We need to get back to the hover car and get out of here. Call in more help."

"They're nearby," Filzbalm said, sticking his head out from Skylar's hood and staring at the tent floor. *"Underground, I think."*

"Filzbalm says they're—" Skylar's words were cut off as a massive quake hit. The tent pole nearest him broke, letting the heavy cloth fall. As he scrambled to keep his footing, the ice below the tent gave way. Skylar found himself falling as the tent, cots, and desk tumbled into a shadowy abyss.

The ice smashed down around him. He instinctively put his arms over his head as he fell.

"Mom!" Solaria screamed. "Skylar!"

Then Skylar stopped falling. Something had hold of him. The ice and debris showered down around him, but he'd stopped moving.

"Help me help Solaria," Filzbalm said. *"We need to join together."*

"Like we've done before." Skylar thrust his mind out to Solaria, lending her his strength as he realized her mover powers were what was keeping him from falling farther down the hole.

"Solaria, lower us down," Felonia said, sounding more than a little out of breath. A light came on in the direction of her voice.

Skylar turned toward the light. She was floating a few feet from him, and Solaria was between them, her eyes closed in concentration. Having a visual on Solaria helped him push more energy toward her.

They slowly resumed their downward trajectory, but most of the ice, snow and items from the tent had already passed them, so Skylar stopped covering his head. He wasn't a mover. Other than lending Solaria power, there wasn't much he could do to help her out.

"We're almost there," Felonia said, sounding encouraging. "You can do it, Solaria."

"She's drawing a lot of power." Flizbalm sounded tired.

"If we don't keep giving it to her, we're all going to drop, unless you can get your wings free of my hood in time," Skylar said, trying to look and see what Felonia was seeing of the ground beneath them. He was getting lightheaded from the energy draining out of him, but it was the only thing he could do to help the situation, so he stayed quiet as she slowly lowered them down.

When his feet finally touched ground, Skylar breathed a sigh of relief. Then Solaria sagged against him. He wrapped an arm around her waist. "Hang on."

Felonia was there, taking some of her weight off him. "You did good, Solaria."

"Thanks, Mom." She grinned slightly. "Movers gotta move."

"Relax. You really exerted yourself there," Felonia said. She handed the light to Skylar. "Look around, see if you can spot anyway for us to get back up." Once he had the palm light, she took all of Solaria's weight off him and gently settled her on a spot on the ground where there wasn't a ton of ice shards poking up, or broken pieces of metal from the debris fall.

Skylar did as she suggested, but he couldn't spot any close walls, or anything beyond the debris. He wandered farther away from Felonia and Solaria, trying to find a way out of the cavern they'd fallen into.

"We're a long way down," Filzbalm said. *"I can feel the wind from the surface, but only barely. There is also a breeze from somewhere else."*

"What do you mean, somewhere else?" Skylar panned the light around, hoping to get a better clue as to what Filzbalm was talking about.

"It's a stale breeze, but moving air has to come from somewhere." Filzbalm eased out of Skylar's hood and perched on his shoulder. *"Maybe I can get a better feel for it out here."*

"Does Filzbalm have any ideas?" Felonia asked.

"He says there's a stale breeze blowing," Skylar relayed as he continued to look for the walls. "But we can't find any obvious openings."

"Then maybe we should follow his stale breeze. See where it leads." She sighed. "I wish we'd brought more lights with us."

"Maybe some fell down with the tent," Solaria suggested weakly from where she lay on the ground.

"Let me see if I can find the desk," Skylar said. "If there would be any kind of light or useful things, they would be in the desk, right?" It made sense to him.

"Sounds good." Felonia knelt next to Solaria. "If you can find a med kit, that might be useful too. I'm not getting anything on my com, even with it rerouted to the spaceport system. We're probably too deep for them to work."

Skylar tried to remember where the desk had been in relation to some of the cots he spotted strewn about the cavern floor. He stopped and then turned to the right. The palm light shone on a crumpled lump of metal that lay under several large chunks of ice. He hurried over to it.

Two drawers were partially open and within reach. He pulled on the first one. It wouldn't open farther. He tried the second one. It was the same. He started to put his hand in the first one when Filzbalm ran down his arm.

"Here, let me." The Solar Drake folded his wings tight against his back and slipped into the drawer. A second later he reappeared. *"Nothing useful in there."* He flowed over the edge of the top drawer and into the one beneath it. Something thudded. Then he came out pulling a palm light in his muzzle. *"There's a large dent in the back of this drawer. I might be able to get into the one below it."*

Skylar took the light from him. "Be careful. Do you need me to shine the light in there for you?"

Filzbalm shook his head. *"My vision works differently than yours. I'll be fine."* Then he turned and disappeared again.

Seconds later there was more banging around. *"Skylar, I think I found something else useful. It's a med kit. But I don't know if I can get it out. I might be able to get it open, though."*

"Try that." Skylar started to push on the large chunk of ice in front of the desk, then stopped. If he caused anything to shift before Filzbalm got out of the desk, he might trap him in there and not be able to get him back out, or worse, crush him if things moved the wrong way.

"It's tight. The kit is nearly as big as the drawer. I can reach a few things inside though. Do you want me to bring it all out?"

Skylar didn't instantly know the answer to that. He glanced over to where Felonia still sat with Solaria. "Filzbalm found a med kit, but we can't get it out of the desk intact. Should he bring everything out piece by piece, or just some of it?" He raised his voice slightly, and it sounded strange as it bounced around the cavern.

"As much as he can get," Felonia replied, her voice just slightly softer than Skylar's had been.

Somewhere nearby, something shifted and groaned. A chill of danger went through Skylar. He didn't want to do anything to cause another cave in. Something told him it wouldn't be hard for him to be trapped in the cavern if any of them made the wrong sound, or moved incorrectly.

"This will take several trips." Filzbalm said, then there was more banging around and the Solar Drake appeared with a couple of med patches in his claws. *"I think these might be stimulants."* He handed them to Skylar.

"Thanks." Skylar took the small wrapped packages and held the light over them as Filzbalm scurried back into the desk. They were stimpatches. Just the thing to give Solaria a boost of energy and maybe help her get back on her feet until they could find a way out.

Filzbalm brought out four more stimpatches and some antiseptic pads. Skylar didn't think any of them had been injured, but since they were in a strange place, he decided to keep the antiseptic pads too, slipping them into the front pocket of his coat.

The last thing Filzbalm dragged out of the drawer was a small medical multi tool—part laser, part forceps, part clamp. He gave it to Skylar, then unfolded his wings and flew up to his shoulder. *"There are a couple other things in the kit, but I can't get the lid open enough to get them out. I'm sorry."*

"Hey, no worries. This stuff will help." Skylar put the tool in the pocket next to the antiseptic pads and hoped they wouldn't need any of them. Then he rushed across the cavern with the stimpatches for Solaria. He

just hoped they would be enough to keep her going until
they found a way out of the cavern.

19
Defining The Problem

SKYLAR WASN'T sure how far they'd walked, but his feet hurt and he wanted desperately to stop. He also didn't want to sound weak around Solaria and her mom, so he kept his mouth shut and trudged along in Felonia's wake.

"Okay, I'm now sure these are thermal vents," Felonia said. "It's the only thing they could be. Tunnels like this shouldn't exist otherwise."

"Then why aren't we roasting?" Skylar asked. He'd already noticed the temperatures were warmer than on the surface, but if they were in some of the tubes that carried the geothermal vapors and gasses that previously powered Wegascu, it only made sense they should still be hotter than the four of them could handle.

"It appears that whatever is taking the power has drained off enough that we're not in any danger." Felonia shook her head. "But that doesn't make any sense either. Something that powerful should be able to be detected from orbit."

"Unless it has some way of cloaking itself from satellites," Solaria said. She paused and leaned on the side of the tunnel.

Filzbalm had picked the passageway they were traveling in, since he was the only one of them who could detect the soft breezes that flowed underground. He'd claimed the other ones didn't have much of a flow, so weren't worth going down if they wanted to find a way to the surface.

"Do you need another stimpatch?" Felonia asked. "We've got two left."

Solaria shook her head. "Just give me a moment. Let's save the patches in case we get into a spot where we need my mover powers." She slumped to the smooth rock floor. "I doubt I can do much without either them or a nice long sleep."

"And none of us are going to get any real rest until we get out of here," Felonia said. "We're not safe down here. We have no idea where the thing that's attacking us is, or when it's going to attack again."

"I bet it won't attack until after dark," Skylar said. "That's what's it's been doing, coming out at night."

"But why?" Felonia asked as she sat next to Solaria. "There's too much we don't know about this thing."

"Other than the survivors in Glacier City kept saying 'she.'" Solaria closed her eyes as she leaned against the tunnel wall.

"She. Yes, I keep forgetting that," Felonia said. "That doesn't give us much more information either. You're right, she does seem to strike at night. But that doesn't help us much at this point, unless she has some kind of aversion to sunlight. There are more than a few creatures in the universe that do. Particularly things that evolved in the depths of space."

"But that wouldn't explain why she's here," Skylar said. Talking didn't help with the deep fatigue he felt, but it did help his brain push back the strange psychic humming they were all hearing. No matter how far they got from the cavern they'd dropped into, the buzzing was the same strength. It was like the geothermal tunnels were alive and broadcasting it, but if that was the case, it would mean Pantheria itself was alive, and everyone knew planets weren't alive in the sense of having psychic abilities or emotions. It shouldn't be possible that people had overlooked life forms as large as planets for thousands of years.

20
Thermal Tunnels

SKYLAR HAD totally lost his direction in the winding passageways they went through. They were following Filzbalm's feeling of the air movements and Felonia, who kept saying that she could feel Aniu reaching out to her. He knew from his classes that most married psychics ended up forming either empathic or telepathic bonds, much like the bonds parents had with their children. Since Solaria agreed with her mother about the direction they needed to go, he just followed along.

"I believe they're this way," Filzbalm announced and pointed down a passageway. *"Fairly close too."*

"Filzbalm says that way," Skylar announced for the others.

Felonia closed her eyes, then nodded. "I think he's right. I can almost touch Aniu's mind, but there's something blocking me."

A lot of debris littered the passageway, even more than the spot where they'd been dropped into the tunnels. The chunks of ice were huge, some of them taller than Skylar and two or three times his girth. More often than not, they were scrambling over huge boulders of ice.

"Too far," Filzbalm said after they had gone a couple hundred feet.

"Need to go back," Skylar relayed.

"But there's no way to get through back that way," Solaria said, then she sighed. "Unless we move all this ice, and it'll have to go down the tunnel one way or the other."

Felonia patted Solaria on the shoulder. "Then we all work together to move the ice. You, Skylar and Filzbalm are used to working together. Let me join the link and we'll be able to lift much heavier loads, and maybe we can push enough ice down the tunnel to reach them. They aren't far now. Your father is coming in strong, even if there is something blocking him. It almost feels like someone is shielding him."

"I think so too." Solaria put her hand on the boulder in front of them. "Okay. Movers gotta move."

Skylar put his hand on her shoulder and let his own energy flow to her. "Take what you need."

"Okay, but we'll try not to take too much." Solaria let out a long breath, then closed her eyes. "Mom's better at fine control than I am. I'm going to let her direct our energy."

Filzbalm's strength flowed into Skylar and he didn't even try to hold it the way Professor Aduncus had been teaching him to. He simply added it to his push out to her. The ice boulder shuddered, then slowly rose off the tunnel floor and floated away from where they'd come from.

When it landed a short way down the corridor, Felonia sighed and the pull of energy subsided. "We don't want to block a passage that we're fairly sure will let us out of here." With a long breath and a creased brow, she went to work on the next chunk of ice blocking their way.

For fifteen minutes they worked, then Solaria collapsed between them.

"You need a rest," Felonia said. "Sit down over against the wall. We've got one more stimpatch. Use it."

Solaria shook her head. "What if Dad or Uncle Phil needs it worse than I do? We're almost there. I can feel them just beyond the ice."

"I can too, and something in there with them." Felonia crossed her arms and frowned. "I think we need all our power to get through the debris, and right now that means you using the stimpatch to get you back on your feet. You know I don't like you using those things, but at the moment, they're a necessity."

Skylar had never had any experience with stimpatches before. He'd always heard they were something that helped psychics more than regular people, or at least that was what his mother had said. "What's wrong with them?"

"They can become addictive," Felonia snapped, sounding tired and stressed. "She's used several right in a row. That shouldn't be enough to start a problem, but we never know."

"Mom, I'm not going to become a stim-addict." Solaria reached for the patch her mother was holding out for her. "And let's face it, if I do, it's for a good cause. We need Dad and Uncle Phil."

Felonia hugged her. "Yes, we do." When she released Solaria, she looked at Skylar. "Sorry for getting short with you, Skylar. I keep forgetting you're new to this world, and you've still got a lot to learn. Most of us know a lot more about what we are before we reach Stars' End."

Over the years, he'd gotten used to his own mother becoming short from time to time when she was tired or stressed, and to his knowledge, she'd never endured anything like their past hours. His mother had also been a lot slower to apologize to him. He really appreciated Felonia saying something. "I understand."

"Thanks." She gave him a quick hug. "You're a good young man."

Solaria took a deep breath. "Okay, Mom, I think I'm ready."

Skylar glanced at her. The stimpatch was on her palm, where the fur didn't interfere with its connection to her skin. "Don't push yourself too much."

"We're in this together," Solaria said.

"And movers gotta move," Felonia added before she could.

THE LAST ice boulder nearly rolled down the tunnel as voices called out from behind it.

"We're back here!" Phil's voice rang out.

"Careful with your voice," Felonia said as the boulder stabilized and floated over to join the rest of the pile.

"Felonia?" Aniu was softer, then emerged from the darkness.

"We came looking for you, and the ground collapsed under us," Solaria explained as she rushed forward to hug her father.

"Same thing happened to us," Phil said as he helped Mayor Lusino and Cafpar O'Byrne forward. "We'd have been killed if O'Byrne hadn't managed to get us all down, then shield us from her mind."

"So it was the same creature that attacked Glacier City?" Felonia asked as she joined Solaria in hugging Aniu.

"Yes." Cafpar O'Byrne was pale and shuddering, leaning heavily on Phil. He pulled at the bottom of his heavy coat, and glanced into his pocket. "She's very powerful. I don't think our current psychic scale is adequate to categorize her. I've never touched a mind so powerful." He looked nervous about something.

"So how do we stop her?" Skylar asked. He wanted to offer to help, but he wasn't sure his lanky build was up to helping a grown man like Cafpar O'Byrne stand, and

Lusino was larger still. There was no way he'd be able to help the Pantherian move around the tunnels. Of the lot of them, the mayor of Wegascu looked to be in the worst shape.

"That's the question on everyone's mind," Phil said. "I hate to say it, but we may have to evacuate Pantheria until we can come up with a plan."

Solaria took Lusino from Phil. "We might have a way to track her."

"Track her?" Phil raised an eyebrow as he adjusted his hold on O'Byrne.

Skylar nodded. "She's absorbing geothermal energy. We can tell where she is by the energy she's stealing."

"And it's showing up on planetary thermal scans." Solaria sighed. "At night."

"Sounds like you kids have been busy," Phil said.

"Absorbing geothermal energy?" O'Byrne muttered. "Then she's a lot more powerful than I thought. We may not be able to stop her. I need to get to my ship and access my databases. If I can't find anything, I'll need to go for help."

"We haven't found a way out yet," Felonia said. "We were lucky to find you."

"O'Byrne has very powerful shields," Flizbalm said. *"I can't reach his mind. I think he's what was blocking Felonia and Solaria from reaching Aniu's mind."*

"It's not nice to try to read minds without permission," Skylar said, but he was curious about the statement. He hadn't tried to read O'Byrne, but then he was a little more tired than Filzbalm from lending Solaria and Felonia his energy to get the ice blocks moved.

"I know, but there is something about him. Something familiar."

"Don't start in sounding like Solaria and saying we look alike." Skylar had to admit their base features were similar, same brown hair and blue eyes, same pale skin

tones. But O'Byrne was a lot more muscular than he was. Skylar wasn't sure he'd have it in him to work out that much, unless a lot of his bulk was his coat, or something else. It was hard to tell.

It was impossible to tell if O'Byrne had heard their mental conversation. He sighed and took a couple of steps away from Phil. "Well, now that I'm not keeping all the ice and snow from crushing us, I can get myself up there. I'll send a search party for you, if you haven't checked in by the time I locate the information I need." Then he vanished in a soft puff of air.

Skylar stared at the spot where he'd been. "Where'd he go?"

Phil frowned. "I knew he was powerful, but there aren't many movers strong enough to teleport."

"I'm not surprised he left us down here," Aniu said. "He's the head of the largest corp in the universe. He's got to save his own hide first. Keep the shareholders happy."

"We should be thankful he didn't desert us when we were caught in the collapse. We'd be fewer people he has to worry about with Council secrets." Lusino spoke for the first time. "My city is gone, isn't it?"

Solaria nodded. "I'm sorry sir, but it's worse up there than Glacier City was."

"We need to keep going if we're going to get out of here," Felonia said. "We can only hope we don't run into any more major ice debris fields. We might not be able to get past them."

"The air was getting better before we turned away to find them," Filzbalm said. *"I think I can find us a way out."*

After Skylar relayed the information, they followed Filzbalm's lead and endured another two hours climbing through the tunnels before reaching a massive cavern.

"I think this is the main chamber at the heart of the local geothermal system," Aniu said as they stood on the rim of a deep hole.

"So how do we get around to keep following the fresh air?" Skylar asked. He peered over the edge, shone his palm light down and couldn't see the bottom.

"We might not be able to," Felonia said. "We might have to try a different way."

"Let me check." Filzbalm crawled out of Skylar's hood and took off flying.

"Filzbalm!" Skylar shouted with his mouth and mind.

"It's warm enough with my ring, I'm fine." Filzbalm was already outside the range of the lights. *"I'll be right back."*

Skylar slumped against the wall of the tunnel they stood at the mouth of. As they'd reached the central chamber, it had become wide and smooth enough for them to walk all abreast, and not single file as they had in some of the tighter places.

"He'll be fine," Solaria said, touching Skylar's shoulder.

"I hope so," Skylar said staring off into the darkness. "If he's not, I won't be." But he was a lot more worried for Filzbalm than he was for himself.

"I know." Solaria squeezed his shoulder.

Without Filzbalm blocking for him, the psychic humming that had been with them since they entered the tunnels was louder and more uncomfortable than ever. Skylar was pretty sure the others were also feeling it, but weren't making any show of being affected. He was determined not to express any discomfort.

"I wish I could tell if this is just residue, or something more," Phil said as he leaned Lusino against the wall opposite Skylar. "It's really irritating. Has the psychic field been down here the whole time?"

"As long as we've been down here, it has," Felonia said. "I figure it's coming from the being that's attacking our cities."

"Skylar and Solaria might be onto something," Aniu said, then tapped the smooth tunnel wall. "It might be about geothermal power. She might be tapping into it."

"But there are no geothermal vents or tunnels near the dig site," Felonia said. "If she was something we awakened, shouldn't she have been near a geothermal site?"

Phil closed his eyes and frowned. "We don't know exactly what we're dealing with here, but if I was going to imprison her, I'd do it well away from somewhere she could draw power. I wish we had a map of the geothermal systems on the planet, something with all the vents, lava tubes, convection zones, the works. That might help us figure things out."

"If we could get a signal out to Del, he could go over things and let us know," Skylar said, desperately wanting to contribute something.

"I think right now we need to focus on getting out of here," Felonia said as a soft buzzing of wings heralded Filzbalm's return.

He landed on Skylar's shoulder and shivered. *"The air comes from above. You might be able to reach it if I fly a rope across to where the opening is, but there's a problem."*

"What kind of problem?" Skylar wished he could just let Filzbalm explain to everyone without having to relay things.

"I have discovered a colony of ice bats living in the tunnel. They are very protective of their territory. They were almost fast enough to catch me."

"We also don't have a rope," Skylar pointed out.

"But we might be able to fashion something," Solaria said. "Is the rope the only problem?"

Skylar shook his head. "He says there's a colony of ice bats over there."

Solaria grinned. "Ice bats are worthy quarry."

"Yes, they are," Felonia agreed. "But we need to get everyone to safety."

"Mom." Solaria rolled her eyes. "I promised Skylar a hunt while he was here. Even though looking for survivors in destroyed cities is close to hunting, it's not the same thing. If we disturb them too much, this could be a good hunt."

"Relying on our primitive sides might help us." Aniu patted Solaria on the shoulder. "But we have to remember, we have injured and Skylar. Safety first, then hunting."

Solaria grinned. "Safety first, then hunting."

Skylar hoped they were all going to get across the chasm in one piece before Solaria and the other Pantherians decided to lose themselves to their animal sides, slaughter all the ice bats, and possibly doom themselves in the process.

21
Killing Bats

SOFT CHIRPS filled the darkness as Skylar let go of the rope Felonia had fashioned from everyone's clothes except Skylar's. Since the Pantherians were used to personal nudity, they didn't seem to mind. The idea of being naked in front of several people he didn't know well—or worse, Solaria—wasn't something Skylar wanted to entertain.

What had been interesting was the way Felonia had reshaped the clothes into a sturdy rope using her psychic mover gifts. She'd taken the opportunity to explain to Skylar and Solaria that sometimes movers weren't just about heavy work, but delicate things too. She'd shown Solaria how to move the molecules of the fibers around in such a way that they could be recombined into something stronger, thinner and in a single strand. It had taken her several minutes to do the work, and they almost didn't have enough raw material for her to work with, but before she'd resorted to asking Skylar for as much as a sock, she had a sturdy, delicate fiber long enough to reach the other edge of the chasm so they could get across.

Filzbalm had flown it across and found a rocky protrusion to tie it off to. Aniu had gone first, to make sure it was safe, then let Felonia know to send them on over.

The hand-over-hand progression across the rope had almost been more than Skylar could bear. His arms and shoulders burned with the effort by the time he reached the far side. Going up had made things that much harder. He wished the line had angled down so they could've all just slid to the next geothermal tube.

"Sounds like there's a lot of bats in here," Skylar said. "At least I think the clicks and chirps are bats."

"That's them," Solaria replied in a hushed voice. "I wish Uncle Phil would hurry getting Lusino over here. I want to get some of them for dinner."

Skylar frowned. "Dinner? We're going to eat bats?" He was still getting used to the idea that Solaria ate just about any kind of meat. At school, she was always going on about how the meat there didn't have the same taste as things she killed herself. It was easier to ignore when she wasn't looking at having something she'd just killed for dinner.

"I bet they're tasty," Filzbalm said before Solaria could add anything.

"If properly prepared, they're delicious," Solaria said. "But it takes a fair number of them to make a good meal."

"Kids, step a little away from the edge." Aniu waved them deeper into the tunnel. "We need to give Phil room."

Skylar turned to look. Phil was just reaching the spot where the light from the palm beam Skylar had handed over to Aniu illuminated his face. He was panting and his hands shook as he drew closer. Lusino clung to his back with his eyes tightly closed and his own breath coming in short gasps.

"You're almost here, Lusino," Aniu urged.

Without needing to be told twice, Skylar stepped back until he was nearly out of the pool of light. The chirping and clicking grew louder. He hadn't seen any of the bats with his own eyes. Filzbalm had told him they were all clinging to the ceiling and walls just a few feet past the edge of the chasm, then shown him a mental image of what they looked like. They were definitely bats, but they were all a strange off-white color close enough to the color of the snow and ice to blend into the surfaces they clung to. Their eyes were a beady red and they were little more than fuzzy white lumps with leathery wings that stuck out above their bodies as they skittered along their perches.

A harsh *oooph* drew Skylar's attention back to Phil. He'd made it to the ledge and let Lusino stand on the rocks there while he put his hands on his knees and panted. "I'm a feeler, not a mover. If being in Intergal Rescue didn't keep me in peak condition, that would've been impossible. Sorry, Lusino, but you need to lay off the farm-raised antelope—they're awful fatty."

"No need to apologize," Lusino huffed out as he sat next to Phil. "From now on, I'm going to start acting like a rural teenager and if I can't catch it, I won't eat it."

"That's a good attitude," Felonia said as she made it across the rope easily and landed on the ledge next to Phil. "But I think before we can start planning the next phases of our lives, we've got to get out of here and stop this entity who's determined to destroy our planet." She wiped a hand across her brow. "Is it just me, or is it warm in here?"

Skylar had been too worried about everything else going on to think about the temperature, but when she mentioned it, he realized it was a bit warmer than the other tunnels they'd been in.

Aniu shrugged. "These are geothermal tunnels, maybe they're building their energy back up."

Felonia shook her head. "I don't know about that. If she's pulling the power out of them, they shouldn't be able to restart, particularly not in just a few hours."

"Of course, if you're right and they are restarting, we might want to get out of here quickly," Phil said, straightening. "Because I don't want to be here when millions of gallons of heated water start rising through that chamber."

"But it didn't happen in Glacier City," Solaria said, walking over to the ledge's edge. "Why would it happen here?"

"Didn't you say last night the geothermal network here was the largest on the planet?" Skylar asked, torn between joining her on the edge and keeping watch for the bats to wake up and swoop down on them.

She nodded. "You're right. Maybe the one here was too much for her to completely drain."

"Let's get moving." Phil gave Lusino a hand up. "Like I said, if we've got hot water returning, we need to get out of here."

"We need to get beyond the bats quietly then," Aniu said, then started past Skylar.

"But Dad!" Solaria sounded mad. "A bat hunt?"

"Safety first." Felonia pushed against Solaria, sending her after her father.

Although he wasn't about to try to explain it to Solaria, hunting wasn't really his thing. Skylar was pretty sure he wasn't missing much if they could get past the bats without having to kill any of them. He kicked a rock that went a little farther than he planned and rolled off the edge of the chasm, causing several other rocks to cascade after it. After a couple of seconds, several jolts of steam rose up.

The palm lights illuminated the bats for a moment before the entire wall shifted and the bats all took to wing. It was like an off-white, living wave dropped down on them. Lusino fell to his knees and put his hands over his head. Solaria cheered as she started snatching bats out of the air and smashing them into the wall beside her.

Skylar put his hands over his head and tried to figure out what he should do.

"Solaria has the right idea," Filzbalm said, and excitement poured through Skylar. *"If there weren't so many of them, I'd help her, but they work as a hive mind. See? They're attacking her and not the rest of us."*

Peering past his arms, if was quickly evident that Filzbalm was right. The bats were mobbing Solaria. The thing was, she hadn't seemed to notice. She was moving with quickly fluid actions, snatching bats out of the air so fast it looked like they were serving themselves to her.

"Did you say 'hive mind'?" Skylar asked.

"Yeah, it's a strange form of mutual consciousness. There appears to be a colony queen." There was a quiet thoughtfulness for a moment. *"Much like with Solar Drakes."*

Skylar hadn't learned much in the way of offensive tactics, but he had an idea. "We need to hit her telepathically. If we can stop her from attacking Solaria, we can get out of here." He didn't wait to get the okay from any of the adults—he pushed out the way he'd done one other time, on accident. But unlike when his telepathic powers had first erupted at school, he had training and understanding about what he was doing.

"Skylar," Felonia shouted. "What are you doing? Stop that."

He ignored her as his mind met with resistance and he thrust harder.

"Skylar, relax." A heavy hand landed on his shoulder and a wave of calm washed over him.

"You're making progress," Filzbalm's thoughts pushed the calmness away. *"Keep it up—I'll block Phil."*

The resistance Skylar had felt dissolved before anyone could do anything else to him. Around them, the bats seemed less organized. They flew in circles, but didn't close in on Solaria any more.

The floor around her was littered with small white bodies. Blood dripped from her hands. Solaria stopped grabbing bats and turned toward him. "No fair using powers to end up with a bigger head count."

Skylar stumbled a bit and broke off the telepathic assault he'd been broadcasting. "Head count? I wasn't trying to kill them." His guts twisted. "I was trying to defend you."

"What did you think you were doing, striking out like that?" Phil asked, lifting his hand from Skylar's shoulder. "Or having Filzbalm block my attempt at calming you?" He eyed Filzbalm suspiciously. "You shouldn't have been able to do that. I guess there's a lot we still have to learn about Solar Drakes."

"Yes, there is," Filzbalm whispered with a slight chuckle.

Bile rose in Skylar's throat. He'd never wanted to intentionally hurt anyone, with the exception of the Boarisk raiders who'd attacked Hummassa and killed his mother. The bats were innocent. They were just doing what bats do and defending themselves. If he wasn't going to eat them, he shouldn't have attacked them.

Phil's calm swept over Skylar. "There's still a lot you have to learn. Something tells me they haven't bothered putting you through psychic ethics classes yet— probably figured you'd have had those when you first got to Stars' End like most of the students do. There's a lot more to being a psychic than just learning to use your powers."

"I don't think this is the right place for an ethics lesson, Phil," Felonia said. "We need to get moving. For good or bad, the bats have been dealt with. Solaria, gather what you can carry. We'll leave the rest and hope there are some scavengers in the tunnels that will make use of them. The temperatures are continuing to rise. Filzbalm, we need you to lead us out of the tunnels."

Filzbalm launched himself off Skylar's shoulder. *"The remaining bats are disorganized enough I should be able to get us out of here without them bringing me out of the air."*

"Just be careful." Skylar forced himself to straighten. Phil's calming presence helped him pull himself together enough to move on down the tunnel.

"Come on," Solaria said, her arms full of bat bodies that were nearly the same color as she was. She followed Filzbalm.

As they went across the area where the bats had been roosting, there were a lot more bodies than could be accounted for by Solaria grabbing and killing the ones she had. The way they lay scattered about, it looked like Skylar had scrambled their hive mind and they'd all flown into the walls in mass confusion, or fear. He wasn't sure if maybe he'd managed to take out the queen of the group and somehow the others hadn't known what to do. He'd never caused such loss of life.

A lightheaded nausea filled Skylar and wasn't sure he'd ever be able to eat anything the resembled the ice bats, and didn't want to use his telepathic powers like that ever again.

When things like this happened, he totally understood why his mother had been so scared of psychics. If he could do that when he was just trying to incapacitate the roost queen, what would he be able to do once he fully learned to use his powers and could focus his will on any mind he chose? He wrapped his arms around his chest and wished his mother was there to hug him and tell him everything was going to be alright, but she wasn't and never would be again. He just hoped he'd never do anything like that in the future. He hadn't meant to kill them. He'd just been trying to save Solaria. It wasn't fair. The bats hadn't deserved to die.

22
Exploding Face In The Snow

FILZBALM LED them out of the tunnel and into the ruins of Wegascu. The afternoon sun was a glow on the horizon. Shadows stretched across the broken ground, casting the whole area in an eerie otherworldly mix of pink and black, shadows and ice.

Lusino dropped to his knees, and wailed. "My beautiful city. She has destroyed my city."

Phil pulled him up. "Come on. We don't know where she is and the sun is going down. We need to get away from here before she wakes up and comes after us. Without O'Byrne, I don't think any of us will survive."

"The hover car is over by the Intergal tents, south of the city," Felonia said. "I can get us there, as long as we don't have any more collapses."

"I'd rather not go through that again," Skylar muttered as they headed through the devastated city, keeping the glowing horizon on their right. He hadn't thought he'd be able to feel worse than he had when he worked Glacier City and found so many dead, but he did. The cold seemed to permeate every cell of his being. It pulled at him and he wanted to find somewhere he could be warm again. But he wasn't sure even a sunny beach on Hummassa would be enough to warm the frozen part of his soul that had killed the bats.

Filzbalm landed on his shoulder, then went and tucked himself at the base of Skylar's neck. *"I'm with you."* He rubbed his head against Skylar's jaw.

Skylar reached up and rubbed his gloved finger across Filzbalm's head, wishing he didn't have the glove on and he could feel the soft warm skin against his. *"Thank you."*

HALFWAY ACROSS the fragmented ice city, Skylar's com beeped. He pulled his glove down so he could see the screen. It was Del.

"Please tell me you've got something," Skylar said as soon as the connection completed.

"That claw symbol, you said you'd seen it before." Del's voice sounded urgent.

"Yeah." Skylar looked at Solaria who appeared tired as she trudged next to him. "Solaria, where was that claw, paw, symbol?"

She walked a little closer to him. "A couple of different places in the dig site. It might've even been on that crystal claw totem thing Chillarni showed us."

"Wait, a totem?" Excitement edged Del's voice.

"Yeah, I thought we told you about that." So much had happened in the past few days… Skylar tried desperately to remember what he'd told who. "It was a long crystal with a paw at the end, complete with claws. I think the symbol was on it. Didn't we send you a picture of it."

"Nope. Look, you need to use that."

The ice and ruins around them exploded, cutting Del's voice off. An invisible force slammed into Skylar, sending him flying. Anger engulfed him.

"Stop!" Filzbalm's voice roared in his head.

As suddenly as it started, Skylar's flight ended, and he hung in the air, just inches from the jagged side of a building. He was fifteen to twenty feet off the ground. Something had stopped the anger too.

Near him, Solaria hung in a similar fashion. Her head was bowed, her brow furrowed, her hands clenched into fists and her eyes closed. A strange haze engulfed her.

"Lend her power or you'll fall to the ground," Filzbalm urged as he scrambled out of Skylar's hood.

"What's happening?" Skylar tried desperately not to panic, but he was hanging in midair and he wasn't sure what he was supposed to do *except* panic.

"An attack," Filzbalm said. *"Now relax and help her keep you afloat."* The Solar Drake tapped into Skylar's power—the gentle tug of it on his energy reserves was something he was beginning to feel.

Skylar did as Filzbalm instructed. He let the power flow easily between them, and hoped it was enough to get them safely down. It was one thing to watch Solaria float around in the nearly weightless environment of the Z-GBall court at the school, but on Pantheria, she was holding them against gravity. From the look on her face, there was more than a little strain.

"Ease the two of you on down," Felonia said evenly from nearby.

Not wanting to take his attention off Solaria and the energy he was pouring between them, Skylar closed his eyes and pushed power toward Filzbalm, who seemed to be amplifying it.

"Leave here!" A voice tore through the area. It hit Skylar's brain so hard he blinked against the pain of it. Ice and snow showered down on him as the closest ice spire shattered.

"We're trying," Phil shouted back. "We have injured."

Skylar dropped several feet in the air before Solaria stopped his fall. She let out a heavy breath as his heart, that had skipped more than a couple of beats, started up again.

"This isn't your planet." The wind seemed to carry the words that shook Skylar both inside and out.

"And it isn't yours any longer," Aniu said.

Skylar wished he could take his concentration off Solaria, but he was afraid if he did it would break the flow of power between them and he'd fall the last ten to twelve feet. He couldn't tell for sure with the broken ice and scattered snow under him.

"If I can't have my home, none of you will." The voice sounded like it was coming closer.

"You're killing thousands of people," Phil said.

"Not my people," the voice replied. It was a fairly neutral-sounding voice, but had a very slight female tone to it.

Skylar slowly drifted downward with Solaria at his side. Filzbalm flew off his shoulder and circled them.

"Your people killed all of mine, so why should I care?" A pair of huge, ice blue eyes appeared in the snow that swirled around them. They were round and pupilless.

"If you don't stop, you're killing more than just the beings who live on this world," Phil said.

"And did your kind worry about that when you destroyed my people?" The voice came closer. Beyond the eyes, the rest of its body came out of the snow and ice. It looked like it was forming itself from the snow and ice blowing around it.

Skylar floated gently down, and another mind joined his and Filzbalm's in trying to keep them all from falling. From their earlier work, he recognized the feel of Felonia's mind. It was almost comforting as the chaos erupted with them in the epicenter.

"We don't even know who your people were," Phil said.

"We ruled this part of space before you came here." She continued to solidify, appearing vaguely human, but in huge proportions. It looked like her body was going to be nearly ten feet tall.

"Easy, we're almost down," Filzbalm said as he returned to Skylar's shoulder.

"Wait." The form that had looked nearly solid as it drew closer suddenly exploded outward. "I will not break my agreement with She Who Holds."

The unseen force that had thrown Skylar into the air vanished. He fell a couple of feet, then stopped.

"Almost down," Felonia said, then Skylar's feet touched something solid.

He put his hands on his knees. A wave of exhaustion hit him. He glanced at Solaria in time to watch her crumple to the ground as her father and Phil rushed forward to catch her. He had questions, but he was so tired he couldn't put them into words before darkness hit him and the snow cushioned his fall.

23
Del To The Rescue

COLD SEEPED through Skylar's thermal suit. The cold made him want to sleep more, but he sat up and stared around. The early morning sunlight was just peeking over the horizon, the light so pure and white Skylar had to look away, toward the area closer to him. They were still in Wegascu, but they were at the crater where the Intergal tents had been. Felonia's hover car was nearby. The cold wind tore at him.

"You're back," Filzbalm cheered. The sound hurt his head.

"Please be quiet." Skylar rubbed his temples. "Where is everyone?"

"Phil and Aniu are trying to get a hover car working, but the EM pulse associated with the telekinetic blasts seems to have fried everything." Filzbalm eased his way to the base of Skylar's neck from where he'd been beside his head. *"Solaria's still unconscious from the strain of blocking the telekinetic blow to us."*

"Is she going to be okay?" Skylar stood and realized the white pile he'd thought was snow next to him was actually Solaria and Felonia.

Felonia slowly opened her eyes. "I think so. She's dreaming right now. That's always a good sign when someone has overstrained their powers. At least she didn't fry her synapses catching both of you and blocking that thing's power."

"Will there be any damage?" Skylar knew psychics could burn themselves out if they did things they weren't trained and strengthened to do. He really doubted that the constant exertion of her powers was something Solaria was ready for. She'd done a lot with her telekinetic powers in a short time, and they'd run out of stimpatches.

"I don't know." Felonia ran a hand over Solaria's forehead, brushing a bit of white hair off her brow. "Lusino didn't make it. Her last attack was too much. We're all lucky to be alive."

Aniu came over from the hover cars. "I want to know who She Who Holds is and what kind of treaty she was talking about."

"We might never know," Felonia said. "Any luck on getting transport running?"

Aniu shook his head. "All the electronics are completely down. We're going to need new parts if we have any hope of getting anything moving, and I don't see that happening any time fast. Even the dermal coms are beyond repair. I'm surprised none of us have burns from the nano circuitry frying." He tapped his wrist and there wasn't a beep or any other indication of the com implanted there responding.

Skylar did the same thing, and there was no response. Since he'd gotten the implant months earlier, he'd always been connected to the universe—somehow it felt odd to not have it there at his touch. He felt cut off in ways that he hadn't before he got the implant. "So, what are we going to do?"

"Phil is trying to see if he can cobble together something from parts that might let us get a signal out." Aniu shook his head. "Right now, I think our best bet is for me to start running and see if I can find a home or settlement that was outside the EM pulse area and come back and get you all."

"Aniu, I don't like splitting us up again," Felonia said. "We're all vulnerable. We should stick together."

"We're all starting to feel the effects of prolonged cold exposure," Aniu countered her. "We need to get out of the elements. If this was winter instead of spring, we'd be dead by now." He leaned over her and gave her a quick kiss, then kissed Solaria's forehead. "I need you two to be safe. I'll be back as soon as I can."

Without another word, he turned and trotted off into the distance. Skylar stared after him until the white glare off the snow became too much and he had to turn away.

THE WAY Felonia took control of their situation reminded Skylar of his mother. It felt good to have her there. It gave him hope that they might actually survive the elements and the being who seemed set to destroy all life on Pantheria. He wasn't sure his mother had had much hope in living through the Boarisk attack.

"Skylar, we need to get the remains of these tents together and see if we can put up enough protection to survive the night," Solaria said as she walked slowly away from their makeshift camp. She hadn't been on her feet long, but was already doing what she could as Phil scavenged farther into the city.

"Not much left," Skylar said as he kept a safe distance from the crumbling edge of the sinkhole that had nearly devoured them.

"But there is a little bit." Solaria led them over to a tent that was still anchored in the ice. The edge of it flapped down into the hole.

Skylar heaved on the edge of the tent, pulling it from the edge of the crevasse. The fabric was a lot sturdier than he'd realized when he'd gone in them before. It was a heavy weave and obviously designed to endure a lot of diverse climates.

"There's a portable heater," Solaria announced from the side that was still anchored. "But it's electric, so I doubt it's working. Her pulses were too powerful."

"There are a lot of things in the universe the humans have forgotten, or been told to forget," Filzbalm said from within Skylar's hood. The Solar Drake had been fairly quiet since Skylar woke up. His mental voice still hurt and Skylar wondered how long it was going to take before the little pains in his brain would stop enough for him to function normally.

"That's becoming obvious," Skylar said as he started folding the tent up. "I think we've got a lot to discover in our universe."

"You wouldn't think so," she said as she lifted her edge of the tent and walked toward Skylar. "I mean we've been out in the galaxy for a long time, you'd think we'd have stumbled across everything there was to find."

"But what about beyond our galaxy?" Skylar wondered out loud. "We live in a vast universe. We may have mapped the Milky Way, but there are other galaxies out there. I wonder if there are already exploration teams trying to find ways to reach them."

"And it's on a need-to-know level of security?" Solaria reached him with her end of the tent and then walked over to another edge to bring it to him. "Probably. They obviously don't want everyone knowing. But when you think about it, that makes sense. How many groups would just go nuts at the idea of expanding the power base of the Galactic Council? A lot of folks would have a fit. Particularly those who weren't included in the decision to explore. We've got a ton of problems in our own galaxy without going elsewhere."

Skylar carried his edge of the tent toward the center. "Things like Boarisk raiders?" The raiders who killed his mother were never far from his mind. But what scared him more was the idea that there might be worse species out there. If they pushed into other galaxies, they might find things that made the Boarisk look tame. Was it worth exploring if that was the case? He was still pretty sure it was. He at least hoped so. Ever since his adventure on Armstrong's Rings, he wanted to find new and different planets. He wanted to go out into space and see what there was to see. Even if he didn't have a ship of his own, he'd decided he had to find a way to make that happen.

"Exactly." She paused and stared at him for a second. "And even things like humans."

Skylar frowned. With the little bit they'd learned from O'Byrne, it sounded like his own people might actually be the original monsters in the universe. How else could using illegal gene tech be explained? And if the Pantherians weren't the original species on Pantheria, if the humans had created the species and seeded them after destroying the natives, that was evil beyond what he could imagine. Every species deserved a chance to live. That was what his mother had always told him. If O'Byrne and his corporation were the ones pulling the strings, they should be stopped.

He sighed. "Yeah, I think you're right there. But you've got some human in you too."

She frowned as she folded the tent closer to the edge. "Don't remind me. You know, we should keep that quiet when we get back to the academy. There's a lot of kids there who aren't that fond of humans to begin with, and this news might start problems."

"Then it's a good thing I'm getting better at shielding." Skylar got his last edge brought over. The tent was a large white lump on the frozen ground. Bits of ice and snow clung to the heavy fabric. He sat down on it and it collapsed a little bit.

"What are you doing?" Solaria stared at him.

"Getting the extra air out. Haven't you used a tent before?" He bounced a bit and it compacted more.

She shook her head. "No. We don't use tents on Pantheria. When we hunt, we just sleep outside. Our fur protects us from the elements."

"On other worlds, we use tents and similar things to help keep us alive. We're not all as rugged as you cat people." Skylar stood. "Now, let's get this back to the hover car for your mom." He bent down and tried to pick up the tent. It was a bit more than he could handle.

"Here, let me help." Solaria stooped and grabbed the edge of the tent opposite Skylar.

Together they lifted it, and he was thankful it wasn't too far from where they stood to the hover cars that sat dead on the snow.

"You know, I think a few stimpatches would be handy about now," Solaria said once they reached the hover car and put down the tent.

It was Skylar's turn to frown. "Really?"

Solaria laughed. "No, silly. Well, yes. But not like you're making it look." She sighed as they started back toward the wreckage of the Intergal camp. "I could use a boost, but it's 'cause I'm bone tired. I'm not getting addicted to them or anything. It would be nice to have enough energy to access my mover skills. As it stands right now, it's going to be hours, up to a day, before I'm able to do anything more than I am now."

"And that's how it's going to stay, young lady," Felonia said as she emerged from under the nearest collapsed tent. "We can do this all the old-fashioned way. The hunter's way."

"By sweat and effort," Solaria finished. "I know. I get it. But it would be nice to get a little boost."

Skylar did his best to make sure his frown didn't show through, but he'd never heard Solaria want to do anything by any way than with brute force. Even when she played Z-GBall, it was with force more than form. He wondered if maybe she was growing addicted to the stimpatches after just a few uses.

Something roared in the evening sky. A small ship drew their attention, and a thrill went through Skylar. With any luck, they wouldn't have to spend a cold night in the ruins of Wesgascu. He just hoped they'd be able to get out of the area before their adversary awoke for the night and damaged the ship so they couldn't get away.

"Careful," Felonia said. "I don't see any markings on that ship."

"Looks new," Solaria said. She pursed her lips and narrowed her eyes. "I'm not an expert in small, long-range ships."

The ship landed a short distance from them. It settled into the snow, kicking up soft powder as it did. After a moment, a ramp extended and a door opened.

"Del?" Skylar hurried toward the craft.

"You're alive!" Del ran down the ramp. Grinning, he stopped just shy of Skylar.

Skylar frowned. "Why wouldn't I be?"

"Your communication was cut off," Melody said as she followed Del down the ramp. "We were really afraid something had happened to you."

Skylar looked from his friends to the ship. "Whose ship is this?"

"It's one of Mom's," Melody said. "I was home when Del called all frantic. I asked, and since Mom had been busy the whole time I was home, she said I could take the ship and get Del and then come to you. We're really lucky the stargate for the museum is so close to the planet. If it had been much farther out, it would've taken us days to get here. Our gate is just shy of lunar orbit too."

"Well, thanks for coming," Solaria said as she walked up next to Skylar. "Maybe we can find my dad before dark."

"Speaking of finding, how did you find us?" Skylar asked.

Del shrugged. "I scanned for Filzbalm. I figured there wouldn't be any other Solar Drakes on Pantheria. There was some kind of ghost image as we emerged from the gate, like he'd just gone into it, but I figured it was a glitch of some kind, since once we cleared the gate's event horizon I was able to get him on the scanner. We came right here."

Skylar punched Del on the shoulder. "So you're getting better at spatial navigation?"

Del blushed and shook his head. "Wasn't me. It was Clive, Melody's mom's pilot. He did all the hard work. Melody and I just worked the sensors and did the logical thing."

"Whoever it was, it doesn't matter," Felonia said as she joined them. "But it's growing dark. We need to get away from here before this nice ship ends up as so much junk. Let's use your sensors to find Phil, collect him and get into the air."

"Let me find Phil." Skylar's head hurt, but it would do him some good to feel helpful. He pushed out his thoughts, looking for Phil in the ruins. Since there weren't any other living beings in the area, it was fairly easy for him to locate Phil's mind.

"Skylar, was that a rescue ship?" Phil asked as soon as their minds connected.

The strength of the connection surprised Skylar. Phil was a high-level feeler, but didn't register on the reader scale. The only explanation he could come up with was Filzbalm was augmenting him, but the Solar Drake was staying quiet.

"Yes—well, sort of. It's Del and Melody. Felonia says we should get in the air before dark." He glanced at the western sky where the sun had disappeared and only a bright orange glow remained.

"I'm coming." Phil severed their contact, but not before Skylar got the impression of him running toward the camp.

"Phil will be here in a few," Skylar said, feeling good at being helpful with something.

"I'll get Clive to prepare for takeoff as soon as he arrives." Melody turned and walked up the ramp.

"While we're waiting," Del began. "When we were cut off, I was trying to ask you about that crystal claw totem thing you found."

"I didn't find it. Felonia's team did," Skylar corrected him. "I saw it in their office."

"Okay. But where is it now?" Del asked, glancing between the ship and the city. He shivered slightly and put the sleeves of the heavy coat he wore together, so they covered his hands.

Skylar glanced at Felonia. "Didn't you tell Chillarni to take the artifacts to the house for safekeeping?"

Felonia nodded. "That's right. Since the being came out of the dig site, I figured it would be safer to move things to the house until we could arrange to get them off world."

"I think we need that totem," Del said. "Melody and I have found several references to it in our study of the writings on the walls. Like I said before, it's all in different languages, but Melody found translations of different parts of the hieroglyphs in some of her mother's ancient books. Her family has quite the extensive library. In some ways, it rivals what I could find at the museum. Between what she found and what I found in the archives, we've been able to translate most of it."

"Get going!" Phil shouted, waving as he ran toward them.

A strange light cut through the twilight behind him.

"Move it," Felonia said with only a little less emphasis than Phil used.

Not needing prompting, Skylar ran up the ramp, but stopped just inside the ship.

Solaria dashed passed him. "Melody, Phil's almost here, but look to the north. We need to be in the air the second he hits the ramp."

The ship shook as it rose slowly.

The glow behind Phil seemed to gain speed as Phil ran faster than any biped Skylar had seen before. Phil was all but a blur as he raced toward the ramp, leaping in the air to clear the last little distance to safety.

Skylar took a firm hold on the nearest hold on the side of the door, reached out and grabbed Phil's arm. Phil clung to his arm as Skylar tried to pull him up. The glow was nearly upon them.

"Up! Up!" Solaria shouted.

The ship gained elevation faster. The ground dropped away. The glow seemed to reach up toward them. Rage hit Skylar hard as he gave a final yank and got Phil inside the ship. The door clanged shut and the ship rocked to the side as it sped away. Skylar managed to keep his feet, but only just as he let go of Phil. He wasn't sure what he would do if something happened to Phil. Without Phil, he wouldn't have made it off Hummassa. He wouldn't have ended up at Stars' End, and his future would be a lot bleaker than it was.

"Thanks, Skylar." Phil clapped him on the shoulder. "Good save back there."

"What was that glow?" Melody asked, emerging from the cockpit.

"I think it's our very angry native," Phil said. "She was weak when the sun was still up, but as the light faded, she grew stronger." He shuddered. "I hate being hunted."

"With you there, Uncle Phil." Solaria frowned. "We're hunters, not prey."

He shook his head. "We all have to remember, everything in the universe has things that prey on them. Even those of us who've hunted for generations have predators, but I don't think that's her sole purpose."

"Where to?" called a male voice from the cockpit.

"We've got to find Dad," Solaria said. "He's running for help."

"Then to the Indruias settlement," Del replied. "We need to find that totem. It might be our best chance to stop her."

Skylar hoped he was right. Del wasn't wrong very often, but if he was wrong about the totem, it could cost them all their lives. They hadn't even seen anything that had stopped the thing of mist and shadows—he wasn't sure how else to think of it.

24
Finding A Lure

THE SIGHT of the lights of the Indruias settlement warmed Skylar as they flew in. Aniu was up in the cockpit, giving Clive directions to the house. They'd found Solaria's father still running nearly twenty clicks from Wegascu. He was tired, more than a little footsore and happy for the lift home. He and Felonia were promising each other they'd start running and hunting more in an effort to get into better shape for future catastrophes.

"So what are we going to do?" Skylar asked quietly when it was just Del, Solaria, Melody, and him around.

"I'm hoping when we touch the claw there will some instructions embedded in it or something," Solaria said.

Del rolled his eyes. "You know things don't work that way."

"I suppose you found something in your translation." Solaria sounded a little snappier than normal, but after everything they'd been through the past few days, he couldn't really blame her.

"A little bit." Del sighed. "Whoever put up the warning was trying desperately to make sure if the right person needed it, the information would be there."

"But they didn't want to make it too easy," Melody said, coming back from the cockpit. "We're about to land, so stay seated." She glanced over at Phil, who looked to be asleep. "He should be okay."

"Maybe. We lost the mayor of Wegascu today. I think he took it hard." Skylar tried not to think about the people he knew who were lost. Lusino and Mutanio were just the latest. They had a lot to do and he didn't want to get depressed when the thoughts of the dead always brought him back to his mother, and Teir, whose fate he still didn't know.

"Uncle Phil doesn't like failing to save people," Solaria said. "It's part of what makes him a good member of Intergal Rescue."

A slight bump signaled that the ship had set down.

"Okay," Felonia appeared out of the cockpit. "We need to find this totem and figure out what we're doing."

An old-fashioned com in Felonia's ear beeped as Melody opened the ship's door. She tapped it to accept the connection. "Yes, Zhetallia." There was no hologram since the com was one that had been in the ship's emergency equipment. Skylar wasn't sure what all was being said—all they could get was Felonia's side of things. "So she's going after Berginna tonight. Another geothermal city…we're fairly sure she's targeting the geothermal areas in an effort to destabilize the planet. Yes, that's why she hasn't gone after the spaceport yet. Give us a couple of minutes and I'll reconnect. We just reached the house."

"Berginna?" Aniu asked as he joined them when they resumed their walk down the ramp.

"Yes." Felonia shook her head. "I wish we had some way of figuring out where she was going in time to evacuate the cities."

"From what we saw coming in, it looks like the whole planet is being evacuated," Del said. "I don't think I've ever seen so many ships heading through a stargate at one time."

"We were the only ship heading toward the planet," Melody added.

"Okay." Felonia opened the door for them. "See if you guys can find the totem you think might help. Zhetallia wants to talk to us right now. I think the planetary council is trying to come up with a plan. We'll come find you when we're done with Zhetallia and the council."

"Are they still on the surface?" Solaria asked.

Felonia shook her head again. "The council is in a ship in low orbit. I bet Zhetallia tried to reach us all day, but with us underground, the coms weren't working."

Solaria patted her arm. "Go call her back and make a plan. We'll find the totem. We've got to stop this before we don't have a planet to call home."

"Thanks." Felonia gave her a big hug. "You've grown into such a responsible young woman." She flashed them all a grim smile. "I don't think of any of you are kids anymore—you're all on the verge of being adults." She stood and followed Aniu and Phil as they went down the hall.

Skylar glanced into the living room. There were more of the polycrates full of things piled around. He pointed toward them. "It's in one of these."

Del grinned. "Wow, it's just like some of the rooms at the museum." He hurried over and opened the closest one.

"This hunt may take a while," Solaria said with a weary sigh.

Filzbalm flew out of Skylar's hood and landed on the back of the couch. *"I'm not sure it's here."*

"What do you mean?" Skylar asked as he made it to a pile of crates on the opposite side of the room from where Del and Solaria were carefully going through things.

"It had a feeling to it. Almost like it was reaching out to the minds around it. I don't feel that now."

Filzbalm stretched his wings before folding them against his back.

"That doesn't mean it's not here," Skylar said as he stared at the instafoam packing material in the top of the crate he opened. "Maybe all the foam and wrappings are muffling it."

"Muffling what?" Melody asked as she pulled the instafoam from the top of her crate.

"Filzbalm says he doesn't feel the totem like he did when Chillarni showed it to us," Skylar explained.

"Who's Chillarni?" Del asked.

"One of the archeologists who works with my folks." Solaria tossed the packing material to the side. "You guys realize we're going to have to go find more instafoam to repack the crates. We'll never get things back in just right to reuse the pieces we have now."

"That's one of the drawbacks to instafoam," Del said as he pulled out a silk-wrapped item. "Things never fit back the same way unless you're very careful with everything."

Solaria sighed. "And we really don't have time to be careful." She tossed more instafoam aside as if to prove her point. "Mom and Dad have a ton of cans of the stuff around. We'll just redo everything after the hunt is over." She sighed dramatically as she pulled things out, quickly unwrapped them, frowned and set them aside with a bit more care than she was showing to the form-fitting foam. "This is going to be worse than a mouse hunt in a room full of holes."

"I guess that's one way to look at it." Skylar lost his wonder at Solaria's ability to turn everything into a hunt reference in one way or another. Skylar looked at the dusty clay bowl he'd unwrapped. It didn't really look special in any way other than it was old.

By the time he reached the lower layer of artifacts, he didn't have anything more than a pile of the clay bowls and wondered how they could be of any interest to anyone, even as Del had to exclaim how interesting everything he unwrapped was and how they all showed evidence of a prehistoric society that was more than just bipedal cats. At least one of them was having a good time as they raced to save Pantheria.

"SOMEONE HAS already opened this box," Del announced as he reached the bottom of his stack.

"How can you tell?" Solaria looked into his box. "Oh, the instafoam isn't there. Maybe Chillarni got into a hurry and missed this one?"

Skylar remembered how fastidious the woman in the dig site office had been. "I doubt that."

Del frowned and reached into the crate. "This might be where it was."

"What makes you say that?" Skylar rolled his shoulders that were aching from digging through the crates. He walked over to Del's latest crate, welcoming the chance for movement.

"Look here." Del traced an indention in the foam. "From what you said this looks like the right size and shape for what you described."

Skylar peered in. The spot was just slightly larger than the crystal claw had been, but with each of the items wrapped before being encased in instafoam, that made sense. "Unless there was more than one of them, you could be right." Skylar wondered who had taken the totem, and how they were going to find it. It was their best chance at saving the planet, even if Del hadn't explained how it worked.

Solaria sighed and put her hands on her hips. "I hate it when prey slips through my claws. But who would've taken it?"

"Are you looking for this?" Aunt Blizza's voice jerked then all around.

Skylar stared as she held up the crystal claw. It radiated a bright light. When he'd touched it back at the dig site, there had only been a little bit of a glow. The totem seemed to be responding to something about the old woman holding it.

"That's it." Solaria jumped over the couch and hugged her great aunt. "Why did you take it out of the box?" She reached for the claw, but Blizza moved it just out of reach.

"It was calling to me." Her eyes didn't seem to be looking at any of them, but were focused on the crystal in her hand. "If I didn't know better, I would swear it's alive. The angry one. It's attuned to her."

"Attuned to her," Skylar said. "The claw is on the same psychic frequency as the thing that's taking out the geothermal areas?"

"More than that," Blizza said. "They seem to be parts of the whole, but I have no idea how that is possible. She's awake again."

"Blizza's been going on about her being asleep all day, then she said she was awake, but Blizza was holding me in her rooms with her," Leonada said, emerging from the hall. Her dark fur made it look like she was emerging from the shadows themselves. "Solaria, I didn't have anywhere else to go, so I came here. I've been helping Blizza as she would let me, but once I was in the house, she wouldn't let me leave. I hope it's okay. My whole family was in Glacier City. I don't have anyone outside of school now."

Solaria moved around Blizza and hugged Leonada. "Of course you can stay with us until we go back to school, and probably afterwards too. We're good at taking in orphans—just ask Skylar."

Skylar didn't like the attention suddenly being directed at him as Solaria, Leonada and Blizza looked his direction. There was something piercing in Blizza's gaze as it moved away from the crystal. She seemed more together than she had before. It was like the crystal had woken something inside her. It made Skylar shiver.

Blizza seemed to look through him. Her gray eyes glazed over for a moment and she shook. "Can you hear the screams? So many are dying."

"Berginna." Skylar's guts knotted. Felonia had said that was the city being attacked. "We need to get to Berginna."

Solaria looked down the hall. "Mom, Dad, and Phil are still talking with the council."

"If what I learned through the hieroglyphs is right, we shouldn't need them," Del said. "We have all the talents represented with just us."

"So why wait?" A thrill went through Skylar. He knew Solaria's folks would be worried, but they didn't have time for them to finish with the council. "Melody, can we take your ship and get there? Maybe we can save a few lives."

"Sure. But we have to try and not destroy this one." Melody grinned and led them out the door. "Mom's going to be really pissed if it doesn't come back exactly the way I left with it."

After spending months cleaning up the farm zone of the school after one of the school's shuttles got destroyed on their last adventure, Skylar didn't want anything to happen to the ship either. He paused at the door. "Shouldn't we at least leave a note for your folks?"

"They're taken care of," Blizza said with an eeriness to her voice that gave Skylar shivers.

He almost ran down the hall to find them and make sure they were okay, but he didn't really think the old woman would hurt them. Maybe she had simply telepathically told them what was going on and just had an odd way of saying that.

"Filzbalm, can you sense anything from them?" He desperately wanted to make sure everyone was fine.

"They are asleep," came his quiet reply.

"Of course they're asleep," Blizza's mental voice burst into their private conversation. *"You didn't think I'd kill my own family? I'm not a human. You might be a light, but you still have a lot to learn."* She didn't even turn toward them as she continued toward Melody's ship.

Her interruption into his private link with Filzbalm gave Skylar chills. Even Professor Aduncus said their link was something he couldn't intrude on. He didn't like the idea of Blizza being more powerful than the professor, but unless he was going to prevent them from finally doing something to stop the carnage, he couldn't say anything. He had to go along with his friends and do everything he could to make the world right again.

25
Into The Cold

THE FLIGHT from Solaria's home to Berginna was unusually quiet. Del and Melody had explained what they had deciphered about the crystal claw. It wasn't as much as Skylar would've liked, but he supposed he should be happy with what they had. The whole time, Blizza clutched the totem like a little girl clinging to a favorite doll.

Strange, wispy lights danced across the sky as they drew near to the city. They were a brilliant mix of green, white, blue and gold.

Solaria stared through the cockpit window. "What is that?"

"Looks like an aurora of some sort," Del said. "You've said she affects the electromagnetic spectrum— maybe the lights are a side effect of that." He frowned "I've never heard of any being who could manipulate electromagnetism. It's one of the primal forces of existence."

"The longer you live, the more you will discover you have never heard of," Blizza said. The closer they flew to Berginna, the more she sounded normal, like her brain was all there and there wasn't anything wrong with her.

"I live for learning new things," Del said.

"And you should," Blizza replied, never turning from the brilliant light display. "Your kind have always been the ones who consume information. You might not always be the ones to discover new and interesting things, but you make sure it's available for everyone else."

She was direct, but something in her words made Del flinch. To Skylar, it was almost like she was insulting something about the Tursiops, but he couldn't exactly put his finger on it.

"Where should we set down?" Clive asked as he banked the ship slightly.

"Wherever looks safe," Melody said.

Clive shook his head. "Nowhere out there looks safe. This light show is playing havoc with my instruments."

The land around the city was dotted with small houses, most of which were dark. A huge fountain of water erupted from the ground near the city center. Berginna was powered with geothermal energy like the other towns had been. There was a good chance they knew where their quarry was.

"She's got to be near there." Solaria pointed toward the geyser. "There's a park just to the north of there."

Leonada shuddered and looked down at her hands. "I can feel her. It's just like Glacier City. She's so angry."

Skylar put a hand on her shoulder. "You can stay in the ship if you want." He didn't like the idea of them having to help Leonada back to the ship if she suddenly stopped in the middle of their attempt to halt the destruction. It might cause the whole thing to fail.

"No." She straightened and squared her shoulders. "I...she needs to pay for what she's done."

Blizza laughed—it was almost a cackle. "Child, how do we know that she's not paying us all back for something that was done to her years ago? We're trying to save our world, but maybe it *was* her world first."

The ship dropped, then regained some altitude. The move made Skylar's stomach bounce and Filzbalm dug into his shoulder.

"That's not possible." Clive pulled back on the steering yoke. "We're not going to be able to get too close. The magnetic fields are too powerful. I'm heading outside the city."

"We don't want to destroy Mom's ship," Melody said quietly, almost as if she was trying to remind herself, or find a reason to fly home.

Solaria growled softly. "There's some ice flats over there." She pointed to the south of the city. "Let's get landed so we can close in on foot."

"Fine," Clive grumbled. He turned the ship and it soared toward the spot Solaria had indicated. He set the ship down without even the slightest jostle.

"I think we should stay fairly close together," Blizza said. "We're stronger as a group." She paused as she walked out of the cockpit. "Even you, pilot. Your skills may be needed before this is over."

"I'm just a pilot," Clive argued and made no move to rise from his chair.

"You're also a mid-range feeler," Blizza countered. "We may need you." She continued walking out of the ship.

Skylar stared at Solaria and almost asked if Blizza had always been so scary powerful, but he didn't want the old woman butting in again, so he kept his mouth shut and his thoughts to himself as they followed her out of the ship and onto the ice flat.

Outside the ship, the winds were fierce. They tore at Skylar's heavy coat and made him thankful for his thermalsuit. Filzbalm curled up at the base of his neck and wrapped his tail around Skylar's throat. Del pulled up his collar and shivered.

"Okay, it's really cold," Melody said. "We need to make those warming rings for all of us."

Solaria rubbed her hands together. "I have to agree. I've never felt it this cold."

"We need to move quickly," Blizza said. "It's only going to get colder."

"It was frigid the night she attacked Glacier City," Leonada said. "It's almost too cold for Pantherians out here."

Blizza sighed. "And complaining isn't making it any warmer. Our prey is this way." She took the lead and never once looked over her shoulder to make sure any of them followed her into the city.

The first ground quake took Skylar by surprise. Somehow, he managed to keep his feet, even as Del, Clive, and Melody fell. The Pantherians swayed and shuffled, but didn't fall. Blizza barely slowed down. She didn't seem nearly as frail as she had around the house.

"What's causing that?" Clive asked as he got back to his feet.

"She's claiming the ground water," Blizza said. "The places where the water was holding up the ground are collapsing. We have to hurry."

"Why?" Skylar asked as he gave Melody a hand up, then really wished he'd kept his mouth shut.

"Because we don't want her getting away," Blizza snapped. "She's growing stronger."

"But I can't feel her," Skylar said. He'd been wondering about that since they got off the ship, but hadn't realized what it was that was missing. The night she'd awakened, they'd all felt her anger and rage. In Berginna there wasn't even a hint of it.

"That's because I'm blocking her from us," Blizza said. "If I let her get to us, we'll all be paralyzed, and we won't be able to do what we need to."

It made sense, and after Skylar helped Del to his feet, he made sure to not voice any further questions. He didn't exactly like the way Blizza was bossing them around, even if she was the senior of the group and the most powerful, but he didn't normally question his elders.

Around them the city continued to shake, and before long, they were all scrambling to keep their footing on the unstable ground. Buildings of all descriptions collapsed, and people called for help. As much as he wanted to stop and lend aid, Skylar knew if they didn't stop the carnage, saving a few people wouldn't amount to much. The idea of the greater good really irritated him sometimes.

The first drops of water hit and Skylar yelped from the heat as it burned through his glove. "How do we deal with this?"

"Movers have to move." Solaria said. She glanced at Leonada, who nodded, and the water stopped hitting them as they continued toward the center of town.

"Very good," Blizza said without breaking stride. "All of you stay close to them so they don't have to protect an overly large area."

"Should we lend them power?" Skylar asked.

"I could without problems," Filzbalm said without moving against Skylar's neck.

"Conserve your strength," Blizza said. "Hot water is going to be the least of our problems really soon."

"You're right, old woman." A voice rolled out of the water toward them. "Your shields are strong, but your body is weak."

Ahead of Blizza, a giant form materialized out of the water. She didn't seem fazed by the boiling bombardment around her. She was more solid than she'd been in the tunnels beneath Wegascu. The water ran down her broad shoulders and cascaded over her breasts.

She was nearly twice the size of any living creature Skylar had ever heard of. He stared up at her.

Blizza raised the crystal claw. "Stop. This is our world now."

The giant woman stared at her. "But this was my system first. Your kind killed all of us." She frowned. Somehow the very human expression looked wrong on the huge proportions. A slight movement on her forehead revealed a third eye, nearly hidden in the heavy creases there.

Rage swelled up and slammed into them. Blizza took a step back and the hand holding up the totem shook.

Without prompting, Skylar reached out to her, as if he was going to catch the old Pantherian before she hit the ground around them. When he touched her shoulder, she latched onto him with her mind and pulled him in. The years of her life bombarded him. He saw everything—the training she'd endured to master her massive talent. The love she'd destroyed without meaning to. The family she'd kept at arm's reach after that. The loss of friends and loved ones, each one tore a piece out of her, leaving less and less of her until she was only a shell of the vibrant young woman she'd once been.

Skylar tried to pull back, but her hold was too strong. He gave her all his power and more as she tapped into Filzbalm, and somehow reached beyond the Solar Drake. The power of all drakes rushed through them and into her.

It was impossible to say who screamed first, Blizza or Filzbalm. The Solar Drake's cry was high and keening. It ripped at Skylar's soul. He couldn't pull his thoughts together enough to help Filzbalm block Blizza's mental hold.

Then Blizza engulfed Del, and the others. They were like one mind being forced into the crystal claw. A bright light flashed out of the totem and struck the giant. Freyandor…the name appeared in Skylar's mind. She had been the last of her kind when she'd been encased in ice. The crystal claw had been constructed to join enough powerful psychics together to hold her and stop her.

She'd been a goddess among her people, the only one capable of stopping the humans when they'd found her solar system and wanted it for their own. But she'd locked the planet's resources away before they'd stopped her by combining their power into an unstoppable force. She'd taken the once vibrant world and stripped it of everything, leaving it a cold, desolate rock. All this poured through the link the claw formed between them.

The image of the Mother of Drakes flashed in Skylar's mind. Through Filzbalm, she was fighting with them, but it was more than that. She'd fought Freyandor before. There had been a drake with the humans who'd first fought for the planet. And there was more, but it flashed by too fast for him to make any sense of it.

Under Skylar's hand, Blizza crumbled. He caught the crystal claw before it dropped.

Freyandor's rage was like a living thing. It lashed at them.

Melody screamed.

As his fingers closed around the crystal claw, Skylar took up the point in the circuit Blizza had been. He became the focus of all their minds, all their power.

Solaria roared in his thoughts.

Leonada echoed her.

"Skylar, push back against her," Del said.

"Listen to him." Blizza's thoughts were weak. *"Every Light needs knowledge."* She surged through him, then out through the totem in his hands. She became the force he was using against Freyandor.

With another roar, Solaria and Leonada's minds rushed through him too. Their mover powers surged after Blizza's thoughts.

Freyandor stumbled backwards, but her rage continued to push against them.

"You will fail." Leonada's thoughts raced out. *"You failed in the past. You will fail now. You have always been a failure."*

Again, Freyandor weakened. Her rage was lessened.

Skylar clutched the crystal claw so hard he was afraid he was going to break it, but he held it high, trying to focus all their might through it. He remembered how Blizza had held them together, and before that, how he would loan power to others—but he'd never been on the receiving end of that power. He gathered everything up and thrust at Freyandor. *"We protect this world. You lost the first fight. You will lose this one."*

Thoughts that weren't his own hit him hard. They weren't even remotely human thoughts. A lush world torn asunder.

The heat from the water faded. He didn't exactly understand how he did it, but he pulled that heat into himself, then pushed it out into the city. The water cooled as it wrapped around Freyandor.

"Lie down, Freyandor," Blizza urged. *"Our time is over."* Then another wave of power surged through Skylar. It felt like Blizza kissed his forehead. Then she was gone.

"Don't lose her power," a distant voice urged.

Understanding, Skylar gathered it up and focused it along with everyone else at Freyandor. Inside he felt sad. Freyandor was just fighting for her lost world, but she was killing people who'd had nothing to do with its destruction. He wished there was another way, but they didn't have time to find it.

He poured the power through the crystal claw that amplified their gifts into something Freyandor couldn't resist. As the cold water fell around her, it hardened into ice. The nature of Pantheria exerted itself and bound her. Her mind screamed as Blizza's power shut her down. Thanks to Clive, Del, and Melody, she didn't have the willpower to marshal her forces to resist them. Solaria and Leonada wrapped the ice hard around her as Skylar continued to hold the crystal claw high and focus their powers as a single unit.

His arm ached as Freyandor fell silent. Then the totem in his grasp exploded and their connection was broken.

Pain lanced through Skylar's hand and everyone screamed.

"You've done well." The Mother of Drakes sounded tired as she broke her connection with him, and Skylar dropped to his knees.

26
Aftermath

SKYLAR WAS thankful he'd been practicing his shielding. The grief blowing around him was touchable. It made the air thick and uncomfortable. He wondered if he'd be able to recover if he hadn't been blocking it as hard as he could. The Unica family stood in a semicircle as the swirl of Blizza's ashes blew into the wind, aided by Felonia and Solaria. It was a fitting tribute to the aged reader that they held her memorial in the gathering twilight two nights after she'd given the last dregs of her power to imprison Freyandor.

Near the family, the various politicians and leaders of Pantheria who had come to pay their respects stood silently as the last light faded and darkness claimed the Indruias settlement. As the steam cleared from Berginna, they'd all showed up to declare Skylar, and his friends, heroes for saving their planet. It had been awkward. He never planned on being a hero. He'd just wanted to have a quiet school holiday. He wasn't sure how to react, so he did his best to ignore most of it.

He also wasn't sure how he should react to the Mother of Drakes joining in their mental gestalt. Filzbalm was being quiet about that. He was the only one other than Skylar who'd felt her presence. Skylar wasn't sure if that was because she'd come through his link with Filzbalm, or that there'd been so much going on at the time.

"Are you ready to go?" Phil asked. "We should get you young people back to the academy." He shook his head. "You're all still kids, but it doesn't feel right calling you that. Kids wouldn't have been able to do what you did. You saved the planet."

Skylar held up his hand and hoped it was going to be enough to stop Phil before he could go on. "Please, can we just go back to Stars' End?"

"Where we're just students," Solaria finished for him. "It's been a hunt I'll never forget, but I think I'm ready to go."

Her mother gave her a big hug. "Rebuilding is going to take years. Go learn everything you can so you can come back and help. We're going to need every mover we can get."

"I will." Solaria hugged her back.

"I will too," Leonada said. "At least I have a planet to come back to." She touched her stomach. "And Mutanio's son will be raised by the old ways. I think he'd like that."

Felonia let go of Solaria and hugged Leonada. "You both will always have a home with us."

"Thanks." Leonada swallowed as she returned the hug, then stepped away.

Phil gave quick hugs and waved the ones heading to the spaceport toward his hover car. "Any of the students who are left and don't stay for the rebuilding will be meeting us at the spaceport in a few hours."

Skylar settled into his seat and looked out the window. There were only a few lights in the settlement. It seemed like there had been more the night they'd arrived, but at least the people there were still alive, unlike the ones in the other cities who had been destroyed as Freyandor grew in power.

Phil started the hover car and drove away.

"Are we really not supposed to say anything about Freyandor?" Skylar asked. Right before Del and Melody had left to head back to the museum, O'Byrne had returned with a squad of lawyers from the galactic council had and sworn them all to secrecy, making them all sign lots of papers in an effort to keep one of the biggest conspiracies in the galaxy from getting out. He'd said something about getting delayed by stargate traffic, or he would've been back sooner.

Melody had acted oddly around him, like she knew him, but didn't want to admit it, or something. O'Byrne had seemed somewhat strange around her too. He acted like he was making a point of staying away from her, after a stiff acknowledgement of her. It made Skylar wonder if may O'Byrne and her mother moved in the same circles or something.

"For now." Phil turned in his seat. The autopilot light shown from the control panel. "That's one of the things you guys are going to learn. There's a lot in the galaxy the government is trying to hide. We're lucky you didn't all end up as collateral damage. I figure O'Byrne didn't make his report to the president in time, or there would've been a team of very powerful psychics on the planet to take Freyandor on, and then wipe her existence from our minds instead of him just showing up with a bunch of lawyers in tow."

"They could try to wipe our minds," Filzbalm muttered from Skylar's shoulder.

"It wouldn't be the first time they've done something like that, and it won't be the last." Phil shook his head. "The people in power aren't always nice, and they do what they think is right for the general populace."

"Even if it isn't right for us," Skylar said.

"Exactly." Solaria frowned. "But we're not ready to take on that prey, or at least that's what Mom told me last night. We've got to mind our tongues and not let anything we know out. They're gathering the information."

"Del says there's a lot of it out on the dark web," Skylar blurted out.

"And don't let people hear any of you talking about that either," Phil said. "We've just had proof of the most dangerous information in the galaxy—humans creating a good number of the bipedal species. When that gets out as more than just rumor, it could tear our society apart. There are reasons genemanip is illegal. More than a few slave races have been created in the past, before there were laws. Once everyone knows the truth, we'll have to deal with the speciesists claiming one species is superior to another, and we all know that isn't true. Our galaxy is changing, and things are only going to get more interesting from here on out."

"And interesting isn't always a good thing," Skylar said, recalling an old Hummassan proverb his mother was fond of saying about living in interesting times.

Phil grinned sadly. "That's very true."

Leonada put her hand on her stomach again. "What's this all going to mean for us?"

"It means we keep our mouths shut and our minds open," Phil replied. A sharp alarm ping made him turn back around in his seat. "That's the best way to keep ahead of the changes." He glanced at the control panel and grumbled, "Like the strange electromagnetic storms that are hitting the planet since you all defeated Freyandor. We don't know if they are remnants of something she'd done, or something else." He took the steering wheel and guided them away from the lights dancing on the horizon in front of them.

Skylar watched the lights until he couldn't see them anymore. They were returning to Stars' End as heroes as opposed to detentionees. He should be happy about that, but he was just sad. He wondered how many other races in the galaxy had suffered the fate of Freyandor's people. The more he was exposed to the universe, the less he liked it, but he wanted to see more. It wasn't necessarily the universe he didn't like, but the people in it.

He scratched at his palm. Ever since the crystal claw exploded, he'd felt like there was something there, something buried deep in his hand. There wasn't any kind of wound or scar, and with everything else going on he didn't want to draw attention to it, but it itched sometimes, and he had to resist scratching at it for fear someone would notice. He wouldn't be surprised if some small piece of the crystal wasn't still with him.

"Do you think we'll beat Del and Melody back to the academy?" he asked when the quiet of the hover car started to get to him.

"I guess it just depends on when the museum lets Del go. Of course, running out in the middle of his internship like he did might cause problems," Solaria said from the front seat beside Phil.

Phil shook his head. "Won't be a problem for him. I made a few calls and gave him a good reference for being out. Your folks also put in a good word for him. He'll be lucky if they don't request him to come back each break until he graduates."

"That'll make him happy." Skylar grinned and settled a little deeper into the plush seat. Del loved the museum, and if he ended up getting a job there, he'd be ecstatic. As the dark frozen landscape of Pantheria slipped past Phil's windows, Skylar knew more than ever, he had to be free to go anywhere he wanted to. Even after what he'd seen, there was still so much more to experience.

"And I'm staying right here with you." Filzbalm rested his muzzle on top of Skylar's ear.

"And I'll be here for you," Skylar replied, scratching Filzbalm's small horns. Beyond knowing Filzbalm was with him, it felt good that Del and Melody would come to his rescue. Solaria would be there for him

too. They were his family, and would always be, ever after he found his father. That would require some effort on his part, and he wasn't sure he was interested in finding someone who hadn't done much for him while his mother was alive. But with so much happening, seeing families destroyed on Pantheria, he was wanting to at least find out who his father had been, and then he'd see about finding him.

There was a wide universe out there, and there was no telling where his next adventure would lie, or how long it would take for him to find it. Skylar hoped it would wait until he knew more and had a greater grasp of his psychic gifts. With luck, it would be something he found on his own, as opposed to something finding him.

Skylar's adventures continue in,
"Skylar Mars and the Mysterious Armada".

If you'd like to stay on top of new releases and upcoming
work by Drew Seren, please join our mailing list at
www.drewseren.com.

And if you enjoyed Skylar's adventure, please leave
a review. It's easy and won't take you very long.

Who is Drew Seren?

Drew Seren was raised on a diet of science fiction, both in print and on the screen. He spent many nights watching Star Trek and Space 1999 with his father. Comic books were a main staple of his reading, and then when he was in high school he started reading *Dragon Riders of Pern* and quickly began devouring any science fiction he could, luckily his father had an extensive library at the time. He started writing soon after that, letting writing help him make it through class. During college and his corporate life, Drew spent a lot of time writing to help him endure the mundane things that gnawed at him. Through his twenties and thirties, comic books and science fiction helped him survive. To this day, he's still reading as much or more than he's writing. He's also an avid gamer, playing first *Dungeons and Dragons*, and currently lots of *World of Warcraft*. He's recently turned his attention to writing full time and exploring the vast galaxy through new and interesting eyes.

Stay in touch with Drew through his website
www.drewseren.com

and Facebook pages
fb.me/drewseren

Feel free to drop Drew an email
drew@drewseren.com

www.ingramcontent.com/pod-product-compliance
Lightning Source LLC
Chambersburg PA
CBHW071149180726
48291CB00007B/2387

LA FANCIULLA DALLA NEBBIA

UN ROMANCE MEDIEVALE

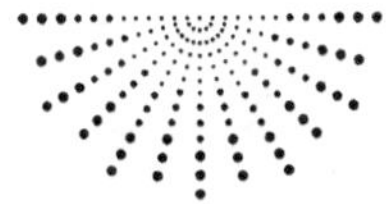

TANYA ANNE CROSBY

Traduzione di
ERNESTO PAVAN

Titolo originale: *Maiden from the Mist*

Copyright © Tanya Anne Crosby

Traduzione di Ernesto Pavan

Copertina © Tanya Anne Crosby

Seconda di copertina: illustrazione di Novel Art Creations; modello: Michael Foster c/o VJ Dunraven Productions

0 9 8 7 6 5 4 3 2 1

❀ Creato con Vellum

LA SCOZIA NEL MEDIOEVO

"Le cose che un uomo ha udito e visto sono i fili della vita; se egli riesce a districarli con delicatezza dall'aggrovigliata conocchia della memoria, chiunque lo desideri può intesserli nella forma di qualunque credo preferisca."

— W.B. YEATS, IL CREPUSCOLO CELTICO

Brilla sul Minch la stella fortunata
che dalla nebbia conduce la dolce fanciulla.
Lunga la chioma e morbida la pelle,
il leone farà uscire dalla tana.
La Profezia della Fanciulla

DUNRÒNAIGH KEEP, ISOLA DI RÒNAIGH, NOVEMBRE 1135

Caden Mac Swein staccò dal muro l'alabarda del suo avo. Fece un passo indietro e la usò per fendere l'aria, valutandone il peso. "Quanti sono?"

"Una cinquantina, a occhio e croce."

Caden sferrò un nuovo fendente a vuoto e imprecò sottovoce. Ricavata da un blocco di robusto legno di frassino, l'asta dell'enorme arma simile a un'ascia superava il metro e venti di lunghezza. La lama era un'ottantina di centimetri di ferro, rinforzata sul filo con dell'ottimo acciaio. In totale, l'arma misurava oltre un metro e ottanta e pesava una dozzina di chili. Soltanto un uomo della stazza e della forza di Caden poteva anche solo sperare di impugnarla, e chiunque si fosse trovato alla sua portata avrebbe potuto attestare la sua capacità nell'usarla.

Sempre che avesse avuto ancora la testa attaccata al collo.

Caden passò le dita callose sulla lama affilata. Preferiva di molto quell'arma vichinga alla spada a due mani. Un tempo, essa era appartenuta al suo bis-bisnonno, Swein del Nord. Si chiamava Bestia e, una volta che si iniziava a maneggiarla, colpiva il bersaglio senza errori.

Vestito per la battaglia, Davino, il 'piccolo Davie',

entrò di corsa nella sala portando con sé la spada di suo padre. A tredici anni, il ragazzo era molto piccolo per la sua età; la claymore lo raggiungeva quasi in altezza. "Si stanno radunando presso la Grotta del Gigante," annunciò. "Andiamo a cacciarli dalla nostra terra!"

Caden aggrottò la fronte. La Grotta del gigante era una grotta marina naturale dalla volta talmente alta da produrre un'eco. Nelle sua profondità potevano trovare posto ben più di cinquanta uomini. Se il nemico si nascondeva al suo interno, sarebbe stato facile sottovalutarne il numero. Era fondamentale sapere esattamente quanti uomini le forze di Caden avrebbero dovuto affrontare quel giorno; non erano abbastanza numerosi da potersi permettere di correre rischi.

"Sono entrati?" chiese a suo fratello, rendendosi conto che Davino doveva aver osservato il nemico dalla torre alta. Costruito dagli antichi, Dunrònaigh Keep era soprannominato 'il *laird* del Mare del Nord'. La sua tenacia era tale da sottrarlo persino all'autorità dei kelpie della tempesta, che governavano sulle acque dello Skotlandsfjörð.

"No," rispose suo fratello.

"Ottimo." Caden annuì. "Ottimo." Per fortuna la grotta vicino alla spiaggia era maledetta e infestata dagli spiriti. La maggior parte delle persone non si sarebbe mai avventurata in quel luogo in cui le ossa di donne e uomini sventurati abbracciavano ancora le stalagmiti vicino alla volta. Intrappolati dall'alta marea, i loro corpi erano finiti troppo in alto per poter essere recuperati. Ora, aggrappati nella morte a quei loro ultimi giacigli, attendevano con ossa tremanti che il mare se li riprendesse. E così sarebbe stato, perché il loro era un mare vendicativo. Nessun uomo che avesse mai solcato lo Skotlandsfjörð avrebbe mai potuto dire che gli Uomini Blu non fossero i più feroci tra i nemici. Tutti gli scozzesi delle Isole Occidentali li temevano, ma a quanto pareva non abbastanza da tenere i loro luridi stivali lontano dalla spiaggia di Caden.

"Andiamo! Sono pronto," annunciò Davie, anche se faticava a sollevare la claymore di suo padre. Lanciando al fratello minore un'occhiata carica di malcontento, Caden disse: "No che non lo sei, Davie."

I grandi occhi azzurri del ragazzo spiccavano da sotto la visiera dell'elmo. "Sì, invece," ribatté. "Non puoi proibirmi di venire, Caden. Sono un uomo adulto." Lanciò un'occhiata ad Alec, nella speranza di suscitare le simpatie del capitano, ben sapendo che era l'unico uomo a cui Caden desse retta; ma Alec ebbe il buon senso di guardare altrove. "Oggi combatterò come un uomo, accanto al sangue del mio sangue," insistette Davie. "Combatterò accanto a te, fratello!"

Caden addolcì il tono della propria voce. "No, giovane Davie. Potrai essermi più utile qui." Dove *qui* stava per 'dentro la fortezza'. Lontano da tutte quelle lame assetate di sangue. Un tempo, in un passato più glorioso, Caden era stato il terzo di cinque figli; ora erano rimasti solo lui e Davino. Il loro avo, Conn Cétchathach delle Cento Guerre, era stato alto re dell'Éire. Davino era solo un ragazzo, ma ciò nonostante aveva visto un quarto delle battaglie che aveva visto Conn. Almeno uno di loro – Caden o Davie – doveva sopravvivere alla giornata sano nel corpo e nella mente. Caden era deciso a far sì che quello fosse Davie.

Il giovane mise il broncio, la mascella serrata sullo sfondo del viso lentigginoso.

"Davie," cercò di ragionare Caden. "Uno di noi *deve* restare a guardia della fortezza. È un compito onorevole, fratello mio. Dunrònaigh Keep è il cuore di Rònaigh e l'orgoglio della nostra gente. Se noialtri dovessimo cadere, chi condurrà il nostro popolo alle navi? Chi li guiderà se io dovessi morire?"

"*Gonadh*! Tu vuoi affibbiarmi un compito da donna, Caden."

Caden appoggiò una mano sulla spalla del fratello. "Proteggere il soglio del capoclan e tutto ciò che abbiamo di caro? No, fratello mio. Questo è un compito da capo."

Poco convinto, Davie fece una smorfia. "Fallo tu, allora!"

Le dita di Caden accentuarono la stretta sulla spalla di suo fratello. Indurì la sua voce e il suo cuore. "Dùin do ghob." *Chiudi quella bocca.* "Uno di noi deve condurre lo scontro e, fino a quando non sarai in grado di impugnare questa alabarda, quel qualcuno non sarai tu. Hai capito?"

Davino sollevò il mento. "Ti supplico, Caden," implorò. "Ti prego. Sono un uomo, ormai. Ti prego!"

"No." Caden si accigliò. "Un uomo non ha bisogno di definirsi tale. Non cambierò idea."

Perdiana, non erano rimaste più nemmeno delle nobildonne tramite le quali stabilire alleanze con potenze lontane. Caden non intendeva mettere in discussione quanto aveva deciso. Suo fratello *non* avrebbe combattuto quel giorno; sarebbe rimasto al sicuro nella fortezza, in modo da poter combattere un altro giorno. Si guardarono negli occhi. Per sottolineare il concetto, Caden porse la Bestia a suo fratello; la pesante arma cadde con un tonfo sul pavimento e i suoi spuntoni di ferro scheggiarono la pietra. Mancò di un soffio il piede di Davie e produsse un frastuono che rivaleggiava con l'eco nella Grotta del Gigante.

Davie fissò l'alabarda vichinga, la fronte aggrottata per la rabbia.

Non c'era bisogno di dire altro. Davie poteva anche essere scontento, ma Caden era riuscito a farsi capire. Il giovane lasciò che recuperasse l'alabarda da terra senza dire una parola. Era ancora cupo in viso quando Caden si avviò verso la porta. Tutti gli uomini in attesa nella sala si incolonnarono dietro di lui. Il suo capitano allungò il passo per rimanere al suo fianco. Solo dopo che furono usciti dalla sala Caden si voltò e disse: "Fa' in modo che mio fratello rimanga qui."

"Tenterò."

"No," disse Caden, la voce che risuonava come un tuono. "Tu *lo farai*, Alec. Se l'ultimo fratello che mi rimane dovesse venire ferito, avrò la tua testa." Nel dirlo, brandì l'alabarda con entrambe le mani.

Era una minaccia a vuoto, che Caden Mac Swein non avrebbe mai messo in atto ai danni del suo più fidato amico e consigliere, ma Alec capiva più di molti altri la risolutezza del suo *laird*. Caden era deciso a proteggere a tutti i costi il più giovane dei Mac Swein dai mali della guerra. Lui stesso portava su di sé una dozzina di cicatrici, dal mento fino ai piedi, ma era meglio che quei segni sfregiassero il suo corpo piuttosto che quello di Davino. Un giorno sarebbe stato Davie Mac Swein a guidare il loro clan, e Caden non sarebbe riuscito a sopportare la perdita di un altro fratello. Ciò nonostante, nemmeno Alec poteva godere del lusso di rimanere nella torre, perché il loro numero si era troppo ridotto a causa delle molte schermaglie coi MacLeod. E tuttavia, se proprio doveva morire, quello era un buon giorno per farlo. Il sole brillava luminoso in un limpido cielo azzurro. Il mare stesso tuonava, facendo della spuma novembrina cristalli di ghiaccio.

In alto sull'antica torre di Dunrònaigh, lo stendardo dei Mac Swein sventolava nella brezza vigorosa: un leone rampante che impugnava un arco. Le possenti mascelle del felino schioccavano e il vento era il ruggito emesso dal suo muso zannuto.

Più in basso, nei pressi della grotta marittima, una torma di usurpatori attendeva di essere cacciata, le armi d'acciaio che scintillavano malignamente sotto il sole spietato.

Tre nuove barche solcarono le onde, andando ad aggiungersi a quelle già presenti. Fortunatamente, vi era un solo punto d'approdo: la piccola, stretta spiaggia sotto le scogliere. L'alternativa sarebbe stata rischiare il naufragio contro gli scogli di Rònaigh.

La forza militare di un'isola tanto piccola era qualcosa di risibile, ma ogni uomo e donna erano in grado di difendersi. Dalla loro avevano il mare e il fatto che, dall'alto della torre, era possibile vedere ogni palmo dell'isola e del mare sottostante. Quel giorno, la cosa migliore da fare era agire in fretta.

"Hai visto uno stendardo?"

"No."

"Razza di briganti," ringhiò Caden. "Scommetto che è di nuovo MacLeod. Brama quest'isola più di un figlio maschio."

"È una questione d'orgoglio," disse Alec. "Vuole dimostrare a tuo padre di essere migliore di lui, anche se egli è già sceso nella tomba."

"Amadain na galla." *Fottuto idiota.*

All'esterno della fortezza attendevano settanta degli uomini di Caden. Lui sollevò l'alabarda di suo nonno verso il cielo azzurro. "Per Dunrònaigh!" gridò.

"Per Dunrònaigh!" risposero gli altri. Poi, insieme, scesero marciando dalla collina di Dunrònaigh, diretti verso la spiaggia dove il mare si agitava con la ferocia infusa in lui dal vento del nord. Era quasi inverno, ma ciò nonostante, ignorando il freddo, Caden si levò il mantello, e assieme a quel mantello appartenuto ai suoi avi si privò delle ultime vestigia di civiltà. Il vento gelido spronò il suo coraggio.

I suoi uomini lo imitarono, non volendo che nulla li intralciasse in battaglia. Come i loro predecessori vichinghi, erano *berserker* nell'anima e non se ne vergognavano. Ciascuno di loro era pronto a difendere la loro terra fino all'ultimo respiro.

Mentre marciavano, lanciarono antiche grida di guerra, agitando le loro armi scintillanti e invocando la furia degli Uomini Blu, quei bizzosi kelpie della tempesta che proteggevano il Minch e, oltre esso, le acque del Nord. Ogni passo era reso più facile dall'inclinazione del terreno, grazie al quale gli uomini si riversavano verso il basso come una mortale colata d'argento. Dal punto più alto dell'isola, in cima a Dunrònaigh Keep, un osservatore avrebbe avuto l'impressione di una marea umana che andava a riversarsi nel mare di un blu profondo.

Per contrasto, gli usurpatori giunsero risalendo la collina, appesantiti nel passo, ma sospinti dall'avidità e dalla sete di sangue.

"Per Dunrònaigh!" gridò un'ultima volta Caden.

"Per Dunrònaigh!" gli fecero eco i suoi uomini.

Il sole splendeva sugli elmi e sulle spade mentre le due forze si scontravano sulla collina di Dunrònaigh.

La battaglia ebbe inizio. Un ruggito assordante, uno spietato clangore metallico. Il sangue imbrattò la terra come una pioggia macabra, tingendo ogni filo d'erba e arrossando il fianco della collina.

Combattendo senza sosta, Caden deviava i colpi del nemico e sventolava l'alabarda come un uomo posseduto dal demonio, abbattendo chiunque arrivasse a portata della Bestia. La battaglia infuriò fino a quando non furono rimasti in piedi che i più feroci.

Caden incalzò il nemico fino a quando le braccia non gli si fecero pesanti. Continuò a combattere anche dopo che il gelido metallo gli lacerò la spalla. Il dolore lo colpì come un fulmine. Una furia nera prese il sopravvento, perché se quel giorno avesse fallito, Davino ne avrebbe pagato il prezzo. No! Non sarebbe venuto meno a suo fratello.

Nell'istante preciso in cui Caden rischiò di essere colpito da un'altra arma, Alec deviò il colpo. La punta della spada di Alec penetrò alla base del cranio del nemico, uscendo dalle narici e inzuppando di sangue il petto di Caden. L'uomo cadde a terra e il suo sangue andò a mescolarsi a quello di coloro che erano caduti prima di lui. Il fianco della collina era un tappeto rosso, lubrificato a tal punto dal sangue che cominciava a diventare difficile rimanere in piedi.

Ruggendo di rabbia, Caden sollevò ancora una volta l'alabarda, trovando la forza nel pensiero di suo fratello. Per Dio, avrebbero dovuto farlo a pezzi per fermarlo. E tuttavia, mentre lui scatenava la sua furia, due nuove barche iniziarono le manovre che le avrebbero portate ad approdare sulla sua spiaggia.

Nuovi guerrieri risalirono la collina per unirsi alla battaglia. Rendendosi conto della rapidità con cui la situazione rischiava di mutare, Caden rinnovò gli sforzi e rafforzò la propria risolutezza. Lanciando un nuovo grido di guerra al cielo, si gettò nella mischia, colpendo ovunque possibile, assistendo ciascuno dei suoi uomini, e ogni vita che prese alimentò la sua follia.

Il sangue gli scorreva a rivoli lungo le braccia, rendendo difficile mantenere la presa, ma Caden manovrava l'ascia come un prolungamento di sé, fendendo con tutta la sua furia e con tutta la sua forza. Lui e la Bestia erano una cosa sola. Ma anche gli eroi potevano cadere in battaglia e la guerra non aveva simpatie per nessuno. Fu trafitto al polpaccio destro e barcollò, urlando di dolore. La Bestia si mosse da sola, come spinta da una furia omicida tutta sua.

Il sole brillò sul metallo argenteo dell'elmo di un uomo, accecando Caden, ma l'alabarda continuò a muoversi, tracciando un semicerchio letale di fronte a sé, tagliando carne e ossa. Caden udì un suono che lo fece esitare, quello della voce di suo fratello, ma non fu abbastanza lesto da capire da dove provenisse.

Gli occhi azzurri di Davie incrociarono lo sguardo dei suoi per un brevissimo istante, colmi di orgoglio. Il giovane aveva abbattuto l'uomo che aveva trafitto Caden alla gamba. Lo aveva trafitto al cuore con la claymore del loro padre e l'uomo aveva mancato il suo vero bersaglio: il cuore di Caden.

Ma l'alabarda non sapeva nulla di tutto ciò. Suo fratello rimase immobile di fronte a lui, sorridendo da un orecchio all'altro, in attesa della sua benedizione... in attesa che ammettesse di aver sbagliato, che lo chiamasse 'uomo'.

In attesa.

Istanti preziosi trascorsero al rallentatore. Un novizio della guerra, Davie non ebbe la prontezza di schivare e Caden non riuscì ad arrestare il fendente fatale della sua lama. Ancora una vola, l'alabarda schiantò carne e ossa, mozzando di netto la testa di Davie. La testa prese il volo, ma Caden non la vide mai atterrare. Un velo nero calò di fronte ai suoi occhi e lui rimase fermo dov'era, prigioniero dell'oscurità, ascoltando le grida degli uomini che gli morivano attorno.

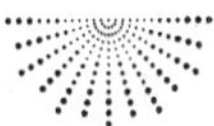

*D*a qualche parte nell'alto della torre, una porta sbatté pesantemente. Qualche istante dopo, i giunchi sul pavimento si mossero agitati dalla corrente d'aria, solleticando le gambe di Alec. Ulteriori porte si aprirono e si chiusero. Si aprirono e si chiusero. *Bam. Bam. Bam. Bam.*

Alec imprecò sottovoce.

Per quanto non avesse buona memoria, non ricordava un altro inverno tanto rigido. Certo, Rònaigh non era che un sassolino in mezzo al Firth, meno di mille acri quando andava bene. Buona parte di quella terra era costa rocciosa, per cui Alec e la sua gente coltivavano quanta più terra possibile e tiravano avanti grazie alla generosità del mare: pesce, uccelli marini e tutto ciò che gli Uomini Blu si degnavano di gettare sulle loro spiagge. Purtroppo, persino negli anni di abbondanza ci voleva gente dura per sopravvivere in quella terra, ed era comunque difficile tirare avanti anche quando tutto erano abili e disposti a lavorare e il *laird* era in grado di guidarli. Ma ora, dopo quella battaglia sulla collina, il loro numero era dimezzato e il benessere di Rònaigh era legato inesorabilmente a quell'insopportabile individuo che se ne stava ai piani superiori. Caden Mac Swein era come un bambino capriccioso e arrabbiato che imprecava contro la sorte. Solo Alec sapeva cosa stava cercando realmente di fare: voleva convincere i membri del suo clan a esautorarlo. Peccato che non sarebbe mai accaduto. Caden Mac Swein era stato il loro campione da che tutti avevano memoria, e as uch Dé, *perdio*, se il destino aveva voluto che solo uno tra Caden o Davie sopravvivesse, Alec era pronto a ringraziare la sua buona stella per il fatto che fosse toccato a Caden.

Davino era stato un ragazzetto fastidioso. Fisicamente piccolo per la sua età, nonché ostinato come i kelpie della tempesta, il ragazzo era nato fragile – il genere di figlio che un nobile vichingo avrebbe probabilmente abbandonato il mezzo alla neve – per non parlare del fatto che la sua legittimità era sempre stata piuttosto dubbia. Il vecchio MacLeod aveva dato inizio alla faida tra i due clan quando, in un momento di rabbia, si era portato via la madre di Caden, e anche se Mary Mac Swein era sfuggita al suo cosiddetto rapitore dopo meno di tre mesi, era tornata a casa con il ventre gonfio come una balena. Se qualcuno avesse chiesto il parere di Alec, lui avrebbe espresso ad alta voce i suoi dubbi riguardo alle dichiarazioni della donna. Aveva il vago sospetto che Mary Mac Swein fosse andata di sua spontanea volontà col vecchio MacLeod, per poi tornarsene a casa dopo essersi stufata di lui. Nessuno era mai riuscito a dirle cosa doveva fare e Alec era abbastanza vecchio da ricordare tutte le volte in cui Mary Mac Swein aveva ballato col vecchio MacLeod. Mary era sempre stata una civetta... proprio come i fratelli di Caden. Soltanto Caden aveva ereditato la bontà d'animo di suo padre. Di conseguenza, nessuno a Rònaigh avrebbe sostenuto che Caden non fosse il migliore e il più promettente di tutti e cinque i giovani Mac Swein, anche se, a giudicare dal suo comportamento attuale, sarebbe stato difficile crederci.

Bam. Bam. Bam. Bam.

Alec strinse i denti e cercò di concentrarsi sui registri.

Uno. Due. Tre. Quattro. Cinque. Sei. Sette.

Far di conto non gli veniva facile come a Caden. A ogni modo, quello era il numero di sacchi d'orzo rimasti. Mancava ancora più di un mese a Calendimaggio, il giorno in cui avveniva la tradizionale benedizione dei campi, e fare alcunché prima di quel giorno avrebbe significato attirare disgrazie sul raccolto futuro. Il problema, ora, era come distribuire quanto rimaneva in modo che nessuno soffrisse la fame... compito in precedenza eseguito dal *laird*. Alec non aveva la più pallida idea di cosa fare, soprattutto perché si trovava in pieno conflitto d'interessi.

Con meno di un mese davanti, avrebbe dovuto probabilmente dare tutto l'orzo, tranne un sacco, al birraio, perché a nessuno piaceva il pane che faceva Bessie. Manco a lui, a dire il vero. Si costringeva a trangugiarlo solo perché provava del tenero per la ragazza che lo preparava. Anche se, naturalmente, Bessie era all'oscuro dei sentimenti di Alec: lui voleva concederle il giusto periodo di lutto, dato che il suo caro marito era stato uno di quei brav'uomini caduti sulla collina. Così come il calzolaio, la cui morte aveva fatto sì che mezzo clan si ritrovasse senza scarpe. Per fortuna aveva iniziato a fare più caldo e i pescatori potevano andare a pesca senza ritrovarsi con le dita dei piedi blu.

Bam. Bam. Bam. Bam.

Al culmine della pazienza, Alec sollevò una mano e fece per chiamare il siniscalco, ma un attimo dopo questi entrò per conto suo. Inchinandosi con deferenza, Afric si avvicinò al tavolo del *laird*... non che Alec ricoprisse quel ruolo. Il siniscalco si era inchinato perché, come tutti i membri del clan ancora in vita, sapeva benissimo che, senza Alec, sarebbe toccato a qualcun altro di loro occuparsi della 'Bestia di Dunrònaigh'. Nonostante la cecità, Caden Mac Swein non aveva perso nulla della sua ferocia.

Bam. Bam. Bam.

"Si può sapere che sta facendo là sopra, sant'Iddio?"

Il siniscalco si strinse nelle spalle. "Perdiana, sembra che più lo ignoriamo e più faccia rumore."

Che il cielo gli cada sulla testa. Era da cinque lunghi mesi che Caden Mac Swein piangeva la morte del fratello. Ma quel che era fatto era fatto. Cosa voleva che facessero, consegnare l'isola nelle mani di MacLeod? Perché, in sostanza, il clan si sarebbe ritrovato a fare proprio quello se non fosse stato Caden, cieco o meno, a sedere sullo scranno del *laird*. Solo Caden aveva il diritto di governare quella terra e nessun altro aveva un lignaggio tanto importante... nemmeno i MacLeod di Skye. Era proprio quello il motivo che Alec credeva fosse alla base della faida. Se il vecchio *laird* non si fosse vantato profusamente col vecchio MacLeod delle proprie nobili origini, forse questi non si sarebbe sentito in obbligo di rapire la madre di Caden. Cristo santissimo, gli spacconi erano la razza peggiore; ma del resto, raramente si rendevano conto di esserlo.

"Si riprenderà," promise Alec; ma diceva la stessa cosa da novembre, quando Caden Mac Swein aveva perso misteriosamente la vista. Lui stesso cominciava ad avere qualche dubbio.

"A Dio piacendo," rispose il siniscalco; poi aggiunse: "Di fuori c'è una donna che dice di dover parlare con voi."

"Con me?"

"Sì, capitano."

"Non con il *laird*?"

Il siniscalco scosse la testa.

"Una donna? Qui? E nessuno ha avvistato una nave?"

"Nossignore."

"E come diavolo ha fatto ad arrivare fin qui?"

Portandosi una mano alla bocca, Afric mormorò: "Non lo so, ma secondo me è arrivata in sella a una scopa, non via mare. Ha una benda su un occhio ed è mezza cieca anche dall'altro."

Alec si grattò la barba e mise giù la penna. Erano trascorsi cinque anni dall'ultima volta in cui il clan aveva avuto l'opportunità di accogliere donne venute da fuori. Un tempo, proprio in quel periodo, il vecchio MacLeod veniva con la sua gente a Rònaigh per celebrare la festa con quello che allora era il suo buon amico, il vecchio Mac Swein. Ma dopo la morte di Mary il vecchio MacLeod aveva dato inizio a una guerra e ora non perdeva occasione per cercare di prendersi ciò che apparteneva a loro. Alec non aveva faticato tanto per tenere nascoste le condizioni del *laird* solo per rivelare il segreto a una vecchia megera vagabonda. Soppesando l'opportunità di apprendere qualcosa di nuovo contro il rischio che la nuova arrivata scoprisse qualcosa, Alec decise: "Mandatela via." Poi avvicinò a sé il registro e tamburellò con un dito su un numero scribacchiato. "Che c'è scritto qui, Alfric? A volte non riesco a leggerli, i tuoi scarabocchi. È un sette questo? E questa piccola riga?"

Il siniscalco parve non udire la domanda di Alec, o quantomeno non se ne curò. C'era uno strano sguardo nei suoi occhi, uno sguardo che Alec sapeva sarebbe stato meglio non ignorare. "Cosa c'è?" chiese.

"Beh, signore... So cosa avete detto a proposito del dare accoglienza agli sconosciuti, ma... quella vecchiaccia sembra dire di avere informazioni utili per il nostro *laird*."

Alec rimase di stucco. "Che stranezza. Una donna cieca che vuole aiutare un uomo cieco?"

Bam. Bam. Bam.

"Molto bene… Immagino sia giusto darle una possibilità." Qualunque cosa pur di risolvere quella situazione. "Falla entrare."

Il siniscalco si allontanò e Alec si alzò dal tavolo per andare a prendere posto sul seggio del *laird* e prepararsi ad accogliere quella bizzarra ospite. Un attimo dopo, una donna piccola e raggrinzita entrò barcollando nella sala, in mano un bastone di legno pallido. Il suo volto era completamente dipinto di blu, con l'occhio buono sporcato di nero per abbinarlo alla benda scura che portava sull'occhio sinistro. Pareva un demonio dai riccioli bianchi e ogni singolo battere del suo bastone sul pavimento di pietra si riverberava come un tuono. Ciò nonostante aveva un'aria fragile, e Alec pensò che una persona tanto debole non avrebbe certo potuto essere d'aiuto al suo *laird*. La sua delusione prese la forma di un sospiro mentre lanciava un'occhiata agli splendidi arazzi che ornavano le pareti. Una volta, tanto tempo prima, erano stati l'invidia di tutta l'Éire. Il Righ Art in persona aveva ceduto la mano della figlia a uno *jarl* vichingo. Pur aspettandosi che l'alleanza sarebbe sfiorita con l'arrivo dei freddi venti del nord, si era ritrovato invece con un alleato a nord: un sovrano vichingo feroce quanto gli Uomini blu e il Minch.

Ahilui, quella donna era una delusione, ma se non altro Alec aveva l'occasione di raccontarle la storia del suo clan. "Benvenuta!" esclamò con un gesto elaborato. "Benvenuta nella sala dei re di Rònaigh."

La donna non parve colpita.

Alec alzò leggermente la voce, certo che dovesse essere sorda oltre che cieca. "Brava donna, voi vi trovate di fronte all'alto soglio da dove un tempo governava Swein del Nord." Alec raddrizzò la schiena, inorgoglito al pensiero di quanto stava per dire. "Sposo della figlia favorita dell'Alto Re dell'Éire, Conn Cétchathach!"

Continuando a sfoggiare un'espressione assai poco convinta, l'anziana disse: "Sì, sì, sì... li conoscevo bene." Poi tirò su col naso a becco e se lo sfiorò con un dito. "Un gran bisbetico, quello Swein."

Alec aggrottò la fronte.

Non era possibile, naturalmente, che quella donna conoscesse quei due personaggi: entrambi erano morti più di mille anni prima. Doveva soffrire di demenza senile. Alec decise comunque di assecondarla. "Già," disse in tono scherzoso. "Dev'essere un tratto di famiglia." Lo stesso Caden era diventato vagamente intrattabile.

"Proprio così," concordò la vecchiaccia, con uno bagliore di allegria nell'occhio buono. "Mi chiamo Biera," annunciò.

Senza che il suo buonumore venisse intaccato, Alec disse: "Benvenuta, Biera, cara amica di Swein. Cosa possiamo fare per voi?"

Senza preavviso, il bastone di Biera si allungò in maniera impossibile attraverso la distanza che li separava e diede un colpetto sulla testa di Alec. "Non ho mica detto che era mio *amico*. Un amico è una persona cara. Io non provavo alcun affetto per quegli uomini. E tu, ragazzo mio, faresti meglio a non abusare di quella parola. Guarda cos'ha combinato l'*amicizia* tra due alleati. Guarda quanto poco contano gli amici nel momento del bisogno!"

Sentendosi rimproverato come un bambino dalla mamma, Alec si portò una mano alla testa e se la massaggiò vigorosamente. Troppo confuso dall'allungamento del bastone di Biera per potersi arrabbiare, lo stupore era comunque evidente sul suo viso. C'era qualcosa, in quella donna, di fin troppo familiare, eppure... non credeva di aver mai visto quel volto arcigno in vita sua.

"Io sono vecchia," proseguì Biera, "e bizzosa quasi quanto il tuo padrone cieco e iracondo. Ma nemmeno Swein avrebbe mai osato prendermi in giro. A ogni modo, non ho bisogno di scope magiche, ma tu potresti essermi utile."

Perplesso, Alec continuò a massaggiarsi la testa. Già sentiva un bernoccolo grande quanto la fibbia di una cintura prendere forma sul suo cranio. Ma come faceva la vecchia a sapere cosa aveva detto di lei Afric? E soprattutto, come poteva una persona tanto fragile fisicamente brandire un bastone in quella maniera? Non avrebbe dovuto poterlo colpire: era troppo lontana. E lui non era nemmeno sicuro di averla vista muoversi. Al contrario, gli pareva che fosse rimasta immobile tutto il tempo a guardarlo storto, attraverso la pittura sul viso, con l'occhio buono.

Che stranezza.

La donna si produsse in un sorriso sottile. "Ora che ho la tua attenzione..." disse, puntando verso di lui l'estremità ingioiellata del suo bastone. Le gemme ammiccarono maliziose, strappandogli un sussulto. Alec affondò nello scranno.

"Tra due notti, dal Minch si leverà una stella fortunata. Dopo di lei verrà una ragazza di nome Sorcha, in cerca di un passaggio per l'Isola di Skye. Voialtri accetterete la sua richiesta, ma invece di portarla a destinazione la condurrete a Rònaigh an Taibh."

Rapire una donna? Alec rizzò le orecchie. "Con la forza?"

"Se necessario."

"Come faremo a riconoscerla?"

La donna sorrise con aria affettuosa. "È impossibile non notarla: ha lunghi capelli soffici e splendidi occhi azzurri. Sarà la più bella giovane che tu abbia mai visto, ma non spetta a te."

Alec fu invaso da un senso di disappunto... fino a

quando la donna non proseguì. "Le sue figlie suggelleranno alleanze secolari e i suoi doni restituiranno al tuo *laird* ciò che ha perso."

Quella donna stava forse dicendo di poter rianimare i morti? A meno che non potesse riportare alla vita Davino, non c'era nulla che potesse fare per Caden. Ma forse, per la sua vista... Alec strinse gli occhi e decide di metterla alla prova. "Dite, mia signora, a cosa vi riferite?"

Di fronte ai suoi occhi, la sagoma della donna parve accrescersi. Raddrizzandosi, raggiunse un'altezza stupefacente, come se nella sua piccola schiena ingobbita avesse celato fino a quel momento la lunghezza della sua spina dorsale.

"Alla sua vista," sibilò la vecchia, le cui parole scivolarono tra i denti come una serpe. "Non devi lasciare che Sorcha lasci Rònaigh, perché se lo farà verrà in cerca di me."

Per un minuscolo istante, Alec ritrovò la combattività. "Perché?" chiese. "Avete forse commesso qualche crimine contro questa povera ragazza?"

L'anziana gli puntò un dito contro. "Amadán!" *Stolto.* "Ciò che lei è per me non è affar tuo. È ciò che sarà per il tuo *laird* a doverti interessare."

Per un singolo istante, l'espressione sul volto di Biera divenne terribile, e brividi percorsero la schiena di Alec. In quel momento intravide l'essenza dell'Universo nelle profondità dell'occhio buono dell'anziana. Costei non era una semplice mortale. Era *altro*.

"Ci siamo capiti?"

Alec annuì. "Sì," disse, per poi raddrizzare subito la schiena. Batté le mani per chiamare il siniscalco. "Portate della birra," ordinò. "Portate dello *uisge!*" Alla sua divina ospite disse: "Abbiamo molto di cui parlare."

"Oh, sì," concordò l'anziana, per poi curvarsi sul suo bastone e dirigersi zoppicando verso il tavolo dove i registri erano rimasti, dimenticati. "Che bravo giovane che sei," gli concesse. "Davvero un bravo giovane. Forza, lascia che ti dica cosa va fatto. L'ultima volta che una stella fortunata si è avvicinata così tanto al mondo, tre sapienti fecero un lungo viaggio per portare in dono a un bambino oro, incenso e mirra."

CAPITOLO DUE

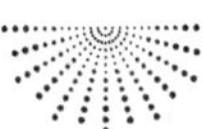

NEL FRATTEMPO, TRA I BOSCHI
DELLA CALEDONIA...

Sbirciando verso l'alto, attraverso il fogliame, Sorcha dún Scoti fissò la bizzarra stella che era apparsa, guarda caso, il mattino prima... proprio quando lei aveva preso in considerazione l'idea di tornare a casa. Ora, più cavalcava verso ovest e più essa le pareva vicina. Era come se Una la stesse prendendo in giro dall'alto dei cieli. "Vieni a cercarmi," le pareva che stesse dicendo. "Trovami, se ci riesci."

"Oh, non temere, ti troverò," disse a denti stretti Sorcha, al che le betulle argentate, con le loro pallide foglie neonate, fremettero per la brezza.

Guardò storto la stella, ma poi il suo sguardo si intenerì. Dopotutto, sua madre aveva preso il nome proprio dalle stelle. Forse quel fenomeno non era opera di Una, ma di Riannag dún Scoti, che la guidava verso la sua destinazione. Purtroppo, di chiunque si trattasse e ovunque intendesse guidarla, una cosa era certa: non restava più nulla per lei nella Valle.

In quel momento, l'aria si profumò di salmastro; un odore familiare per Sorcha, che aveva trascorso parecchio tempo nell'Ailginshire. Ormai suo fratello Keane doveva aver avuto notizia della sua partenza. Anche lui si sarebbe messo a cercarla?

Non gliene importava nulla. Non aveva bisogno di persone che non esitavano a mentirle... nemmeno di Una.

Una, che aveva tutte le risposte.

Una, che li aveva cresciuti da quando erano nati.

Una, che era là fuori... da qualche parte.

Sorcha se lo sentiva fin nelle ossa. *Perché? Perché? Perché?* si era chiesta molte lune prima, quando la montagna nella loro Valle era crollata distruggendo la reliquia sacra del loro popolo assieme alla grotta di Una. La Pietra di Scone era stata l'unica ragione dell'esistenza dei Guardiani nella Valle... una prigione naturale, secondo il nuovo punto di vista di Sorcha. Ma ora era perduta, sepolta sotto una montagna di rocce assieme alla Madre del suo popolo. Perché, allora, si erano reclusi per proteggere un'inutile pietra che gli dei avevano deciso di riprendersi? *Quale futuro attende i guardiani, ora?*

Ma a turbare Sorcha più di ogni altra cosa era un dettaglio: perché Una aveva rimosso il proprio grimorio e la propria *keek stane* da quella grotta?

Perché sapeva.

E se sapeva, perché aveva lasciato quegli oggetti preziosi a lei e se n'era tornata alla grotta in attesa della morte?

Perché non era andata così.

Ora Sorcha ne era sicura. Non c'era da stupirsi che non riuscisse a provare dolore. Una era viva; se non fosse stato così, lei lo avrebbe di certo avvertito. Ne era certissima: l'astuta vecchia non era sepolta assieme alla Pietra di Scone. Era là fuori... *da qualche parte.*

"Ti troverò," disse Sorcha, agitando un pugno contro la stella.

Ma *loro* non avrebbero trovato lei, giurò. Viaggiando da sola, sapeva bene di dover evitare le strade del Re. C'era il rischio che fossero pattugliate dagli uomini di David, per non parlare del fatto che, se ci fossero stati dei briganti, era proprio lì che si sarebbero appostati. E poi, non era stato un problema evitarle: Sorcha conosceva i boschi meglio di molti altri. Era una figlia del vento, dopotutto. Una figlia della foresta. Lei e i suoi consanguinei erano gli ultimi dei Pitti, *bla bla bla*... tranne per il fatto che Sorcha non udiva più il battito dei cuori dei suoi avi nelle vene. Non era più una dún Scoti, ma una Caimbeul, figlia illegittima di un uomo che era cresciuta odiando. E tutto il suo clan – persone che aveva sempre amato e di cui si era sempre fidata – lo aveva sempre saputo. Sorcha non voleva avere più nulla a che fare con loro.

Sputò per terra, rinnegando i *Guardiani* e le loro favolette. Avrebbe dato inizio a una storia nuova, tutta da sola...

Ormai suo fratello, il *laird*, doveva aver mandato degli uomini a cavallo a Keppenach e a Dunràth.

Non importava: sarebbero tornati a mani vuote e senza saperne più di prima. Sorcha aveva imparato molte cose dai suoi fratelli. Da Keane aveva appreso a cacciare e a seguire una pista. Da Lael a maneggiare una lama. Da Cailin a tirare con l'arco. Da Catrìona a sfruttare il proprio fascino. E grazie a Lìli – sì, Lìli era sua sorella – aveva perfezionato la sua conoscenza delle erbe. Ultimo, ma non meno importante, da suo fratello il *laird* aveva imparato a mentire. Una rabbia nera come i capelli sulla testa di suo nipote sbatté le ali nella sua cassa toracica. La verità era che le avevano mentito *tutti*.

Tutti.

Tu non sei la figlia di un Guardiano, la sfotté una vocina nella sua testa; parole che le fecero venire la nausea. Scacciando calde lacrime, osservò la stella dalla lunga coda che attraversava come un serpente il cielo ventoso. Aveva la strana sensazione che, se avesse raggiunto il luogo in cui lo strascico scintillante dell'astro toccava la terra, lì avrebbe trovato tutte le risposte che cercava.

A ogni modo, se Una ancora viveva, Sorcha credeva di sapere dove avrebbe potuto trovarla. Ogni primavera, in quell'esatto periodo, l'astuta vecchia lasciava la Valle, diceva, per esercitare la sua professione presso i clan vicini. Ma Sorcha cominciava a sospettare che li avesse abbandonati per ben altra ragione...

Secondo una delle storie scritte nel grimorio che Sorcha portava in saccoccia – il libro che Una le aveva dato il giorno prima di 'morire' – ogni primavera, a Calendimaggio, la Cailleach in persona tornava a bere dalle polle fatate sull'Isola di Skye, trasformandosi nella propria sorella estiva.

Era proprio lì che Sorcha stava andando: non da Padruig, ma nell'unico luogo in cui nessuno avrebbe mai pensato di cercarla, perché la brava gente timorata di Dio non credeva più nelle vecchie leggende. Erano marionette nelle mani di un sovrano che aveva rinnegato le divinità dei loro avi. Ma lei credeva ancora in esse. E quella stella lassù pareva condurla direttamente da Una. *Come un faro*. Brillava giorno e notte – giorno e notte – e Sorcha era convinta che brillasse solo per lei... per condurla alla Cailleach.

Cavallo e cavallerizza continuarono al trotto e le anemoni a forma di stella chinarono le loro piccole teste bianche al loro passaggio.

Piegandosi all'indietro, Sorcha lasciò cadere la *keek stane* ormai inutile nella sacca della sella. Fino a quel momento l'aveva tenuta in mano, nella vaga speranza che il cristallo si degnasse di parlarle nuovamente. Ma più luminosa si faceva la stella, più la *keek stane* esauriva la sua luminosità, fino a quando non era divenuta che un cristallo lucido.

I suoni della notte erano come musica nell'aria. Un

lupo ululò in lontananza. Le fronde verdi lasciarono presto il posto all'immenso cielo aperto e Sorcha tirò le redini del cavallo in cima a una collinetta che sovrastava il villaggio di Lochinver. Nel corso degli ultimi giorni aveva viaggiato per valli e colline, dal Mounth fino al mare... e ora era arrivata fino a dov'era possibile senza avere accesso a una barca. L'indomani avrebbe dovuto trovare un modo per attraversare il mare; ma, ahilei, con cosa avrebbe potuto pagarsi il viaggio?

Certamente non con la *keek stane*. Né con il libro che teneva in borsa. Non possedeva altro di valore, se non la sua dolce e fedele Liusaidh.

Smontò e osservò il paesaggio. Dal suo punto di vista sopraelevato riusciva a vedere miglia e miglia di mare verde e crudele, con onde spumose che parevano minacciarla. "Vattene," sembrava dicessero. "Non osare venire da questa parte." Ma Sorcha avrebbe osato eccome. E chiunque la conosceva avrebbe potuto testimoniare che non era così facile dissuaderla. Se Una era là fuori, lei l'avrebbe trovata.

Come per rassicurarla, Liusaidh le sfregò il muso sulla spalla, avvicinandosi un poco come per abbracciarla. Sorcha accarezzò con rimpianto il suo caro cavallo, rendendosi conto che presto avrebbe dovuto dirle addio.

"Io. Ti. Troverò," mormorò ancora una volta; poi rabbrividì, ma non perché avesse paura. Non ne aveva. Né aveva freddo. Un invisibile mantello di furia ardente la scaldava fin nel profondo.

Un silenzio eterno e senza età fu la risposta che ottenne. Si appoggiò alla sua giumenta e ne accarezzò il folto pelo bianco. L'indomani mattina, presto, si sarebbe separata da Liusaidh per ottenere un passaggio su una nave. Quando qualcuno avrebbe scoperto la sua vera destinazione – ammesso che succedesse – lei sarebbe già stata lontana. Oltre il Minch, sull'Isola di Skye.

Al diavolo suo padre. Al diavolo la gente. La verità era l'unica cosa di cui le importava, ora.

❧

DUBHTOLARGG

Non per la prima volta e con sommo rammarico Aidan dún Scoti si preparò alla guerra.

Aveva commesso l'errore di credere che sua sorella sarebbe tornata a casa di sua spontanea volontà. Col senno di poi, era stato un errore non inseguirla non appena aveva intravisto la luce ribelle nei suoi occhi. Solo una volta, in passato, aveva visto un'espressione del genere sul volto di un consanguineo, ma aveva erroneamente creduto che la sua mite sorella minore non avrebbe mai fatto ciò che aveva fatto Lael: andarsene dalla Valle senza guardarsi alle spalle.

Ora Sorcha se n'era andata e Aidan non poteva biasimare altri che se stesso.

Avrebbe dovuto dar retta a sua moglie. Avrebbe dovuto raccontare a sua sorella la verità: che suo padre era l'uomo che aveva ucciso il padre di Aidan e violato la loro nobile madre. Ma poiché non lo aveva fatto, la domanda che lo spaventava di più era quella che detestava porsi: Sorcha avrebbe ucciso quel bastardo del proprio padre?

Padruig Caimbeul era un farabutto. Aidan detestava l'idea che sua sorella lo affrontasse da solo. Avrebbe voluto che Una fosse ancora viva, perché la scaltra vecchia sapeva sempre cosa fare.

Una volta, non molto tempo prima, Una aveva formulato una profezia terribile... che Aidan aveva ovviamente ignorato. Aveva detto che i lupi di Pechtland si sarebbero sparsi ai quattro venti. In quel momento, Aidan la trovò una previsione decisamente azzeccata, perché erano rimasti solo lui e Cailin, e quest'ultima avrebbe prima o poi sposato Cameron MacKinnon, se quell'imbecille avesse mai trovato il coraggio di chiederglielo.

Undici anni prima, sua sorella Catrìona era stata la prima ad andarsene, rapita dal proprio letto nel cuore della notte da re David. Nonostante le circostanze della sua partenza, Cat non era mai tornata alla Valle. Lael se n'era andata per aiutare Broc Ceannfhionn a ricatturare Keppenach e lì era rimasta, sposata col Macellaio di re David. Ora anche Keane se n'era andato, naturalmente contro il volere di Aidan, e si era venduto l'anima a David mac Mhaoil Chaluim in cambio di una sposa... una principessa di Moray, senza dubbio, ma ormai quel che era fatto era fatto. E ora Sorcha...

Fino a quella mattina, Aidan era stato sicuro che si sarebbe diretta verso nord in cerca di Keane e di sua moglie. Ma non era quello il caso. Lael e Keane vivevano entrambi a pochi giorni da Dubhtolargg e gli uomini da lui inviati erano già tornati da Keppenach e da Dunràth senza aver trovato Sorcha. Aidan era dunque preoccupato. Si allacciò il cinturone della spada e infoderò l'arma. Lìli entrò nella stanza mentre il buon acciaio si infilava nel suo fodero.

"Vengo con te."

"No."

"Aidan, ti prego! Padruig è mio padre. Tu non hai alcun diritto di tenermi qui."

Aidan si voltò verso sua moglie e le rivolse un'occhiata come non le aveva mai rivolto prima. "Ho tutto il diritto: sono tuo marito e il tuo *laird*."

Per nulla scoraggiata, lei lo afferrò per un braccio e strinse dolcemente. "Ti prego, Aidan," implorò. "Non mi fido di lui."

"Una ragione in più per evitare che tu lo incontri," disse Aidan. Si riferiva, naturalmente, al genitore di Lìli, quell'odioso furfante che aveva concepito non una, ma ben due delle donne che lui adorava. Borbottò un'imprecazione, pentendosi profondamente di aver infuso nelle sue donne un coraggio tale da far sì che queste riuscissero a contrastarlo così facilmente, quando uomini forti e robusti non avevano mai osato farlo.

Perché, in nome della Cailleach, aveva tenuto nascosta la verità a Sorcha tanto a lungo?

La futilità di quello sforzo non gli era mai parsa tanto evidente come in quel momento, mentre incrociava lo sguardo amorevole di sua moglie. Sorcha non somigliava per nulla a lui e moltissimo a Lìli. Avevano persino gli stessi capelli di rame e gli stessi inquietanti occhi viola. Quanto tempo era trascorso dall'arrivo di Lìli prima che lui stesso iniziasse a mettere in discussione quanto aveva sempre creduto? Eppure, assolutamente fiduciosa, Sorcha non aveva mai osato mettere in discussione l'identità del proprio padre. Si era affidata completamente a coloro che l'amavano. E ora, Aidan detestava pensare a come doveva sentirsi.

Tradita, quantomeno.

"Aidan," disse Lìli, pronta a una discussione, "non è per me stessa che temo. È per te, amor mio... e per Sorcha. Non lo sapevi?"

"In tal caso, non hai nulla da temere," le assicurò Aidan. "Se qualcuno dovesse morire oggi, non si tratterà di me."

"Le ultime parole famose, marito mio! Tuo padre deve aver detto lo stesso quando ha lasciato che una serpe gli si insinuasse in casa! E ricorda: non puoi sfidare Padruig senza un buon motivo. Egli è protetto da re David. Se dovessi ucciderlo senza ragione o provocazione–"

Aidan la interruppe. "David è ed è sempre stato uno stolto. Non mi importa se è riuscito ad accattivare l'intera Scotia alla sua causa."

Purché ciò non compromettesse la pace tra i clan, Aidan non avrebbe mai seguito un usurpatore inglese. Non amava la politica, ma come si poteva chinare il capo di fronte a un uomo cresciuto da un re inglese, tornato in Scotia per esautorare il legittimo conte di Moray e insidiare al suo posto un burattino degli inglesi, uno scozzese talmente vile da inginocchiarsi di fronte a un uomo il quale, secondo alcuni, aveva ucciso suo nonno?

"Aidan… ti prego. Tu non lo conosci."

Aidan si voltò di scatto, reso furioso dalle parole di Lìli. Si toccò il petto con un dito. "Non lo conosco?" chiese. "*Io* non lo conosco? Per la pietra, Lìli, ha ucciso mio padre di fronte ai miei occhi e ha violato mia madre mentre era ancora sporco del suo sangue. E tu dici che non lo conosco?"

Lìli sbiancò. Aidan non aveva mai parlato in maniera così diretta dei crimini commessi dal padre di lei nei confronti suoi e del suo popolo. Non lo aveva fatto perché la amava, si rese conto Lìli, e perché sapeva che lei era consapevole più di tutti di ciò di cui era capace Padruig Caimbeul. "Non ti lascerà mai entrare nella sua sala," insistette, temendo ciò che sarebbe potuto accadere se non lo avesse seguito. "Non senza privarti di tutto ciò che hai con te. Ti lascerà indifeso e si circonderà di guardie. E se tu dovessi perdere la pazienza–"

"È proprio per questo che non voglio che tu venga, Lìli." Era raro che Aidan discutesse con sua moglie, ma ora vederla lo infastidiva, perché in quel momento la donna gli ricordava tutte le menzogne per cui avrebbe dovuto fare ammenda. Non solo era identica a Sorcha, ma anche a quell'infame del suo babbo. Aidan scosse la testa, in parte per il disgusto provocato dal ruolo che lui stesso aveva giocato nelle disgrazie di sua sorella. *Come ci si sente a sapere di essere figlia di una carogna?* Voltando le spalle a sua moglie, riprese a vestirsi.

Un attimo dopo, Lìli trovò il coraggio di toccargli la parte inferiore della schiena, un gesto timido che gli fece venire le lacrime agli occhi. Incapace di resisterle, si voltò, allargò le braccia e ingoiò le parole dure con cui avrebbe voluto insultare suo padre. Prese sua moglie tra le braccia e le ravviò i capelli dal viso, parlando con un tono di voce più dolce. "Non posso permettermi di lasciarti correre dei rischi, a ghrà mo chroí." *Amore del mio cuore.* "Hai già sofferto abbastanza per mano di tuo padre."

Lìli gli rivolse una nuova occhiata implorante. "Ti prego, Aidan... non è stata colpa tua. Se lui dovesse fare del male a Sorcha, non potrei mai perdonarmelo. Ti prego," implorò. "Lei è anche mia sorella."

Un fatto tanto semplice quanto nauseabondo.

Che razza di tela di menzogne avevano intessuto. Sua sorella minore era anche la sorella di sua moglie, un fatto difficile da accettare. Aidan prese i lunghi capelli scuri di Lìli tra le mani, la attirò a sé e la baciò con dolcezza sul naso, preparandosi a dirle di no. Ma, ahi-lui, si rese conto che la donna aveva detto il vero: sarebbe riuscita a decifrare meglio di lui l'atteggiamento di Padruig. Rassegnatosi, appoggiò la fronte contro quella di lei. Ogni singola parola che usciva dalla bocca di quell'uomo andava presa con le pinze. E tuttavia, Lìli avrebbe capito d'istinto quando suo padre avrebbe detto la verità. As ucht Dé – *per Dio* – la vita di Sorcha era preziosa e Aidan non poteva ignorare qualunque opportunità di salvarla.

Tornando mentalmente sui propri passi, baciò ancora una volta sua moglie, questa volta sulla fronte, temendo il peggio: che il padre di lei sarebbe in qualche modo riuscito a strappargli la sua amata, senza la quale vivere sarebbe stato insopportabile.

Fortunatamente, o forse no, Lìli conosceva Aidan meglio di chiunque altro e interpretò il suo silenzio per quello che era: un momento di debolezza. "Ti prego… *devi* permettermi di venire con te. Se mio padre tiene prigioniera Sorcha, io lo capirò."

"E se così fosse? Lui non ti darà retta. Non la lascerà andare solo perché glielo chiedi tu."

Lìli lo implorò con gli occhi. "Sì, ma forse mia madre lo farà." Lady Saundra era ancora viva e c'era la possibilità che avrebbe fatto sentire la propria voce a favore della figlia perduta. Ma lo avrebbe fatto per salvare la progenie bastarda di suo marito?

Insieme nella riservatezza della loro stanza, mentre il resto della casa era in preda al caos, Aidan e Lìli tacquero per un istante; poi, poco dopo, Lìli lo abbracciò all'altezza del petto. "Vorrei che potessimo evitare di farlo sapere a lui."

Bontà divina. Padruig non avrebbe avuto bisogno di sentirsi dire alcunché: gli sarebbe bastato posare gli occhi sulla sua prole per rendersi conto di avere due figlie. E dire che non meritava nessuna delle due.

Padruig Caimbeul era un marrano fatto e finito. E Aidan doveva mettere a rischio una sorella per salvare l'altra? Era una posizione insostenibile, ma Lìli aveva detto il vero. Aidan doveva portarla con sé ad affrontare il suo babbo. Deciso, la spinse lontano, ma non in maniera brusca. "Va' a parlare con Cailin," disse. "In nostra assenza, è lei la responsabile della Valle. Di' a Ria di badare a sua zia e preparati a partire."

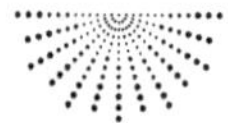

Il mare in tempesta sbatacchiava le navi per tutta la baia. A differenza di certa gente, che si spaventava al primo alito di vento, gli uomini di Rònaigh non avevano paura. Loro preferivano attendere in mare che la tempesta passasse. Ma non potevano ancora andarsene...

Non prima dell'arrivo di Sorcha.

E ora eccola lì... con i lunghi capelli lucidi raccolti in una spessa treccia, che raggiungeva la baia a cavallo di una splendida giumenta bianca diversa da qualunque altro animale Alec avesse mai visto. Cavallo e cavallerizza avevano la testa alta, e il fuoco nell'anima di lei era visibile dal modo in cui agitava la coda... l'animale, naturalmente, non la donna. La vecchia Biera aveva raccontato una storia incredibile, ma ora tutto si stava svolgendo esattamente come lei aveva previsto.

"Che sia lei?"

"Voi che ne pensate?"

I due uomini osservarono la ragazza condurre il bell'animale fino all'estremità del lungo molo e mormorarle qualcosa all'orecchio. Era davvero bella... e Alec non stava pensando solo all'animale, in quel momento. Per un attimo gli dispiacque non poter fare sua quella donna.

Sorcha accarezzò a lungo il collo della giumenta e Alec si chiese cosa avrebbero detto i suoi consanguinei quando avrebbero visto quella bella puledra scendere dalla sua nave. A onor del vero, non sapeva cosa lo entusiasmasse di più: ciò che la vecchia aveva decantato della giovane o la sua cavalcatura. In molti, a Rònaigh, non avevano mai visto un cavallo, men che meno un cavallo del genere. Quegli animali erano di scarsa utilità sulla loro isola, se non per tirare l'aratro. La scuderia di Dunrònaigh aveva qualche maschio e una manciata di femmine, ma l'unico animale di un certo pregio era quello di Caden.

E la ragazza... beh, non era certamente mostruosa. Anzi, aveva il portamento di una regina, e se la vecchia aveva detto il vero, presto nelle sale di Dunrònaigh sarebbero tornare a riecheggiare le risate, i bambini avrebbero ripreso a giocare per i campi e, soprattutto, Caden Mac Swein sarebbe tornato all'antica gloria. Ma prima di tutto bisognava portare la ragazza a Rònaigh e per farlo c'era bisogno di aiuto.

"La rapiamo?"

"No." Alec guardò storto il capitano della nave. "Abbiate pazienza."

Aveva già pagato i pescatori in modo che negassero un passaggio alla giovane, e sarebbe stato meglio se fosse salita a bordo di sua spontanea volontà. Aveva bisogno della sua fiducia per ciò che aveva in mente.

A ogni modo, dubitava che altre navi avrebbero preso il largo quel giorno, col clima in quelle condizioni. L'oceano stesso era come una donna, con il suo carattere bizzoso, e la luna e le stelle esercitavano a loro volta una forte influenza. La nuova stella che aveva iniziato a brillare nel cielo sembrava aver scatenato un bel putiferio. E poi, nessuna delle altre navi era ben equipaggiata come la loro.

Nonostante fossero passati molti secoli, la gente di Alec utilizzava ancora la tecnica dei propri avi vichinghi; non i *drakkar* dalle prue a forma di drago, un tempo molto temuti, ma le mezze navi usate dai mercanti vichinghi per trasportare le loro merci. Con i loro scafi più ampi e profondi delle navi da guerra, tre *knörrs* avrebbero potuto facilmente evacuare tutto il loro villaggio, e loro ne avevano quattro. Per quanto furiosi fossero gli Uomini Blu, la loro nave avrebbe retto alla tempesta senza alcun problema. E nessun inganno dei signori del mare avrebbe potuto impedire loro di trovare la strada di casa, perché le fanciulle che li guidavano attraverso la nebbia erano amiche dei Pinnuti.

"È belloccia… potrebbero essere tentati."

"Non lo saranno."

"Come potete esserne certo?"

"Ho raccontato loro una storiella."

"Cioè?"

"Ho detto che quella donna era figlia della Cailleach e che l'avrebbero riconosciuta dalla sua giumenta. Ho detto a tutti che si tratta di una sposa vergine, promessa al *laird* di Dunrònaigh, e che se qualcuno dovesse impedirle di seguire la stella fortunata che la porterà dal suo amato, la Cailleach in persona aizzerà contro di loro i kelpie della tempesta. E viste le condizioni del mare, dubito che qualcuno vorrà correre il rischio."

"Alla faccia della storiella. Ma, e se non vi credessero?"

"Non dire sciocchezze! Quante ragazze credi arriveranno qui su un destriero bianco come la neve? E quella stella? No, la vecchia Biera aveva previsto il suo arrivo ed eccola lì."

Il capitano della nave sollevò lo sguardo. "È la cosa

più dannatamente assurda che io abbia mai visto," concordò. Tuttavia, chiese preoccupato: "E se parlassero con qualcun altro?"

"Bah! Che facciano quello che vogliono. A noi importa solo di portare la ragazza a Rònaigh. Tutto il resto andrà come andrà."

Più in là, la donna in questione si voltò. Pareva intenta a soppesare le navi nella baia... solo tre delle quali erano in grado di salpare e nessuna migliore della loro.

"Presto," disse Alec al capitano della nave. "Preparate gli uomini. Partiremo entro un'ora." L'atmosfera si stava facendo carica di energia. Rònaigh non era mai stata così vulnerabile. Ma se la vecchia aveva detto il vero, la ragazza avrebbe fatto ben più che restituire la vista a Caden: avrebbe riportato i Mac Swein alla grandezza.

"Non ti dimenticherò mai," disse Sorcha a Liusaidh. "Sei la mia più cara amica."

La sua *unica* amica, a occhio e croce, vista la falsità dimostrata dai consanguinei di Sorcha. Purtroppo il grimorio e la *keek stane* erano troppo preziosi per separarsene e, comunque, nessuno avrebbe riconosciuto il loro vero valore. Anche se, fosse stato per lei, li avrebbe sacrificati entrambi pur di tenersi il cavallo. Purtroppo Liusaidh era l'unica cosa di valore che potesse scambiare.

Sospirando, accarezzò la guancia dell'animale, di cui sentiva già la mancanza. Ma procrastinare non avrebbe reso la separazione meno dolorosa. Più decisa che mai ad arrivare a destinazione, prese la borsa con i preziosi oggetti che portava con sé e se la mise in spalla. Poi legò le redini del cavallo a un paletto e ignorò la domanda espressa da quei grandi occhi marroni. Dopo aver lanciato un'occhiata all'onnipresente stella, si avviò lungo il molo fino a raggiungere il primo pescatore la cui barca pareva in grado di navigare. Non un singolo uccello solcava il cielo tempestoso, solo nuvole nere e quella stella dalla lunga coda. Alcuni gabbiani si erano riparati vicino a una struttura per sfuggire al vento. Una nebbiolina salata le accarezzò le guance e Sorcha esitò, ma poi si costrinse a proseguire. "Scusate, signore," disse, interrompendo un uomo che stava abbassando le vele. "Vorrei affittare la vostra barca."

L'uomo la guardò con aria perplessa. "Ma le hai viste quelle onde? Io non vado da nessuna parte oggi. Non è un tempo da cristiani, questo." Lanciò un'occhiata a Liusaidh, poi tornò a occuparsi delle sue vele. "Torna domani," le suggerì, senza tuttavia mostrare particolare interesse.

Sorcha non poteva aspettare fino all'indomani. Avvertiva un forte senso d'urgenza. Doveva partire subito. *Oggi.* Non sapeva quanto a lungo la stella sarebbe rimasta a farle da guida e, se avesse atteso fino all'indomani, essa sarebbe anche potuta svanire. Aggrottò la fronte.

Dopotutto, pensò, quella barca era pure piccola. Passò all'imbarcazione successiva, decisamente più grande. "Scusate, signore, vorrei pagarmi il passaggio sulla vostra barca."

"Ma come! Non conosci la differenza tra una barca e una nave? *Questa* è una nave, non una barca. Nessuna barca potrebbe mai navigare il Minch in una giornata così. Diventeresti cibo per i Pinnuti, magari nella pancia di un grande pesce."

"Scusatemi," si corresse Sorcha. "Vorrei pagarmi il passaggio sulla vostra *nave*."

"No," rispose subito l'uomo, senza nemmeno prendersi la briga di chiederle dove fosse diretta. Ma poi si guardò attorno e posò lo sguardo su un'altra nave all'ancora dall'altra parte della baia e Sorcha avvertì in lui una certa esitazione, per cui disse: "Vi prego, signore. In cambio del passaggio vi darò la mia giumenta. È giovane e sana, con degli ottimi denti."

L'uomo smise di fare quello che stava facendo e lanciò un'occhiata a Liusaidh, forse in preda al dubbio; ma poi disse bruscamente: "Non sfiderei il Minch nemmeno se mi offrissi in cambio un'intera scuderia di cavalli rubati. Non oggi."

Rubati!

"Buon signore," ribatté Sorcha, "Liusaidh non è stata rubata! È nata e cresciuta…" Si interruppe prima di tradire la propria provenienza. "Nel Mounth. È forte e molto obbediente. L'ho allevata io stessa, sapete. Le ho ferrato gli zoccoli e l'ho domata. Non vi venderei mai un cavallo rubato."

"Beh, in ogni caso, forse non hai notato che questo qui è il Minch. A noi non servono cavalli, buoni o cattivi che siano. Sono le navi che servono, e io non metterei a rischio la mia per nulla al mondo. Questo è quanto, ragazza. Preferisco vivere che renderti un servizio. Ora vai, su. Imeacht gan teacht ort!" *Vattene e non tornare mai più!*

Il vento le spinse in faccia i capelli. Era vero: l'oceano aveva un aspetto minaccioso. Ma quegli uomini non le sembravano il genere di persone che temevano un po' d'acqua e di vento. Liusaidh era un cavallo prezioso. Un'opportunità del genere non capitava tutti i giorni; proprio per quella ragione lei si era tenuta il più possibile al riparo dei boschi. Una donna sola in groppa a un cavallo del valore di Liusaidh era un bersaglio allettante.

Frustrata, Sorcha osservò la baia e vide che c'era soltanto un'altra nave all'apparenza in grado di sfidare il mare burrascoso. Ancora una volta, sbirciò la stella, chiedendosi se la sua presenza non avesse in qualche modo provocato l'ira degli dei. Del resto, se era davvero opera della Cailleach, probabilmente l'intento era proprio quello. A ogni modo, per nulla intimidita, Sorcha girò attorno alla baia per raggiungere la nave più grande in essa ancorata: un'imbarcazione splendidamente ornata, a bordo della quale un uomo robusto si stava avvolgendo una corda attorno alla mano. "Scusate, signore, avete intenzione di salpare quest'oggi?"

L'uomo gonfiò il petto. "Ma certo!" disse sorridendo. "La mia gente ha sangue vichingo. Un po' di burrasca non ci fa paura."

Alto, possente e biondissimo, l'uomo era di una bellezza quasi pari a quella della sua nave. Il suo atteggiamento non faceva pensare che fosse un poco di buono, ma c'era comunque qualcosa di bizzarro in lui... qualcosa su cui Sorcha non poteva permettersi di soffermarsi, non avendo grandi alternative. *Doveva* trovare un modo per attraversare il Minch. "Ditemi, signore... quanto dista l'Isola di Skye?"

L'uomo si strinse nelle spalle. "Con questo tempo? Almeno mezza giornata di viaggio."

Sorcha si morse il labbro. "Così tanto?"

"Oggi siamo alla mercé del Minch, ragazza. Se non hai mai avuto la disgrazia di avere a che fare con gli Uomini Blu, non puoi sapere quanto siano intrattabili.

Gli Uomini Blu?

Sorcha non aveva idea di cosa stesse dicendo quell'uomo. Non sapeva chi fossero quegli uomini blu o perché mai bisognasse avere a che fare con loro. *Pinnuti. Uomini Blu.* Era una strana lingua quella che parlavano quei capitani. Ma un'occhiata sul ponte della nave rivelò un equipaggio di uomini dai capelli chiari, tutti al lavoro sulle vele e nessuno con la pelle blu. "Beh," disse Sorcha, tentando un azzardo, "vorrei pagarmi il passaggio a bordo della vostra nave. Ma vi prego, ascoltatemi prima di rifiutare. Posso offrirvi in cambio un cavallo prezioso."

L'uomo smise di fare quello che stava facendo e guardò in direzione di Liusaidh, che era rimasta esattamente dove l'aveva legata Sorcha, la splendida criniera mossa dal vento. "È quello laggiù?"

"Sì, proprio quello."

"E non vorresti altro in cambio?"

Sorcha prese fiato. "No."

"Si innervosisce facilmente?"

"No."

Diversamente dagli altri, costui parve prendere in considerazione la proposta di Sorcha. Lei trattenne il fiato.

"Credi che riuscirà a viaggiare a bordo di una nave?"

Sorcha si voltò per lanciare un'occhiata a Liusaidh mentre rifletteva sulla domanda dell'uomo; quando si voltò, avvertì al tempo stesso entusiasmo e tristezza. "Non vedo perché no."

"Come si chiama?"

"Liusaidh," rispose Sorcha, sorridendo. Era stata lei a darle quel nome. "Significa guerriera." E di sicuro Liusaidh ne aveva l'aspetto mentre se ne stava lì, tutta sola e pronta ad affrontare qualunque cosa il mondo le avrebbe scagliato contro. Sorcha non aveva mai dubitato della devozione di quell'animale... diversamente da certa gente.

L'uomo si asciugò la fronte con l'avambraccio e parve meditare sulla proposta di Sorcha mentre osservava Liusaidh. "Ha tutti i denti?" chiese in un tono di voce che sembrava speranzoso.

"Sì, signore."

"Ed è stata ferrata?"

"Sì. I ferri sono nuovi."

"Che mi dici del suo carattere?"

Nel dirlo, l'uomo la guardò in maniera particolare,

squadrandola, il che la spinse a chiedersi se si stesse riferendo al cavallo o a lei stessa. Fortunatamente, il suo sguardo non mostrava tracce di lussuria; ma se aveva voglia di litigare, lei non si sarebbe certo tirata indietro. Sorcha e le sue sorelle non erano gente che si lasciava calpestare. Tanto per stare sicura, disse: "È buono. A meno che non venga provocata."

Un attimo dopo, l'uomo scosse la testa come per dire di no. "Ahimè, ragazza mia, il mare è di pessimo umore oggi. Non sarebbe un viaggio piacevole."

"Per favore!"

L'uomo inclinò la testa e parve soppesarla nuovamente. "Hai gambe da marinaio?"

Sorcha aggrottò la fronte; non conosceva quel linguaggio. "Non so cosa vogliate dire, ma sì, ho ottime gambe."

L'uomo fece un largo sorriso. "Quello che volevo dire è: soffri il mal di mare? Io ho molto da fare e a bordo non c'è nessuno che voglia far da servo a una signorina di buona famiglia come te."

Di buona famiglia? Costui non aveva davvero idea di chi fosse Sorcha, e se l'avesse avuta, probabilmente le avrebbe sputato addosso. Lei stessa odiava l'uomo che l'aveva concepita al punto che si sarebbe sputata addosso da sola. Ma per un attimo le parole dell'uomo le diedero sollievo, suggerendole che poteva ancora convincerlo. "Non temete: non ho bisogno di essere servita da nessuno. Per quanto riguarda le mie gambe, ho vissuto quasi la mia intera vita in una casa costruita su un lago e non ho mai vomitato, se non quando avevo bevuto troppa birra."

L'uomo ridacchiò e si sfregò la mascella barbuta. "Siamo in due, ragazza, siamo in due. Dicevi di essere diretta all'Isola di Skye?"

Sorcha fu colta da un impeto di ottimismo. "Sì."

L'uomo strinse gli occhi; poi, dopo un lungo istante

carico di tensione, annuì. "Forza, allora: prendi il tuo cavallo e portala qui. La convinceremo a salire in barca e partiremo."

Aveva detto 'barca', non 'nave'. Sorcha non riuscì a celare la propria gioia. Avrebbe potuto baciare quell'uomo, se non altro perché le aveva concesso dell'altro tempo da trascorrere con la sua amata Liusaidh.

Corse a riprendere la giumenta e non vide mai l'occhiata soddisfatta che si scambiarono i marinai. Una volta salita a bordo, l'uomo con cui aveva contrattato venne a offrirle una fiasca. "Il viaggio sarà più gradevole con un po' di *uisge* nello stomaco." Lui stesso bevve e, dopo aver fatto una smorfia, passò la fiasca a Sorcha. "A proposito, il mio nome è Alec. Benvenuta a bordo del Veliero di San Ronan."

"Grazie," disse Sorcha, accettando l'offerta dell'uomo. Aveva effettivamente una gran sete, e anche una gran fame. Da quando aveva lasciato la Valle si era nutrita quasi solo di bacche e funghi. "Il Veliero di San Ronan? È un nome gradevole, ma non capisco il riferimento."

"San Ronan è il patrono della mia terra," rispose l'uomo. "Per coloro che seguono la religione del Re, perlomeno. Per quanto mi riguarda, preferisco la Cailleach. Qualche giorno fa, quando non sapevo che pesci pigliare… ma non importa. Bevi. Abbiamo già alzato le vele."

Sorcha non conosceva bene la religione del Re, né le importava chi pregasse quali divinità. Ma quell'uomo non aveva idea di quanto lei fosse vicina alla Madre del Creato. Decise che li avrebbe presentati. Entusiasta all'idea dell'avventura e di aver fatto un passo verso la riunione con la sua mentore, prese lo *uisge* offertole dall'uomo e ne bevve un lungo sorso, per scoprire che era persino peggiore dello *uisge* della sua dispensa. Ma in modo o nell'altro, voleva dimostrare una volta per tutte di non essere una mollacciona. L'uomo sorrise con aria di approvazione quando lei inghiottì senza esitare; dopodiché Sorcha gli restituì la fiasca.

"Nah, tienila," disse lui. "Ne avrai bisogno. Il viaggio non è lungo, ma un pisolino ti farà bene. E non c'è niente di meglio di un goccetto per dormire come si deve."

Sorcha sapeva che era vero. Anche se, naturalmente, nemmeno lo *uisge* era riuscito a farla addormentare dopo che aveva scoperto le menzogne raccontatele dai membri del suo clan. Temeva che avrebbe potuto trangugiare l'intero contenuto della fiasca e rimanere sveglia e tormentata. Ringraziò Alec e si mise comoda vicino a Liusaidh…

NEL SOGNO COME NEL RICORDO, PADRUIG CAIMBEUL incombeva come una figura enorme. All'epoca della gioventù di Aidan, l'uomo era stato un essere temibile, con la lunga barba spruzzata di rosso e la spada assetata di sangue. Ma ora, colui che gli sedeva di fronte somigliava a un rospo rigonfio, con il triplo mento e la pancia che sporgeva oltre i braccioli del trono. Il distante genitore di Lìli era il tiranno di Caisteal Inbhir Nis, che aveva ereditato da suo padre, e il cui possesso gli era stato confermato da David mac Mhaoil Chaluim come pagamento per la sua partecipazione al complotto per uccidere Aidan… complotto del quale la presenza dello stesso Aidan nella casa dell'uomo testimoniava il fallimento. E tuttavia, tutto l'oro che Padruig aveva estorto a David in cambio della propria perfidia non era servito che a comprargli una fine prematura. A giudicare dal pallore untuoso della sua pelle, l'uomo aveva già un piede nella fossa.

Ciò nonostante, la sua corte era splendente, con

arazzi indorati e mobili di legno intagliato sulla piattaforma. Non c'erano giunchi sui pavimenti e il granito era lucidato a specchio. Colonne che Aidan non aveva mai visto prima marciavano lungo il perimetro della stanza fino al seggio del signore sulla piattaforma rialzata. Era una scena degna di un piccolo sovrano. Tra di loro erano frapposte guardie in livrea, uomini che, immobili, non guardavano che Aidan. Ma nulla di tutto ciò aveva lo scopo di far colpo sugli attuali ospiti di Padruig. Al contrario, Aidan aveva la sensazione che Padruig li avrebbe sbattuti volentieri in cella e avrebbe buttato via la chiave se ciò non avesse rischiato di attirare su di lui le ire di David. Infatti, pur essendo egli stato al suo servizio, sembrava che il sovrano avesse deciso di prendere le distanze dagli uomini disonorevoli... un fatto che, sebbene fortunato per la Scotia, non aveva certo spinto Aidan a considerare David il suo unico e vero Re.

Il gruppo di cinque persone, che includeva la figlia dello stesso Padruig, era circondato dalle guardie, che impugnavano lance dalla punta d'argento. Aidan si rese conto nell'istante stesso in cui ammise il motivo della loro visita di aver fatto uno sforzo inutile. Non solo Padruig non sapeva dove si trovasse Sorcha, ma palesemente non aveva idea del fatto di esserne il padre. Era un gran peccato, perché Aidan sarebbe stato ben contento di vivere ancora vent'anni e basta se ciò avesse significato non vedere mai più quel brutto muso.

Padruig agitò un dito grassoccio e unto verso di lui. "Vorresti dirmi che *io* ho una figlia?"

Lasciò la domanda in sospeso, perché Aidan gli aveva già dato la risposta e non intendeva ripetersi.

"Ho una figlia e tu non ti sei mai degnato di dirmelo?" L'uomo fece una smorfia. "Non c'è da stupirsi che vi chiamino selvaggi; non sapete cosa sia la cortesia."

Aidan serrò una mano a pugno di fronte a tanta arroganza. Padruig sedeva sul suo trono dorato in cima alla piattaforma e gli parlava come se Aidan fosse stato poco più che una bestia... dopo aver violentato e percosso sua madre. E osava ancora chiedere *perché* lui non gli avesse rivelato le origini di Sorcha?

Lurido porco.

"Nel caso ve ne foste dimenticato, avevate anche un'altra figlia, che eravate disposto a mettere a morte. Capirete che non c'era molto da fidarsi."

Aidan stava parlando di Lìli, che era stata inviata a Dubhtolargg per assassinarlo nel suo letto... cosa che, senza dubbio, il caro babbo avrebbe negato. Ma Aidan aveva la parola di Lìli al riguardo e, nonostante il sangue che scorreva nelle vene di sua moglie, si fidava di lei senza alcuna esitazione.

"Capisco," disse Padruig, trafiggendolo coi suoi strabilianti occhi viola. "Ora vorresti dirmi che diamine vuoi?" Prese una prugna da un vassoio accanto al trono e la gustò lentamente, guardando al tempo stesso Aidan dall'alto in basso. Fece spettacolo di ogni morso, lasciandosi colare il succo lungo i denti. Aidan tacque, trattenendosi fino a quando non ce la fece più.

"Avete o no fatto prigioniera mia sorella?"

"Sorcha?"

"Sì."

"Che bel nome," disse Padruig, continuando a gustare la sua succosa prugna. "Ella brilla luminosa come suggerisce il suo nome? Nella vostra lurida lingua non significa forse qualcosa come 'luce splendente e radiosa'? Qualcosa del genere. Curioso come se ne sia andata proprio alla luce di quella strana, nuova stella. Non lo trovi affascinante?"

Qualcosa, nell'atteggiamento dell'uomo, suggerì ad Aidan che egli aveva iniziato a tramare nel momento in cui aveva appreso la notizia. Padruig si volse per dire qualcosa alla donna seduta accanto a lui: presumibilmente la madre di Lìli, anche se non pareva aver nulla da dire alla figlia da tempo perduta, la quale era in piedi e in silenzio alle spalle di Aidan. Non aveva chiesto dei nipoti o sorriso, nemmeno di nascosto. Lìli, per fortuna, non aveva ancora detto nulla, e Aidan sperava che avrebbe continuato così: nonostante fosse disarmato, avrebbe strozzato Padruig se questi avesse osato offendere la donna che amava. Era quello il motivo per cui non aveva voluto che Lìli lo seguisse. Ma era evidente che, nonostante tutto, sua moglie aveva preferito rimanere in silenzio di fronte al padre. Aidan si chiese se avesse sperato che la riunione con la madre potesse produrre qualcosa di piacevole: una mesta presa d'atto del loro alienamento, magari un'espressione di rimorso per quanto era accaduto. Ma niente.

Padruig mormorò con veemenza alla donna seduta accanto a lui; poi si voltò nuovamente di fronte al gruppetto scarsamente benvenuto, guardando alle spalle di Aidan e rivolgendosi alla figlia. "Guarda che ti vedo, Lìleas. Vieni a salutare tua madre. Ti abbiamo insegnato le buone maniere." Quando Lìli non obbedì immediatamente, l'uomo aggiunse: "O sei diventata una selvaggia come quello che hai sposato?"

Tremando, Lìli si fece avanti, ponendosi accanto ad Aidan e prendendolo per mano. Lui le diede il sostegno tacitamente richiesto, noncurante di ciò che suo padre avrebbe potuto pensare del gesto. Se dubitava della forza di Aidan, che la mettesse alla prova. Lui non era più il giovane indifeso che, un tempo, non aveva potuto far nulla contro l'uomo che gli aveva ammazzato il babbo. "È vero?" chiese il padre di Lìli. "Sorcha è figlia mia?"

Lìli sollevò il mento. "Sì, signore... è mia sorella."

Padruig scoppiò in una risata sguaiata e continuò a ridere, come se trovasse l'idea molto divertente. Poi si schiarì la voce e disse: "Bene bene... peccato per te, mia cara. Avevo paura a lasciarti alcunché, visto che tu lo avresti dato a quel buzzurro che hai accanto. Ma ora il problema non si pone più." Sorrise in maniera grottesca. "Forse tua sorella si dimostrerà più… malleabile. E se è pepata come la sua nobile madre, forse riuscirò anche a ricavarne un bel gruzzolo."

Aidan avvampò. "Vi assicuro che mia sorella non è per nulla malleabile," disse a denti stretti. "E comunque, se non è con voi, qui abbiamo finito. Arrivederci."

Padruig strinse gli occhi. "Sai una cosa, bamboccio? Rimpiango di non averti ucciso quand'eri ancora un ragazzino."

Aidan strinse la mano di Lìli. "Potete sempre provarci."

Ancora una volta, Padruig rise. "Parole forti per un *ospite* disarmato. Dimmi, o Re delle Colline, cosa mi impedisce di farti uccidere seduta stante? Sarebbe mio diritto." Accennò con la mano alla sua corte e alle sue guardie. "Potrei dire che mi hai minacciato e nessuno dei presenti lo negherebbe."

Aidan strinse i denti. "Dubito che riuscireste a staccarvi da quella sedia in tempo per salvarvi la vita."

"Razza di…" Padruig si alzò dal trono molto più in fretta di quanto Aidan avrebbe immaginato.

Avrebbe fatto meglio a non provocarlo finché Lìli era lì al suo fianco, ma era difficile controllare la rabbia. "Per rispondere alla vostra domanda," lo interruppe, "devo avvertirvi che non sono venuto da solo."

"Ho visto, brutta canaglia. E tuttavia, mentre tu sei accompagnato dagli uomini di David, dimmi, dún Scoti, chi c'è a sorvegliare la *mia* piccola Sorcha?" Agitò una mano per accennare al firmamento. "Lei è la mia stellina. Se dovesse accaderle qualcosa, ti riterrò personalmente responsabile."

Aidan strinse i denti, non volendo rivelare all'uomo quanto quella domanda lo turbasse. Era vero: era venuto seguito da un esercito. Ma Sorcha era ancora là fuori, da qualche parte, sola e indifesa. E ora si era verificato il peggio: quel demonio di suo padre ne era venuto a conoscenza.

"Levati di torno," disse Padruig, tornando a sedersi e congedandolo con un gesto. "Sta' sicuro che non risparmierò gli sforzi per cercare la *mia* bambina. Rivolterò ogni singola pietra..." Assunse un'aria di preoccupazione palesemente fasulla. "Ritroverò e mi riprenderò la mia cara piccina, e poi—"

"Padre," singhiozzò Lìli.

"Zitta, tu, donnaccia!" esplose Padruig, alzandosi nuovamente in piedi. "Hai rinnegato il mio nome – e tutto ciò che possiedo – il giorno in cui sei andata a letto con quel lurido abitante delle colline. Ascoltami bene, figlia mia: non commetterò lo stesso errore con tua sorella. Dio ha voluto concedermi una seconda occasione. Troverò *mia* figlia e farò in modo che mi dia degli eredi, a costo di generarli io stesso!"

Infuriato da quella minaccia, Aidan scattò verso la piattaforma. Subito fu bloccato dalle lance degli uomini di Padruig, che si incrociarono di fronte a lui, bloccandolo. Lìli non volle lasciare la sua mano, il che gli ricordò della sua presenza. Non avrebbe certo fatto un favore né a lei né a Sorcha finendo trafitto dalle preziose lance degli uomini di Padruig.

"Aidan!" gridò Lìli.

Padruig rise in maniera oscena.

"Andiamo," mormorò Lìli. "Ora! Lui vuole solo provocarti." Ma poi, quando Aidan fece per allontanarsi, lei si lanciò una lunga occhiata alle spalle, verso la donna seduta accanto a suo padre; e quando quella donna si voltò, Lìli emise un suono strozzato e terribile. Il cuore di Aidan si spezzò per la sua dolce moglie. Per non dare al padre di lei la soddisfazione di vederla piangere, la condusse fuori dalla porta. Avrebbe voluto potersi prendere il tempo per consolarla, ma un istante dopo essersi abbassata, la saracinesca si rialzò e sei uomini a cavallo uscirono galoppando dalla fortezza.

"Stanno andando a cercare Sorcha," disse Aidan, sapendo d'istinto che era così.

Nonostante le sue conquiste, a Padruig Caimbeul mancava una cosa per salvaguardare il proprio retaggio: un erede. Aidan si rese conto di dover trovare Sorcha prima degli uomini di Padruig. Diede a sua moglie un rapido bacio sulle labbra, le disse che la amava e la rimandò a casa scortata da alcune guardie. Prese poi con sé il resto dei suoi uomini e quelli fornitigli da Jaime Steorling e David mac Mhaoil Chaluim, e rivolse lo sguardo a ovest.

CAPITOLO QUATTRO

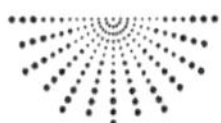

*S*orcha si svegliò con la bocca asciutta.

Era come se avesse trangugiato degli stracci appallottolati. Le doleva la testa e aveva paura di aprire gli occhi alla luce... se, come credeva, era giorno.

L'ultima cosa che ricordava era di essere salita a bordo di quella nave. Nell'istante in cui erano partiti avevano incontrato una tempesta. La nave rollava e beccheggiava, rollava e beccheggiava...

Ma no... dev'essere lo uisge.

Spalancò all'improvviso gli occhi quando si rese conto che era la sua testa a girare, non la cuccetta su cui giaceva.

Si trovava in una stanza bizzarra, arredata spartanamente come una cella, le pareti ornate solo di ragnatele e ben poco a scaldarla. Il letto era grande a sufficienza per ospitare tre uomini adulti e un'occhiata in giro rivelò la presenza di uno sconosciuto nudo: un uomo robusto come il capitano della nave e con i capelli altrettanto dorati. Somigliava a un orso, seduto su quella sedia dall'altra parte della stanza, le braccia incrociate e gli occhi chiusi, le spalle nude appoggiate alla parete. Nel sonno, il suo volto era comunque atteggiato a un'espressione dura e Sorcha pensò per un istante che doveva essere il suo carceriere; ma poi la sua mente annebbiata dall'alcol fece due più due. Uno sconosciuto nudo, il letto disfatto... Sussultò e si affrettò ad alzarsi. Sollevò immediatamente le coperte e controllò se vi fosse del sangue, ma le lenzuola erano pulite.

Inoltre, non si *sentiva* violata. E se un uomo di quella stazza le avesse usato violenza, lei se ne sarebbe di certo accorta. Confusa, lasciò cadere le coperte e si voltò verso lo sconosciuto nudo tenendo le mani sui fianchi. "E voi chi sareste?" chiese.

Il colosso aprì gli occhi: brillanti occhi azzurri che si volsero nella sua direzione, ma leggermente fuori fuoco. Sorcha fu colta dalla tentazione di sventolargli una mano davanti al naso.

"Chi siete *voi*?" ribatté l'uomo. "Ma soprattutto, cosa ci fate nel *mio* letto?"

Sorcha non era più esattamente *nel* letto dell'uomo, ma non avvertiva la necessità di puntualizzare. Del resto, la cosa era evidente. "Che vuol dire 'chi siete voi'?"

"Non mi sembra di aver parlato per enigmi."

"Dov'è Alec?" chiese Sorcha. Era Alec quello che voleva vedere, ora: l'uomo che l'aveva raggirata.

"Dovevo immaginarlo," esclamò disgustato lo sconosciuto nudo.

"Cos'è che dovevate immaginare?" Sorcha era del tutto confusa. Soprattutto, aveva la sensazione di essere ben lontana dall'Isola di Skye. "Dove mi trovo?" chiese, questa volta in tono decisamente più irritato. Qualcuno avrebbe dovuto rispondere della doppiezza di Alec.

"Nella *mia* stanza," rispose l'uomo, come se lei fosse stata una *eegit*.

Sorcha lo fulminò con lo sguardo. "E dove sarebbe la vostra stanza?"

"A Dunrònaigh Keep."

E come diavolo faceva lei a sapere dov'era?! *Respira,* ordinò a se stessa. *Respira.* Era possibilissimo che ci fosse una spiegazione ragionevole per tutto. Il fatto che i suoi consanguinei l'avessero tradita non significava che tutti gli altri fossero propensi a fare lo stesso. "D'accordo, allora ditemi... per caso Dunrònaigh Keep si trova sull'Isola di Skye?"

"No," rispose l'uomo. Si alzò di scatto, nudo come il giorno in cui era nato, senza vergognarsi di avere il membro al vento. "E ora, se avete finito di occuparmi il letto, vorreste lasciarmi riposare?"

Come se lei avesse potuto andarsene! Se costui non era il suo carceriere, dovevano essere entrambi prigionieri.

L'uomo percorse la stanza con fare deciso, diretto verso il letto che aveva rivendicato come proprio, e Sorcha si levò di scatto dalla sua strada, rimanendo sorpresa quando egli non si voltò a guardarla lascivamente. Nella foga, per poco non inciampò nella manica di... per la Cailleach, cosa aveva addosso?

Un abito nuziale? Lungo e fluente, con lunghe e ampie maniche che toccavano terra, era azzurro ghiaccio e dal ricamo complesso. Chi glielo aveva messo addosso? Ma soprattutto, *perché* qualcuno le aveva fatto indossare un indumento tanto elaborato? E già che c'era, se non era sull'Isola di Skye, dove si trovava? "E voi vorreste dormire?" chiese furiosa una volta che l'uomo si fu messo comodo sotto le coperte.

Lo sconosciuto si voltò su un fianco, rivolto verso il muro. "A meno che voi non abbiate qualcosa di meglio da proporre." Ma non fece nulla che mostrasse l'intento di mettere in atto quella velata minaccia.

"Provateci e vi strappo gli occhi," lo mise in guardia Sorcha.

"Non servirebbe a nulla," ribatté l'uomo.

Perché non la voleva? O perché lei era già sua? A ogni modo, Sorcha si scoprì più furiosa di prima. *Che diamine stava succedendo?* Dove l'aveva portata Alec?

Scambiandosi di posto con lo sconosciuto, Sorcha si sedette sulla *di lui* sedia e cercò di capire cosa stesse accadendo. Dopo un lungo istante, l'uomo nudo si mise a russare, e pure della grossa.

Suo fratello Aidan le aveva detto di non fidarsi mai degli sconosciuti, ma nella sua determinazione di raggiungere Una, Sorcha non aveva nemmeno preso in considerazione l'idea che qualcuno avrebbe potuto giocarle un brutto tiro. Si credeva forse immune ai pericoli a cui era soggetta una donna sola? Era stata così arrogante da credere che non potesse accaderle nulla?

Era una Guardiana – una prescelta – ma ciò non significava che non potesse essere ferita. Ciò nonostante, considerate tutte le sue capacità, Sorcha non era una fanciullina indifesa. Non le avevano insegnato a chinare il capo di fronte alla paura.

Cercò di ricordare quanto possibile, ma non riuscì ad andare oltre lo *uisge*. L'uomo di nome Alec le aveva dato la fiasca e lei, naturalmente, l'aveva accettata, non avendo motivo di credere che il contenuto fosse diverso da ciò che egli aveva dichiarato. *Dopotutto, perché avrebbe dovuto mentire?* Sorcha gli aveva già dato tutto quello che aveva di valore. E non aveva mai avuto intenzione di bere più del dovuto.

Non poteva esserci altra spiegazione: lo *uisge* doveva essere stato *drouged*.

A pensarci bene, l'uomo le aveva concesso quel passaggio un po' troppo facilmente...

Quell'"Alec' l'aveva forse lasciata chissà dove per fuggire col suo cavallo? L'aveva venduta a un viscido *laird* celibe? O peggio ancora... la nave era affondata e Sorcha era stata trascinata a riva dalla corrente, unica sopravvissuta su un'isola dimenticata?

Perdiana. Avvertì un primo sentore di paura al pen-